CW01024434

The
WARTIME
NURSE

BOOKS BY IMOGEN MATTHEWS

The Girl from the Resistance

The Girl with the Red Hair

WARTIME HOLLAND SERIES

The Girl Across the Wire Fence

The Hidden Village

Hidden in the Shadows

The Boy in the Attic

IMOGEN MATTHEWS

The
WARTIME
NURSE

bookouture

Published by Bookouture in 2024

An imprint of Storyfire Ltd.
Carmelite House
50 Victoria Embankment
London EC4Y 0DZ

www.bookouture.com

Storyfire Ltd's authorised representative in the EEA is Hachette Ireland
8 Castlecourt Centre
Castleknock Road
Castleknock
Dublin 15 D15 YF6A
Ireland

Copyright © Imogen Matthews, 2024

Imogen Matthews has asserted her right to be identified as the author of this
work.

All rights reserved. No part of this publication may be reproduced, stored in any
retrieval system, or transmitted, in any form or by any means, electronic,
mechanical, photocopying, recording or otherwise, without the prior written
permission of the publishers.

ISBN: 978-1-83525-311-3
eBook ISBN: 978-1-83525-310-6

This book is a work of fiction. Whilst some characters and circumstances
portrayed by the author are based on real people and historical fact, references
to real people, events, establishments, organizations or locales are intended only
to provide a sense of authenticity and are used fictitiously. All other characters
and all incidents and dialogue are drawn from the author's imagination and are
not to be construed as real.

PROLOGUE
SEPTEMBER 1944

Will

Straight ahead, a luminous pale-yellow moon hung in the clear night sky, providing clear visibility. So far, so good. Will adjusted his goggles, checked the position of the bulky Dakota he was piloting against the other planes flying in formation. Relieved the worst was over, he nodded to himself that every-thing was as it should be. Far below, he could just make out the shapes of dozens of parachutes swaying and gently bobbing down to earth. He gave a silent prayer that the men would be delivered safely into the hands of those who'd been primed to pick them up.

Beside him sat Jack, his co-pilot and best friend since school, good with numbers and a stickler for detail. He'd been at Will's side for every one of the paratroop drops they'd made these past days into Holland. Below the cockpit in the body of the plane was Sam, the wireless operator, who transmitted all messages to and from their base. Nick, the navigator, had the crucial job of keeping the plane on course, pinpointing the target for the drop-off and returning to home base. They'd bonded over their work and were all good friends. Each one was essential to the success of every mission from the moment they lifted off from RAF Saltby to touchdown some eight hours later.

Will's eyes kept flicking to the dials in front of him, alert for any sudden changes that might spell trouble. Apart from the infernal drone of the engine and incessant rattling of the metal seats, more an irritation than anything to be concerned about, everything was working fine. He waited on an instruction from Nick on when to turn the plane and bank away towards the Dutch coast. Back home to England.

'By my reckoning, we should get back to base by nine p.m.,' Jack shouted over the roar of the engine. 'I made sure the mess kept back enough lamb stew and dumplings for us. I don't know about you, but I'm starving!' He turned to Will with a toothy grin.

'Me too. And I could murder a beer.' Will laughed.

'Or something stronger,' said Jack, staring out of the window at one of their planes also tracking east below them. 'Sparky should be back at base before us. He's managed to get hold of whisky. I'm sure he won't refuse us a tipple.'

'We'd better get back quick then,' said Will with a smile, and the two men fell silent as they studied the instrument panels and waited for Nick's signal to change direction.

Minutes passed and Will felt the first flicker of anxiety that something was amiss. He sensed more than heard it. A split second's loss of concentration was all it took. Will was rammed back to the present by Jack yelling, 'Watch out... planes approaching on your left!' just as a stream of bullets hammered the metal fuselage and made everything shake violently.

'Oh my God,' Will muttered to himself, as a spider's web of cracks spread rapidly across the windshield. A crackle burst forth from the radio, followed by Nick's urgent voice giving instructions on how to take evasive action. Then, as suddenly as it had started, his voice cut out, leaving a long loud hiss of static.

Jack was now screaming something that Will couldn't make out as the plane suddenly plunged into a nosedive with an ear-splitting whine. They were losing altitude, and fast. From their left, several German fighter planes were flying right up to them. They came so close that Will caught sight of the manic grin of one of the pilots. He would have been able to hear the German's shouts had it not been for the roar of his own failing engines. 'Bastards!' he spat, trying desperately to bring the nose of the plane up and out of the dive.

It happened so fast, but he knew it was all over when a bright light flashed at the corner of his vision, followed by a deafening crunching sound. Everything went dark and silent.

Will sensed something was terribly wrong. He tried to lift his head and open his eyes, but his head hurt like hell and he'd lost feeling in his right leg. He took a sniff in, then another, and gasped – he smelt gasoline. His senses suddenly on full alert, he saw he was still in his seat and so was Jack. But relief turned to panic when he realised that Jack wasn't moving.

'Jack?' he said. There was no response. Then, more urgently, 'Jack!' He grabbed his co-pilot by the lapels of his flight jacket and shook him as hard as he could. 'We've got to get out of here before she goes up in flames.' Will slapped Jack hard across both cheeks, but there was no response. Panicking, Will realised he had to get out before the whole plane blew up. With a strength he didn't know he had, he wrenched open the hatch above his head and sucked in great lungfuls of fresh air. Hoisting himself onto his elbows, he looked all around and saw the plane had crash-landed into a clump of trees and the port wing was smashed to smithereens. His breath came in jerky sobs and then he saw a flicker of flame rise from the wing, turning rapidly into a sheet that came rolling towards him. With a superhuman strength he managed to free himself from the hatch, but as he jumped down he lost his balance and hit his head hard on the ground. Flames flickered at the corner of his vision as he rolled himself towards some nearby bushes for protection. Sobbing and gasping for breath, he waited for the explosion. When it came it was deafening. Instinctively, he curled himself into a ball as scraps of flaming debris rained down all around him. Screwing his eyes tightly shut, he had the sensation of falling, falling, falling, but never hitting the ground.

A voice was calling, 'Hello? Is anyone there?'

There was a rustle of leaves. Was it footsteps? Will managed to open his eyes a crack. Two boots appeared inches from his face. Someone was shaking him.

'Piet! *Kom snel!*'

Will froze at the realisation that he was hearing German, but he was unable to move. He shut his eyes again, fearing the worst.

'Are you English?' came another man's voice.

Will opened his eyes. Two young men crouched over him.

'Yes. English,' he croaked.

'*Hij leeft!*' cried one of them, and Will felt a warm rush of relief that these men weren't speaking German after all. He guessed the words meant 'he lives'. He looked up into the man's face and was confused to see he had tears in his eyes.

'I'm Piet and this is Hans. We saw you come down and didn't think anyone could survive that. Are there any others?' He spoke perfect English.

'There are four of us,' Will managed to say with difficulty. The image of Jack's lifeless body swam across his line of vision before he lost consciousness.

Will became aware of a man and a woman speaking in soft but urgent tones close by. Where was he? He noticed there was a strong smell of something medicinal... was he in a hospital? His right leg felt heavy but he was too exhausted to find out why. It worried him how little he remembered, but he felt soothed by the woman's voice, even though he didn't understand a word she was saying.

Gradually, he blinked open his eyes. The man, a doctor he guessed from the white coat, was walking out of the room, while a nurse in a blue dress with a white apron and matching cap stood at the foot of his bed writing on a clipboard. He watched her, taking in her small, confident stature and dark-blond hair tied loosely in a bun at the nape of her neck. She hummed softly to herself and he found he was unable to tear his eyes away from her. When she had finished what she was doing, she replaced the clipboard. Then, turning to face Will, she saw he was awake and she gave him a smile so sweet it made his heart swell. Moving closer, she placed a cool hand on his forehead. Will gazed up into her kind face, noticing the dimples on either side of her mouth. Her soft brown eyes locked on his and were full of concern.

'Hello. How are you feeling?' she said in heavily accented English.

Will opened his mouth to speak, but his mind went blank. It was as if he'd forgotten how to.

'Perhaps you can tell me your name,' she urged gently, and kept looking into his eyes.

Will tried to nod, but it hurt his head to do so. 'Will,' he managed to say, then added, 'Cooper.'

'Will Cooper,' she repeated carefully and nodded.

He loved the way she said his name. Still unable to find the words to form a proper sentence, he kept staring into the eyes of this angel he was convinced had come to save him.

ONE

HAARLEM, SEPTEMBER 1944

Freddie

Freddie was woken by the persistent rumble of engines and the clack-clacking of many ancient bikes being ridden past on wooden wheels outside her dormitory window. She had no idea what it was about and found herself shaking with fear. Could it be the Wehrmacht moving reinforcements into the city? But this seemed hardly possible in the light of yesterday's news, which had given the first inkling of an end to the war in more than four years. The nurses had all crowded round Freddie's wireless set, the one she'd managed to keep hidden from the Germans under the floorboards, and collectively held their breath as the news unfolded on Radio Oranje: the Allies had taken Brussels from the Germans, Antwerp would follow on and soon their troops would make it over the border of Holland and push back the Germans for good.

But now, as Freddie listened to the rumbling in the street below, a terrible thought came to her – maybe these stories of liberation were too good to be true and the Germans still had the upper hand. And maybe what she was in fact hearing was their latest attempt to demonstrate that they were the ones in power and intended to remain so.

She slipped quickly out of bed, dashed across the bare floorboards to the other side of the room and shook Inge awake. 'Something's happening out there. Can't you hear it?'

'It's so early,' Inge said with a groan and rolled over with her back to her.

'Listen to me. Something serious is going on,' said Freddie urgently, and rushed to the window to confirm what she suspected with her own eyes.

She gazed down, spellbound, on an extraordinary sight. The road was filled with a long procession of all kind of vehicles – army tanks, armoured cars, ordinary cars, trucks, German soldiers on bicycles with bulging saddlebags. They were all heading in one direction, and that was eastwards. And it could only mean one thing, Freddie realised, her heart lifting as it dawned on her what she was seeing.

She turned her head and cried out to Inge, 'Come quick! The Germans are leaving.'

One by one all the other girls woke up and wanted to know what was going on.

'Come and see for yourselves,' said Freddie, beckoning them all over. 'The Germans are leaving. They're actually going back home!'

Once the procession had passed through, people started pouring out onto the streets. At first they stared silently as they tried to comprehend what was unfolding before their eyes – could the enemy really be in retreat? Then, as it dawned on them, they broke into joyful whoops and shouts of laughter, and began slapping one another on the back. It was as if someone had loosened a pressure valve on a tap and the water was rushing out in an enormous whoosh. But some people still stood in stunned silence, not quite believing their eyes. Could this terrible war – the occupation of Holland by the Germans – actually be at an end?

Freddie and her nursing friends rushed into the street to join in the celebrations, hugging strangers and singing and dancing impromptu reels, while orange, white, red and blue confetti floated down from open windows and swirled all around them. She marvelled at the number of people waving flags – Dutch flags; it was such a small act of defiance that only hours ago would have been punishable by the occupying Germans with imprisonment –or worse: death.

'Isn't it wonderful?' laughed Inge, taking Freddie by both hands and swinging her round and round.

'I feel like I'm in a dream. I can't quite believe it,' gasped Freddie, out of breath from her exertions.

'Perhaps they'll give us all a holiday. God, do we need it,' replied Inge, then threw her head back in laughter.

'What's a holiday?' joked Freddie, feeling so light and care-free as she went off to skip round and round with strangers in another reel.

Their wish was granted: most of the nurses were given an immediate two-day leave. The skeleton staff left behind were also promised time off when their colleagues returned.

All Freddie could think of was going to see Trudi. It had been weeks since she had seen her sister, and she couldn't wait to spend this short break with her, relaxing and celebrating like they had always promised each other they would do.

Trudi lived in a shared house that overlooked a communal courtyard in the centre of Haarlem. To get there, Freddie had to fight through throngs of revellers that had congregated in the central market square. She didn't mind as the atmosphere was so good-natured and everyone was hell-bent on enjoying them-

selves. There was music and dancing and strangers invited her
to join in, which she did, though she stopped herself from
accepting a swig of jenever from a bottle that was being handed
from person to person.

Still elated, Freddie arrived outside Trudi's house, and was
about to ring the bell when Trudi came up behind her, calling
her name.

Freddie swung round and threw herself into her sister's
arms. 'Can you believe the *moffen* have been defeated?' she said
breathlessly.

Trudi smiled but didn't seem to share her sister's exuber-
ance. 'Come inside,' she said, and put her key in the lock.

Freddie's mood instantly dropped. She sensed that something was up. She waited till they were inside Trudi's room on
the first floor, then spun round to face her.

'What's the matter with you?' she hissed, irritated to be
denied her long-awaited moment of fun.

'Don't be annoyed, but it's not over yet.'

'How can you say that?' retorted Freddie. 'Haven't you seen
what's happening out there?'

'Yes, of course I have. Now listen to me.' Trudi laid a
placating hand on Freddie's shoulder.

Freddie stiffened as all the old feelings she'd had as a young
teenager came flooding back, when Trudi always knew best. It
had taken Freddie a long time to shake off her belief that she
should always do what Trudi said simply because she was two
years older. And she was in no mood to be dictated to today of
all days.

She still remembered clearly the day she'd decided to
change her name. It was when she'd turned fifteen and was
acutely aware that she still looked young for her age – she was
small and wore her thick dark-blond hair in two long braids.
She'd fully expected Trudi to mock her when she told her she
wanted to be known as Freddie from that day forward, as she'd

so often teased her when they were growing up. But Freddie
had been ready to tell her sister she'd given the matter of her
name a lot of thought. The country was at war and Freddie had
been just as determined as her older sister to join the local resistance group to become couriers of classified information that
could help bring down the Nazis. If she were to join the group,
which was all men, she worried they would tease her for being a
girl, but if she changed her name from Frida to Freddie – a boy's
name – she knew she was sure to be taken seriously. More than
anything, she'd wanted Trudi to agree she'd made the right decision – her opinion had always mattered.

'I've decided my name is Freddie, so I'd appreciate it if you
call me Freddie from now on,' she'd said, sounding more confident than she felt, for she still secretly craved Trudi's approval.

'Yes, Freddie. I promise I will.'

Freddie had flushed with pleasure at being called by her
new chosen name. She'd only been a little let down when Trudi
commented that her braids made her look young. 'It's no bad
thing,' Trudi had added. 'When you're working for the resistance, the *moffen* won't suspect you of a thing.'

Shortly after this conversation, Freddie was asked by the
friend of a friend to go out on the streets and stick pro-resistance
posters on walls. It felt like the right thing to do, a small act of
defiance that she hoped would persuade enough people to take
a stand against the German occupiers. Soon, she was distrib-
uting copies of *Trouw*, the Protestant underground newspaper,
and she asked Trudi for her help. The two worked as a team,
with Freddie usually on lookout in case anyone caught them at
it while Trudi slipped copies into the bags of unsuspecting
passengers waiting at bus stops or at the train station. Then one
day they were invited along to a meeting of the local Haarlem
resistance group, the RVV, who were looking for new recruits. It
had sounded exciting, though daunting, and Freddie was
grateful that Trudi would be with her for support.

From the moment she adopted her new name, Freddie's confidence blossomed. Eager to show her worth, she volunteered to work as a courier as soon as she joined the RVV. She would stow anti-German pamphlets in her satchel, which she wore over one shoulder, and crossed Haarlem at speed on her bicycle, her plaits flying out behind her. She knew all the shortcuts and kept a sharp eye out for any Germans as she zigzagged through side streets, bumping over cobblestones and scooting down alleyways barely wide enough for her to pass.

The only time she nearly came unstuck was when she was stopped at a roadblock by a young German soldier who looked about her own age.

'Where are you going in such a hurry?' he'd demanded in passable Dutch. 'Have you got something to hide?'

'Not at all,' Freddie had replied, making herself meet his penetrating gaze. 'I'm late back from school and my mother is expecting me home.' She'd paused, then added, 'I'm fifteen.'

He'd looked her up and down, seemed to accept her explanation, then waved her through.

Freddie was in fact cycling to the house of a resistance member, with a sealed envelope hidden at the bottom of her satchel containing intelligence about a planned takeover of a Dutch factory by the Germans. She'd hoped that her bold action would prevent this from happening.

Soon Frans, the leader of the RVV, came to rely on the two sisters who worked so well as a team and were quick and efficient at delivering important items in Haarlem and further afield. The Germans were fooled by the two women and their cover stories out on their bikes moving top-secret documents and packages between resistance cells planted all along the north coast. From here, this vital cargo would be passed into Allied hands and would possibly be instrumental in preventing German attacks on Dutch property and people.

Freddie had let her attention drift. She came back to the

present when Trudi asked, 'Are you going to listen to what I have to say?'

'I'm sorry. I was miles away,' said Freddie. 'But let me guess – you've been talking to Frans, who doesn't believe the war is over, and he wants us to keep chasing after enemy targets. Well, I don't want to any more, but don't let me stop you.' She folded her arms and stared at her sister.

Trudi sighed and gave her a pleading look. 'I admit I've just been speaking to Frans. As soon as he heard the news this morning he called me to a meeting, along with everyone else in the group. He thinks we should take advantage of all the upheaval and target a traitor who's been on his radar for months. Other resistance groups have tried and failed, but we have a chance now that everyone is so distracted. You may have heard of him: Jeroen Krist. He's head of the Haarlem police, but he's also an NSB member and has a reputation for tracking down Jews.'

Freddie nodded, knowing that those who joined the NSB, the Dutch political fascist party, were considered as dangerous as the Germans who occupied the country.

Trudi went on, 'Even if the war is over, people like him need to be brought to justice. Freddie, I'd really like you to be part of this initiative. You've always been so good at scouting out traitors and passing on information. Honest, it'll be for the last time. Please say yes.'

The noise in the nearby market square rose to a crescendo and Freddie could just make out voices singing the Dutch national anthem. How she longed to be down there, participating in such a historic occasion. But where was the fun if Trudi wasn't beside her sharing the moment? She considered what her sister had just told her about the treacherous police officer – even if the war was over, there was a strong possibility he still posed a danger. She met Trudi's gaze. 'All right. I'll do it,' she said. 'I've two days' leave, but I can't take any more time off.'

'I knew I could rely on you,' said Trudi, and gave her a hug. 'We must hurry before this Krist gets it into his head to flee. The railway station is already full of NSB families wanting to get away from Holland into Germany. But we have to take extra care. He's a dangerous man and will stop at nothing if he suspects us. One last push, Freddie, and then it'll be over.'

TWO

Despite her reservations, Freddie was excited to be back amongst those she had grown to trust and playing the role she was well suited for. She knew every street and alley in Haarlem like the back of her hand and never needed to consult a map. This was handy as it gave her a time advantage, allowing her to dash off on her bike to find her target. Then she would race back to tell the others where they needed to launch their attack. But on this occasion she had her work cut out, for she had learned that the fascist supporter Krist would be at the town hall, right in the middle of the market square, where crowds of people were celebrating. It would be impossible to follow him on her bike.

Trudi and her colleague Cor had been assigned to shoot the man, but that couldn't happen here in front of hundreds of witnesses. Freddie had instructed them to lie in wait away from the crowds at the back of the cathedral.

Freddie entered the square and weaved in and out of groups of revellers until she found a position in a doorway where she could remain half hidden with a clear view of the town hall.

From here, she kept her eyes fixed on the steady stream of people going in and out through the main door. She knew exactly who to look out for, but no one fitted his description.

The cathedral clock struck eleven. Freddie was growing impatient, and she knew Trudi and Cor would be wondering where she'd got to.

Just then a middle-aged man with thinning light brown hair dressed in police uniform came hurrying towards the entrance of the town hall and disappeared inside. She knew it was him, and she would need to be ready when he came out.

It only took a few minutes. He appeared at the door and as suddenly disappeared into the crowd.

Freddie sprang from the doorway, trying to catch sight of him, but every square inch of the marketplace was covered with revellers. Two hours ago she'd been overjoyed to join in, but now she found the throng a hindrance as she pushed her way through, crying out, 'Excuse me!' to anyone blocking her path. It seemed to take forever to reach the other side of the square. Suddenly, she became aware of Trudi calling her name.

Trudi and Cor were standing in full view of the square. Irritated, she hurried over to them. 'What are you doing here? You don't want to be seen.'

'We came to see what had kept you,' said Trudi, sounding affronted.

'Have you seen what it's like out there?' Freddie retorted.

'Be quiet, you two. Is that him?' said Cor, his eyes fixed on a man who was marching in their direction.

Freddie felt her heart lurch as she turned her head and recognised him.

Trudi took the initiative. 'Pretend we're having a good time. Laugh, smile.' She let out a tinkling laugh and started gabbling nonsense at Freddie, who knew instantly to join in. Cor pinned a smile on his face, but Freddie saw his eyes track the traitor, who was only feet away. Surely Cor wouldn't attempt to shoot him here in front of all these people? She gave him a warning prod.

But the man didn't even look in their direction as he walked past, heading towards a bicycle rack in front of a building. He calmly picked out a bike, mounted it and began to ride towards an alley to the side.

'There's another alley that runs parallel. I'll run down it and intercept him at the end. You two follow on.' Freddie didn't wait for an answer, just sprinted away, her arms pumping. Fortunately, the alley she'd chosen was quiet, so she didn't have to slow down to avoid anyone. She knew it curved round and came out on to the street where her target would be emerging any moment now. She got there seconds before he did; she ran into his path and caused him to wobble and almost lose his balance.

'What the hell?' he cried out. He managed to gain control of his bike and, swerving round her, leaned low over his handlebars and pedalled away furiously.

Two shots rang out, one after the other, but they came too late. He'd got away.

Seconds later, Trudi and Cor turned up, both holding pistols.

Freddie stood bent over with her hands on her knees and slowly shook her head. 'It was so close,' she said, looking up at them.

'You did well to slow him down. Someone like him knows all the tricks. He's evaded assassination on a number of occasions, so you mustn't blame yourself,' said Cor, putting away his pistol and nodding at Trudi to do the same.

Trudi went over and put an arm round Freddie and spoke consolingly. 'We did what we had to. There'll be other occasions.'

They looked up as a group of revellers, all young men, came

swaying unsteadily down the street. They were singing the Dutch national anthem at the top of their voices and swigging from beer bottles.

'Let's go and join in the fun,' said Trudi with a smile, and the three of them retraced their steps back to the market square.

THREE

After the celebrations of Dolle Dinsdag, or mad Tuesday, it became apparent that the war was far from over and that large areas of the Netherlands remained under German occupation. Far from retreating, the German forces regrouped under new leadership and retained their iron grip on the Dutch population.

It was a bitter disappointment. Freddie went back to her nursing duties at the hospital and in her time off worked on assignments with Trudi and their friend Hannie, who was a fearless and dedicated resistance fighter and the only other woman in their resistance group. Their assignments grew in intensity and danger, and usually involved cycling cross-country with guns hidden in saddlebags and working on teams to flush out rogue police officers suspected of passing information about Jews to the Germans.

Freddie's role as the eyes and ears of each operation suited her well, because she wasn't keen on the idea of being in the thick of an attack on a suspected collaborator and expected to shoot. It wasn't that she disagreed with the principle of taking out people who were prepared to betray their own countrymen, but she didn't want to be the one to pull the trigger. Despite her reservations, Frans insisted she learned how to use a gun properly and safely, for she might never know when she would be called on to do so. She was quick off the mark and able to speed ahead and assess a scene before others arrived. If there was even the slightest whiff of Nazi activity in the vicinity, she would warn the others to abort, and they respected her decision. On more than one occasion, she prevented the group from walking straight into the clutches of the Germans.

One time, Freddie and Trudi were sent by Frans to plant an incendiary device in a theatre showing Nazi propaganda films. As they approached the place, they found the doors being heavily guarded by German soldiers with rifles keeping an eagle eye on people arriving. They were also checking bags and turning away anyone they didn't like the look of.

'Let's chat and laugh to each other. Pretend this doesn't bother us,' said Freddie quietly, taking a chance that the Germans would never give two women enjoying an afternoon out the slightest bit of notice. She began telling Trudi a joke and feigned she hadn't seen the guard until she was standing right next to him. His gaze was stony at first, then he flicked his eyes from one to the other as if deciding whether to question them. Still pretending to laugh at the joke, Freddie clapped her hand over her mouth as if to suppress her giggles. He raised his eyebrows and jerked his head towards the door. They were through. Inside, they joined a crowd of people waiting to go into the auditorium.

'My heart's going like the clappers,' whispered Trudi against Freddie's ear.

'Mine too. But never mind that. You go through the left-hand door and find us two seats at the back. I'll go in the door on the right and come to you when I'm finished.'

Freddie stepped inside the auditorium with the device primed in the deep pocket of her coat. She wasn't going to let nerves get the better of her. Taking advantage of the fact that it was pitch dark, she felt her way to the front, and was able to plant it just beneath the stage without anyone noticing. The theatre was filling up and she slipped towards the back, looking for Trudi, who was waving at her from where she was keeping two seats for them.

'Over here!' she called. When Freddie got to her, she grabbed an armrest to steady herself. Doubling over, she began to retch.

'Are you unwell?' Trudi said, loud enough for those around her to hear.

'I think I'm going to be sick,' Freddie croaked.

'Excuse me, Excuse me,' said Trudi and helped Freddie through the throng of people still making their way into the theatre. In the foyer, Freddie's distress appeared to increase. The German on the door looked over in alarm at the sight of the young woman who seemed to be about to throw up.

'I'm so sorry. We have to leave. My friend has suddenly been taken ill,' said Trudi, as she came towards him supporting Freddie. He stared at the woman who minutes before had been in such high spirits, and quickly stepped aside to let them through.

Out on the street, they ran as fast as they could away from the theatre, only stopping when they could be sure they were a safe distance away.

'You're a natural. Did you see the look of disgust on his face?' said Trudi with a laugh. 'More importantly, I don't think he suspected a thing.'

'More fool him,' said Freddie, suddenly fully recovered. 'Now we just have to wait for news.'

Later, they heard that the device had gone off moments

before the film reel began and that the theatre had been rapidly evacuated. No one had been hurt, but the disruption had enraged the Germans, who never could have guessed that behind the planting of the firebomb was a woman.

Whenever Freddie scored a victory against the Germans, however minor, the rush of adrenalin she felt was huge, but nothing compared to the sense of purpose she got from when she was doing the 'tulip run', so called because it took her out to the bulb fields, where farmers still grew a large variety of colourful tulips, daffodils and hyacinths in the early years of the war. How she'd loved the feeling of freedom as she cycled as fast as she could between the endless striped fields of every colour imaginable, her braids lifted by the wind and flying out behind her.

It was a rich agricultural area and these days Freddie visited farms to collect food for families in need. Potatoes, carrots, beets and turnips; in fact anything she could lay her hands on would do. Not everyone was willing to extend the hand of friendship to those less fortunate than themselves, but Freddie soon got to know the farmers who cheerfully put by a little for her each week. With her saddlebags laden with produce, she then cycled back to Haarlem and distributed it to families sheltering Jews and *onderduikers*, the people who needed to hide from the German authorities. She was humbled by the kindness and generosity of farmers, who were feeling the pinch themselves but gave willingly. Everyone was going short these days for the simple reason that the Germans were restricting the supply of food into the shops. Not only that, the enemy was taking from the farmers themselves and demanding they hand over the hard-earned fruits of their labour. No one dared refuse, for they knew the consequences would be dire.

One day, Freddie turned up at a farm she'd visited many times before. She knocked on the door, but there was no answer, so she tested it and found it was open.

'Hello... is anyone in?' She walked through into the empty kitchen, expecting the farmer's wife to be cooking a meal at the stove. It was normally so warm, but today there was an unwelcome chill about the place. Freddie put her empty bags down on the kitchen table and went over to the back door. Outside, she found the farmer and his wife crouching on the ground sorting a few measly-looking potatoes into an empty crate. Spotting her, the farmer's wife looked flustered and quickly got up.

'Hello, my dear. I clean forgot you were coming. But it's lovely to see you. Come into the house and I'll put the kettle on.'

'I'll go and see if there's anything left in the barn,' said the farmer, heaving himself wearily to his feet with a tired smile.

'What's happened?' said Freddie, once they were inside and with cups of tea in front of them.

'We were woken at five by the sound of a truck driving into the yard. I immediately guessed it was the *moffen*. Who else would come calling that early? They banged on the door and demanded to be let in. Kees and I came downstairs and were still in our nightclothes. It wasn't even light. There were four of them with guns and they ordered Kees to fill the back of the truck with root vegetables. I couldn't do anything except stand by and watch. It seemed too much of a coincidence that we'd only finished digging our crop out of the ground the day before. They left us hardly anything and it broke our hearts to see months of hard work disappear like that. We can barely afford to feed ourselves and now there's nothing left to see us through the winter.'

'I'm so sorry this has happened to you. They didn't hurt you, did they?' Freddie asked, appalled to hear how badly they'd been treated.

'No, thankfully.'

'How can they be so cruel? Is there anything I can do?' Freddie felt torn as she caught sight of her empty bags on the table and thought of all those people expecting her to turn up later with food for the next few days. What could she possibly do to help this kind farmer and his wife when she had effectively come to beg for food for others?

'I'm sure it won't be as bad as it seems right now,' said the farmer's wife with forced brightness. 'We have a small store of things hidden away in the barn for emergencies, and Kees will give you whatever he thinks we can spare.'

'No, I couldn't possibly take any. Not after what's happened —' began Freddie, but the farmer's wife held up a hand.

'I promised you I'd help and I don't break a promise. Those people need all the help they can get. We can always manage.'

At that moment Kees came in through the back door holding the crate he and his wife had been filling earlier. It was now filled with potatoes and turnips. He managed a smile as he placed it on the table next to Freddie's bags.

'Not as much as usual but I'm sure my friend Jan up the road will make up the shortfall.' He kept his eyes on her and she knew she couldn't refuse. As he began filling up her bags, Freddie bit her lip, her eyes welling up with tears. Did the Germans have any idea what suffering they were causing, she thought bitterly. Did they even care?

Freddie was still unable to put the whole sorry business out of her mind when she arrived later for her shift at the hospital to be told by a senior nurse that she must report immediately to the matron's office.

'Do you know why?' she asked, with a shiver of worry that she must have done something wrong.

'If I knew I would tell you. But you're not the only one,' said her superior with a placating smile, and she mentioned the names of several nurses who had also been summoned. One of them was Inge. Knowing she'd be with her friend, Freddie walked away feeling slightly better about what was to come. The two of them had been friends since school and, however bad the news they were about to receive, at least they would be in this together.

FOUR

It had all happened so fast that Freddie had no time to process the sudden move to Arnhem, which felt like a million miles away from home. The night before, Trudi had come with her to the train station to see her off and they'd clung to each other, tears flowing down their cheeks. Freddie promised to write as soon as she got settled, unable to admit how scared and nervous she was at what lay ahead. Matron had told the dozen nurses so little about what to expect other than that they would be working under difficult conditions that were likely to be the most intense and gruelling they had yet encountered.

Freddie's only consolation was that Inge was alongside her. They were part of the contingent of nurses drafted in at short notice and she knew that had it not been for Inge, her best friend and confidante during the darkest times, she might well have given up nursing long ago. In fact, had it not been for their chance meeting Freddie might never have even considered a nursing career.

It was a full three years ago that Freddie had been locking up her bike in the market square in Haarlem, when totally lost in thought she'd heard her name being called. Looking up, she saw a young woman with short blond hair and dressed in a long grey woollen coat striding purposefully towards her. For a moment, she didn't recognise her, then saw it was her old schoolfriend.

'I thought it was you,' said Inge with a tinkling laugh. Freddie was instantly transported back to the classroom and happier times.

'Inge! What a lovely surprise,' she said, as the two friends leaned in for a kiss – one, two, three on each cheek. 'What are you doing here?'

'I could ask you the same. I saw you from across the square and had to come and say hello. Have you time for a coffee?'

'Well, yes. But only if you do. You look as if you're going somewhere.'

'Do I?' Inge looked down at her coat and brushed away a piece of imaginary fluff. 'Come on, there's a café I like near here. I'm dying to hear what you've been up to.'

Freddie smiled, knowing she had better be careful with how much she told Inge. Since school, they had gone their separate ways and lost touch. Much had happened since then, but nothing she was able to talk to Inge about. She'd been sworn to secrecy by Frans over her resistance work and knew she must abide by it. Still, she was pleased by this chance encounter, as they'd always got along well. Both girls had a similar temperament and had been high-spirited in class, which had sometimes got them into trouble. But what Freddie remembered most was the laughs they used to have, and she realised how much she missed all that. What with the war and everything, life had become just a bit too serious.

'You haven't changed a bit,' said Inge, perusing Freddie's face, once they were sitting down with a cup of ersatz coffee in front of them.

Freddie could feel herself blush. Back then, she still wore her hair in plaits, and she was acutely aware that she must still look like a schoolgirl. She'd been meaning to cut her hair but hadn't got round to it. 'It's not that long since we saw each other,' she said with an embarrassed laugh. 'But you've changed. You look so... chic. And your hair. You used to wear it long.'

'Do you like it?' Inge said with a frown, and Freddie was pleased her opinion still mattered to her.

'I do. Shorter hair makes you look older and more sophisticated.'

Inge beamed at the compliment. 'I had it cut when I started my job at the hospital. What with all the early starts, I don't have the time to deal with long hair. It's just easier short.' She shrugged. 'Are you working, Freddie?' Her pale blue eyes were as penetrating as ever. Freddie always did feel that Inge could read her thoughts, but she had to stay silent, however much she was dying to confide in her about her work with the resistance.

'No. Not at the moment.' She sighed. 'I haven't decided what I want to do.'

'But it's more than a year since I last saw you. You must have some idea.' Inge stirred her coffee, smiling, as she waited for an answer.

'Not a clue. Tell me more about what you do,' said Freddie, desperate to change the subject.

'I'm a trainee nurse,' Inge said, before adding, 'but I want to be a doctor. You know my father's a surgeon. Where he works there's been a shortage of nurses and he thought it would give me a good grounding in medicine before I go to medical school. Whenever that is, thanks to this wretched war. You know, I thought I'd hate nursing, what with all the long hours, and I was sure I'd faint at the sight of blood, but I'm used to it now. I work on a general ward and we get all kinds of patients: young, old, some very sick, some recovering from operations. There's never a dull moment. The saddest thing is when a patient passes away, especially the ones you care for.' She paused a moment, gazing away into the middle distance. When she looked back at

Freddie she said, 'The hospital where I work needs nurses. If you like, I could help you get a position. What do you think?'

'Me, a nurse? I've never thought about such a thing. Surely you need qualifications. You know I don't have any.'

'Neither do I, remember? Look, if I managed to pass the interview, I'm sure you can too. And I can put a good word in for you with the senior nurse. And if you get in, which I'm sure you will, you can move into the nurses' accommodation where I live. There are always beds going. Go on, Freddie. It'd be so much fun having you around.'

Freddie found herself warming to the idea of becoming a nurse. By the time they'd finished their coffee and gone their separate ways, she was feeling much more optimistic about her future. A future where she could help sick people and do something worthwhile with her life.

FIVE

Freddie blinked against the sun's rays that shone through a slit in the curtain, and rubbed her eyes. It took a moment or two to remember where she was. Then it came back to her. She was no longer in her dormitory in Haarlem opposite Inge, whose solid presence always reassured her. She was in a new place, about to start a new position, and the thought filled her with apprehension. Not because she didn't think she was up to the job – she'd more than proved herself to be a capable nurse – but because it was the first time she'd be working on the front line in a busy emergency department of a large military hospital.

As Freddie contemplated her new surroundings, she could only guess at what her role as a staff nurse would entail, especially after everything had gone so terribly wrong after Dolle Dinsdag. The Allies had been so sure they were about to liberate the entire country and drive the Germans out, but they had failed. Not only was the war far from over, but it was looking likely that hostilities were about to intensify. As a result, the medical staff at Arnhem's military hospital had been put on full alert, and Freddie learned that they should expect the worst. Major cities like Amsterdam and Rotterdam were still very much under the control of the Germans and it seemed inconceivable that they would soon be free. Even if liberation was close at hand, the loss of life was likely to be great. Hospitals up and down the country were being primed for casualties.

Freddie had experience in treating the victims of bomb attacks, including broken bones, serious flesh wounds and head injuries; she knew she would be able to deal with the most serious cases, but it was the scale of the operation that made her nervous. No numbers had been offered since the situation was so fluid, but the Arnhem hospital where Freddie was about to start was bringing in extra nursing staff by the day.

Initially, Freddie was posted on the general ward doing routine work similar to what she'd been doing back in Haarlem. The hospital was still treating the general public but they'd been told it would soon be turned over exclusively to military personnel. So far, the hospital had admitted only two Canadian airmen who had sustained light injuries during the course of their exercises. But the mood amongst the nurses was tense as everyone speculated on an imminent Allied bombing campaign planned in the area. Why else the urgency in bringing them over to this provincial hospital in a part of Holland most had never been to?

Freddie had been working in Arnhem a couple of weeks when she went to the nurses' station to familiarise herself with the patients' paperwork. It was early and no one was about when she heard footsteps coming down the corridor towards her. Hidden behind an open cupboard door, Freddie heard two people deep in conversation. She heard them come to a halt at the desk. From his voice, Freddie recognised the man who had addressed them when they'd first arrived; he was talking to the matron in charge of the wards. They were literally feet away from where she was standing but hadn't noticed her. Keeping very still, Freddie craned her neck to hear his low voice.

'I've heard from London, who say that the British are bringing in troops by plane. Dozens of men are being parachuted close to the bridges. This isn't some small-scale skirmish but an all-out attack to defeat the Germans.'

'Have they given us any idea of the number of casualties we can expect?' said the matron, a sombre-faced middle-aged woman Freddie had never seen smile.

'Nothing's been confirmed yet, but we've been told to expect casualties to be in the low hundreds. If you want my honest opinion, I think there'll be considerably more, so we must prepare for the worst. If the Germans catch wind of the Allied plan, they're not going to take this lying down. They'll be ruthless and I've no doubt our hospital will bear the brunt of their aggression. We need to prepare for the maximum number of casualties and will need everyone to pull together. Can I leave it up to you to organise the nursing shifts so that we're primed and ready?'

'Yes, of course. I'll implement the rotas right away,' said Matron.

'Good. Whatever it takes. I want to make sure that we have the capacity to deal with this crisis.'

Freddie waited tensely till she could be sure they had walked back down the corridor before setting off for the ward.

Inge was just arriving. 'Hello, you. I wondered where you got to. We're on bed-changing duty this morning,' she said with a cheery smile.

'I've something I have to tell you,' Freddie whispered urgently as they hurried to start at one end of the ward. She was desperate to tell Inge what she'd just heard.

'You've gone quite white in the face. Is it bad news?' said Inge, stopping a moment to face her.

'I'm afraid it might be,' said Freddie, then noticed the senior nurse was marching towards them. 'I'll tell you later.'

'Nurse Oversteegen,' she said, addressing Freddie, before turning to Inge. 'And Nurse Janssen. There is to be no gossiping on the ward. You know the rules. I want these beds changed as quickly as possible. Then you're to attend a meeting for all nurses at nine a.m. sharp in the canteen.'

'Yes, Sister,' they said in unison.

They started on the first bed, where a man in his sixties was sitting up. He smiled at them expectantly. 'Have you two lovely ladies come to pay me a visit?' he said.

'Something like that,' said Freddie, returning his smile. 'Now if we could just move you over to the chair, then we'll make sure your bed is all fresh and neat for you.'

His smile dropped. 'But I'm to be discharged this morning. That's what the doctor said. Do you know when he'll be here?"

'I'm afraid I don't know.' Freddie quickly exchanged a look with Inge. 'Doctor's busy doing rounds this morning and I'm sure he'll be along as soon as he can,' she said, though she suspected the doctor had more important things on his mind at that moment.

After they'd finished with him, they continued up one side of the ward, until they came to a bed where a young man was lying on his back with his eyes shut.

'Shall we leave him to sleep?' said Freddie. It seemed cruel to wake him when he looked so peaceful.

'No, Sister will be furious and accuse us of shirking our duties,' replied Inge, just as the young man opened his eyes.

'Why, hello,' he said in English, looking from one to the other.

Freddie was unable to place his accent but guessed he must be from England. Glancing quickly at the patient card at the end of his bed, she said, 'Hello, Mike. How are you feeling?'

He grinned. 'Thank God. Someone speaks English round here.'

'We both do, actually. We learned it in school,' said Inge, giving Freddie a wink. 'We've come to change your sheets. If you would allow us.'

'So soon? I only got here this morning and I'm in pain,' he said. 'Can't you leave a poor chap to rest?'

Freddie showed Inge the details on the card, which gave the time of admission as six a.m. that day. He had sustained extensive bruising to the chest and was waiting for X-rays to see if he had any internal injuries.

'All right. We won't change your bed today. But is there anything you need... maybe painkillers?' said Freddie.

'Would you? I thought you'd never ask.' He winced and screwed up his face in obvious pain.

'I'll fetch some aspirin,' said Inge. 'You make sure Mike is comfortable.' And she gave Freddie another wink.

'Where do you come from?' asked Freddie, adjusting his pillows to allow him to sit up more comfortably.

'A small town on the south coast of England. It was my first flight and the engine failed. The pilot managed to land it no problem, but it came down with a huge thump and I was thrown forward. Those planes are not very forgiving.' He laughed, then pursed his lips into a thin line as he clutched his side protectively. 'I'm hoping it's just a cracked rib and nothing worse. Can you find out for me?'

'I'm afraid you'll have to wait for the doctor to examine you. The painkillers will help in the meantime.'

Inge arrived with the aspirin and waited until he'd swallowed them down. 'If we see the doctor, we'll send him your way,' she said sweetly.

He nodded, then caught Freddie's eye. 'Before you go, there's something I want you to see.' He jerked his head in the direction of the jacket hanging over the chair beside his bed. 'You'll find it in the inside pocket.'

Freddie went over, noting that the jacket was dark blue and had two chevron stripes denoting his rank on the sleeve. She didn't feel comfortable searching through this man's possessions, in case she found something she shouldn't know about, but he had asked her to. Tentatively, she felt around for the pocket, which rustled when she touched it. She pulled out a newspaper of some kind that had been folded in four. Opening it out, she saw written across the top in big letters: *De Vliegende Hollander*. She looked up quizzically and said, 'It's Dutch for the flying Dutchman. What is it?'

'That's right,' said the pilot. 'We've been dropping copies all over the Arnhem area this past week. Its purpose is to inform the Dutch people about the progress us Allies have been making during the war. This edition is really important as it gives some vital details of what's happening in the coming days. I'm afraid I can't read it, but I'm guessing you can.' He smiled expectantly at Freddie.

Freddie scanned the words written in bold on the front page. The Allies were mounting an attack on the bridge in Arnhem and calling it Operation Market Garden. They were confident that this would be the turning point in the war for the Germans, who would beat a retreat back to Germany. Hitler was expected to be defeated.

'So he was right...' she murmured in English.

'Who's right?' said Mike.

'Who's right?' said Inge at the same moment, in Dutch.

Freddie shook her head and said to Mike, 'Thank you for this. We don't get told very much, so this is really helpful.' She held it out to him, but he shook his head and said she could keep it. Gratefully, she folded the paper up along its creases and slid it into the pocket of her apron.

They moved on to the next patient and Freddie took the

opportunity to whisper to Inge about the conversation she'd overheard between the doctor and Matron that morning. 'This news-sheet – *De Vliegende Hollander* – pretty much confirms what they were talking about and that we're about to bear the brunt of the casualties. The battle for Arnhem is going to be brutal.' She looked up to see the senior nurse marching towards them. 'I'll show you it later,' she said hurriedly and smoothed down her apron.

'Hurry up, you two. I've been keeping an eye on you and saw you chatting to that patient. It's against the rules, as you know perfectly well,' the senior nurse said, her face like thunder.

'The patient was talking to us. It would have been rude not to reply. We're almost finished, as you can see,' said Inge calmly.

'Very well. But don't let me see you doing it again,' said the nurse. She clapped her hands. 'Now, finish off quickly. You're expected in the canteen in ten minutes.'

SIX

Within the hour, Freddie and Inge were working in the emergency department and the casualties started arriving. At first there was a trickle, but by the end of the day the place was on full alert as ambulance after ambulance pulled up outside with the first victims of the Allied attack on the bridges of Arnhem. Every single one of the patients brought in was a young man, and many were in a distressed state, with broken limbs, chest and head wounds or other, unseen, injuries that had rendered them unconscious.

Freddie was rushed off her feet, with no time to consider the seriousness of the situation before she was called to attend to yet another victim. The ones with broken bones she could deal with quickly, but it was the ones whose injuries were so bad that they were unlikely to survive that upset her the most. One young man, a Canadian, she was told, lay unconscious with his entire middle soaked in blood. Her job was to cut the clothing from his body. She tried to be as gentle as possible so as not to hurt him, but when she lifted his blood-soaked shirt aside she was horrified to find that his abdomen had been ripped open, exposing his intestines.

She looked up and saw a duty doctor working frantically on another patient who lay motionless on a makeshift stretcher.

'Doctor! Can you come here immediately?' she called out, trying to keep the panic out of her voice. Never had she seen anything so terrible as the scenes unfolding here. Nothing she'd learned in training had prepared her for this.

'Five minutes,' shouted the doctor, and all Freddie could do was hold the patient's hand and speak soothingly to him.

After a few minutes the doctor came over and nodded at her to stand aside. The patient gave a low moan. 'He's coming round. Administer morphine,' he ordered, and began to work on stemming the bleeding and closing the wound.

The man began to scream. Freddie's hands trembled as she hurried to prepare the injection. It seemed to take forever, but she managed to inject him and within minutes he had calmed down. While the doctor worked, she wiped the patient's brow with a cool damp cloth and whispered quietly to him. 'You're in safe hands now. Everything's going to be all right.'

No sooner had the doctor finished than she was called to the next casualty. When eventually there was a brief lull, she went to find out what had happened to the patient with the terrible abdominal wound. She'd so hoped he would turn a corner, but in her heart of hearts she knew that he hadn't survived.

There was nothing more for Freddie to do except carry on, almost robotically. The only way she could work was to block out the cries and moans that filled the crowded space. By midnight, she'd lost count of the number of limbs she'd set in plaster, the wounds she'd cleaned, dressed or bandaged, and the painkilling injections she'd administered. Whenever there was a brief pause, rather than take a rest she rushed to the storeroom to replenish her medical supplies. She knew if she stopped she would find it hard to get going again. Most of all, she hated not being able to spend time with each patient to care for his needs before she was called to another, often more urgent, case. Twice, her path crossed with Inge, who looked as exhausted as she felt, and yet they managed to exchange an encouraging smile or a pat on the arm that said, *We're in this together. We'll get through this.*

At nearly one in the morning, they were finally allowed to go back to their quarters to grab a few hours' sleep, before reporting back for their next shift, which started at eight a.m.

'Let's see if we can get a cup of tea. I'm too wound up to sleep,' said Inge.

Freddie was too tired to object. Suddenly, the idea of a soothing cup of tea was all she could think of.

The canteen was empty, lit by one bulb that flickered and cast a ghostly glow over the place. Never had Freddie seen it look so uninviting. Undeterred, Inge went over to one corner, where a metal tea urn and china cups and saucers were laid out on a table. She filled two cups with a weak brown liquid and stirred a teaspoon of sugar into each of them. 'Sorry, it's the best on offer,' she said, and handed one to Freddie with an apologetic smile.

Freddie sank onto a chair and took a sip of the sweet lukewarm tea, then another. Then she remembered the copy of *De Vliegende Hollander* that she had stuffed into her apron pocket. 'You should read this. I fear that what we've seen today is just the start.' She looked at the blurred picture showing hundreds of parachutists descending from the sky. 'I wonder how many of those men we've treated today,' she said, handing it over with a heavy heart.

'And there'll be many more by the sounds of it,' said Inge, scanning the front page. 'Whoever wrote this is obviously trying to give the impression that the Allies are about to break the Germans. Even if it's true, it'll come at a heavy human cost.'

Freddie thought back to the casualties whose injuries she'd treated, and felt guilty about walking away when many more were still in need of urgent attention. 'It's only when I stop that I'm able to think what those poor men have gone through on our behalf only to end up in here. I wish there was more we could do to alleviate their suffering.'

'I do too, but you'll drive yourself mad if you allow yourself to think too much about it. We just have to do our best and hope it's enough.'

Freddie watched Inge get up to pour them another cup of tea. When she came back, she draped her arms round Freddie's shoulders and held her against her.

'Get this tea down you and then let's go and get some sleep,' she said. 'We'll need it.'

SEVEN

The next morning came round all too soon and Freddie woke worrying about how she was going to get through the next twelve hours. If only there weren't so many admissions so she could attend to yesterday's patients. She had no time to dwell on it as she pushed open the door of the emergency room and was thrust into the present by the chaos that faced her. There were more patients than the night before – some were sitting on plastic chairs nursing broken limbs and in obvious pain, while others were lying quietly on trolleys, waiting to be attended to. She stepped back as a hospital porter and two nurses came dashing past at speed, pushing a trolley with a patient whose head was bound with a bloodied bandage; another bandage covered one eye and his arm was attached to a drip.

Freddie took stock. She'd never seen so many members of staff on duty, but it still didn't seem to be enough. Head down, she hurried to the nurses' station to receive instructions on where she should go first. The hospital emergency manager, a woman in her forties with grey-flecked hair, looked frazzled and barely glanced at Freddie as she thrust a sheet of paper with the names of patients at her.

'The last shift went off an hour ago and now we've a backlog of patients waiting to be seen,' she said as if it were Freddie's fault. 'Make sure that everyone is checked in with details of their injury, then report back here. Every station is under-staffed, so be prepared to work wherever I send you.'

'Yes, ma'am,' Freddie said, and ran her eyes down the list of men, noting their names and nationalities, date and time they'd been checked in. She noted England, Canada, America and Poland. But one, at the top of the list, had no name and was described only as 'white male, mid-twenties (?), Rank: officer?' The day's date and time of arrival was recorded, but there was no further information about him.

'Excuse me, but do you know why there's no name given for this patient?' she said, pointing at the entry.

Her superior was busy briefing another nurse and didn't take too kindly to being interrupted. 'I have no idea. He was probably rushed straight to surgery. It's your job to keep track of who's who on your list, so go and find out.'

Freddie felt herself bristle at being dismissed so rudely, but held her tongue. Surely it was her manager's job to tell her which patients she should be attending to, not hers?

At that moment, Inge passed by and lightly touched her arm. 'Is everything all right?' she said with a look of concern.

'Thank goodness you're here. Tell me I'm not going mad.' Freddie gave her a weary smile and showed her the list. 'There's no name here or any information about where this man comes from. How am I meant to find him in all this chaos?' She gazed around at the waiting room, where every seat was taken; she despaired at finding him.

'I'd try the cubicles at the far end first. You might have some luck there. I'm sorry, but I have to get back before I'm missed. See you at the end of the shift?' She gave Freddie's arm a squeeze.

'Thanks, Inge,' said Freddie gratefully. She didn't feel

terribly optimistic about finding the patient, and wondered if it might not be easier to work her way through the rest of the list first. But she wasn't someone to leave a job half done, and was determined to get to the bottom of who this nameless man was.

There was a row of four cubicles, which were curtained off from the rest of the department. She approached the first two and found them empty. In the third, a young man was sitting on the side of the bed while a doctor in a white coat listened to his chest. The man's left eye was swollen shut and he had bruising across one shoulder.

'I'm sorry to interrupt, but I'm trying to find a patient whose name isn't on the list,' Freddie said, with her hand on the curtain.

'I can't help, I'm afraid,' said the doctor. 'Have you tried the end cubicle?'

Freddie gave the young patient a sympathetic look and let the curtain drop back in place. She went over to the last cubicle in the row and moved the curtain aside an inch. Peering in, she saw a patient lying flat on his back with his eyes closed. The doctor attending to him was tall with wavy white hair and wearing steel-rimmed glasses. 'Can I help you, Nurse? Come in,' he said, turning to her with a kindly expression.

'I'm Nurse Oversteegen. I'm looking for a patient who was admitted this morning, but I don't have a name for him,' said Freddie, stepping into the cubicle and drawing the curtain shut behind her. She looked at the patient. He had a gauze dressing attached to the side of his head with tape, but there were no other outward signs of any injury. She showed the doctor her list.

'Ah, I think you're in the right place,' he said. 'This young man was unconscious on arrival. We don't have many details about him, but from his uniform we know he's a British officer. Hopefully he can tell us who he is when he comes round.'

Freddie nodded. 'Thank you, Dr Akkerman,' she said,

reading the name on his white coat. Glancing at the patient, she said, 'Can you tell me anything else about his condition?'

'Certainly. He's been unconscious since he arrived and I'm keeping him under observation till he wakes. He appears to have suffered a blow to the head, but we won't know if he has any other injuries till we can examine him thoroughly. He's stable, so I don't have any concerns. I was just about to leave when you turned up. I'm needed in surgery.' He replaced the clipboard with the man's details at the end of the bed and adjusted his glasses, which had slipped down his nose. 'Nurse Oversteegen, if you have time, you might want to stay with him. I'm sure he'd prefer to have someone with him when he comes round.'

Freddie glanced at her watch and knew she should say she was too busy, but she was reluctant to leave this young man in case he woke in distress. 'I can spare a few minutes,' she said with a smile, and the doctor left.

She went and stood beside the bed and waited, watching the man's face, which looked so serene in repose. His eyelids flickered and she moved closer, but he didn't wake. Minutes passed as she kept an eye on him, noting each flicker of his eyelids and movement of his head. As she gazed at him, she wondered what terrible accident had happened to this young man that had led to him ending up here in a hospital bed. She monitored his pulse, which was normal, and then went to the foot of the bed to read the notes on his card. It didn't seem as if he was going to wake and she knew she couldn't stay by his bedside indefinitely – time was pressing and she was growing anxious to go and see to her next patient – but she didn't want this man waking up all alone, not knowing where he was. Sighing, she lifted her head, to see that he had opened his eyes and was staring straight at her. She felt a jolt of happiness, as if she'd had some part to play in his awakening. She replaced the clipboard and went over to him with a smile. Placing a hand on his forehead to check for fever, she stared down at him. His dazzling blue eyes locked on to hers and she felt a jolt of something she'd never experienced before. It was as if she'd always been waiting for this moment, and it made her melt inside. For a moment, she found it hard to tear her eyes away, then, remembering the job she was there to do, she said in English, 'Hello. How are you feeling?'

He didn't reply, just kept his eyes locked on hers, and she wondered if he had amnesia.

'What's your name?' She gave a tentative smile.

He responded by smiling back. 'Will,' he said in a croaky voice. 'Cooper.'

'Will Cooper,' she repeated and felt herself blush under his gaze. 'My name's Freddie. I'm the nurse looking after you. You've had a bad accident and you were...' she searched for the English word, 'unconscious.' She wished she could have told him more.

He blinked rapidly. 'You speak good English.'

'Just what I learned at school. I'm practising,' she said with a little laugh.

'I have a brother called Freddy. It's a boy's name.'

She laughed again, wondering why he wasn't more concerned about where he was. 'I know. But that's my name too.' She pulled herself together and dropped her eyes to his notes. 'It says here that you are an RAF officer. Is that right?'

He didn't answer but kept on staring at her.

'Can you remember anything about what happened?' she goaded gently.

He blinked several times and screwed up his face as if trying to remember, then let out a sigh. After a long moment, he said, 'Yes. I was piloting the plane and was about to turn back to England when the gunfire started. Jack... my co-pilot... my friend...' He took a gasping breath. 'The plane started to lose height. I don't remember what happened after that. I'm sorry.' He appeared confused. 'Where am I?'

'This place is Arnhem. Does that ring a bell?'

He closed his eyes briefly, then nodded. He seemed to be gathering his thoughts. 'Yes, of course. The mission was going so well. I watched the men descend after they jumped out of the plane. They were meant to be picked up by our contacts. We're part of a bigger operation to capture the bridges at Arnhem. Do you have any news on what happened?' he asked anxiously.

'I wish I did, but no. I think it's best if you try to rest. I'd like to check your temperature and blood pressure. Nothing to worry about. It's all routine.'

When she'd finished, she packed away her instruments and said, 'Everything is normal. I must go now, but a doctor will see to you soon. Is there anything else I can do for you before I go?'

'Must you go?' he said, a look of panic passing across his face.

She hesitated, torn between wanting to stay and knowing she'd be in trouble if she didn't get on with her work. 'I have to see to my other patients. If you need any help, you can press this button.' She laid the cord with the call button on the bed, then gently guided his hand to show him how to use it. His hand was warm and she felt him move it beneath hers.

'I don't want you to leave me. Can't you stay?' he implored.

'I have to go.' She didn't retrieve her hand for a long moment, not wanting to let go. 'I promise I'll be back.'

EIGHT

Freddie hurried away as if walking on a cloud of air. Had she imagined it, or had something really passed between herself and the enigmatic Englishman? They'd barely exchanged more than a few words, but she couldn't forget the way he'd looked into her eyes with an intensity that felt like an electric shock. But she knew it was unprofessional to allow her feelings to get the better of her and that she must pull herself together.

'Nurse Oversteegen! Will you come here at once?' she heard a voice bark.

She swung round at the sound of her name, suspecting that she was in for it. Glancing at the large clock above the nurses' station, she realised how long she'd spent with Will when she should have been attending to the other patients on her list. She quickly retraced her steps to where her manager was waiting and braced herself for a telling-off.

Her superior was flicking through some forms with an exaggerated flick of the wrist. 'I'll be with you in a moment,' she said, and gave Freddie a look that sent a shiver down her spine.

Chewing on her lip, she thought of Will lying on his own and wished she hadn't been so hasty in leaving him so soon after he'd come round. She had so many questions she wanted to ask him, and none were of the medical kind. Maybe after her dressing-down she'd slip back and check on him.

But she didn't get a chance, because one of the doctors appeared, his white coat open and flapping. He marched over to address her manager, saying he needed all the help he could get at the burns unit, where a number of casualties had just been admitted. Brought back to reality, Freddie knew she must throw herself into this new emergency.

'I've had special training in looking after burns patients,' she said to the doctor. 'I can go right away, that's if I'm allowed.'

The manager didn't look at all pleased, but she agreed to let Freddie go. 'I'll consult the rota and see if I can spare anyone else,' she said, pointedly addressing the doctor.

'Excellent. Come with me right away, Nurse Oversteegen, and I'll explain the extent of the men's injuries.'

Freddie followed him with a mixture of relief at being let off the hook and anxiety at the likely traumas that lay ahead.

She had never seen such horrifying injuries from burns in all the time she'd been a nurse. It was a miracle that any of these men had survived. The doctor had briefly explained that they'd been picked up at the site of a plane crash in the early hours of the morning. It was hard to imagine that they were the lucky ones and Freddie could hardly bear to think of the others who had lost their lives. Once she'd got over her shock at their disfigured faces, her nursing instincts took over and she worked diligently alongside her team to treat the men as best she could. First, they needed to establish the extent of their burns, for the men's faces had been darkened with black greasepaint and their eyebrows and hair were singed. The smell of burnt hair and flesh filled her nostrils as she worked steadily and gently to clean the muck away. She knew only too well that these men would bear scars for the rest of their lives – that was, if they lived. Refusing to let this thought take hold of her, she worked alongside the doctor until every man had been cleaned up and made comfortable with soothing antiseptic creams and soft bandages. She wished there was more she could have done for them; she could only imagine the pain they must have felt.

It was early evening and the worst was behind her. The last of the men had been transferred to the general ward to rest from their injuries. All that was left for the team was to clear up, disinfect the instruments and scrub down the operating table. It had been the worst of days, with no relief from the acute suffering they had witnessed.

The doctor in charge was at the sink, scrubbing his hands and arms up to the elbows. He spoke over his shoulder to the exhausted team. 'Today's been a tough day and a mammoth effort on everyone's part, so well done. Tomorrow is likely to bring more suffering and heartache. After all we've done to treat the casualties, it would be a tragedy if they were to fall into the hands of the Germans. We must do all we can to prevent it, but that's a problem for another day. For now, you all deserve a break. Get yourselves a hot meal in the canteen and some rest.'

Almost dizzy with exhaustion, Freddie trooped into the canteen with the rest of the burns team. Nobody had the energy to speak to one another as they queued in silence for the thick bean soup and hunks of bread, then fanned out to sit and eat by themselves. She had no desire to hold a conversation with anyone and was grateful to be left in peace to eat her meal. It was the first time she'd sat down since she'd grabbed a quick breakfast in here nearly twelve hours ago.

When she got up to go, she was cheered to see a shaft of

sunlight falling through the window and bathing the canteen in soft evening light. She made up her mind to go into the hospital garden to breathe in the scent of late summer flowers, for she needed to get away from the smell of disinfectant that clung to her nostrils and the constant hum of voices and beeping of machines that had accompanied her every waking moment.

Freddie had discovered the garden after one of her first shifts. A refuge for staff and patients alike, this peaceful space was full of shrubs and flowers, with wooden benches positioned in various places beneath shady trees. She chose a seat next to a bank of rose bushes with an abundance of fragrant blooms and sank down. She took a deep breath, inhaling the sweet scent of the roses, and closed her eyes. Immediately, the British officer swam into her mind's eye giving her an unexpectedly warm feeling as she thought of his mesmerising clear blue eyes and his cropped fair hair that framed his handsome chiselled face. She tried to remember what little she knew about him: he was a British pilot, an officer with the RAF, who had been flying his plane back to England. But what had gone so wrong as to cause such a catastrophic crash?

'Fancy seeing you here,' said a familiar voice.

Freddie looked up and saw Inge striding towards her with a wide smile on her face. She sat down and slotted her arm through Freddie's. 'How was your day?'

Freddie made a face. 'I spent the afternoon treating a group of men for severe burns. Their plane went up in flames, but they were lucky. They don't know it yet, but apparently half their unit was killed. What about you?'

Inge winced. 'I didn't fare much better. The soldiers I treated have all suffered gunshot wounds to the chest and abdomen. Apparently, they were part of the airborne operation to capture the bridges in Arnhem, but things didn't go according to plan. The Germans caught wind of it and began shooting the parachutists out of the sky – and we're now bearing the brunt of the casualties. Poor fellows. Most of them didn't stand a chance. It's really tough.' She hung her head and they sat for a moment in contemplation.

'Inge, there's something I have to tell you.' Freddie stared down at her hands clasped in her lap. It didn't seem right to be talking about her feelings with so much awfulness around them, but if she couldn't talk to Inge then who could she talk to? She found herself unable to hold back any longer; she was desperate to share her thoughts.

Inge swung her head round and looked at her in alarm. 'What's happened?'

'You know that patient, the one I didn't have a name for?'

'Oh yes, I meant to ask you about him. Did you find him?'

'Yes, I did. He was brought in unconscious, which is why I didn't have a name for him. Anyway, he came round while I was there and he told me his name was Will.' Just saying his name gave her a rush of warmth. She hesitated, struggling to put into words the way she was feeling.

'Go on,' said Inge, scrutinising Freddie's face carefully.

'Well,' Freddie began, a smile lighting up her face. 'We looked at each other and it felt as if I'd known him all my life, and all I wanted to do was to stay and care for him. It was like nothing else mattered. The thing was, I think he felt the same way about me.' She caught sight of Inge's incredulous expression. 'I know it's ridiculous and I probably imagined it, but I haven't been able to stop thinking about him. I meant to go back to find out what's happened to him, but I've been run off my feet all day. I promised him I would.'

'Goodness, that's the first bit of positive news I've heard all day. Tell me more. Is he Canadian or British?'

Freddie giggled at Inge's excitement, matched only by her own. 'I barely know a thing about him except his name and that he was knocked unconscious when his plane crash-landed, but I do know he's a British officer with the RAF. Inge, I think I—'

'You've fallen in love?' Inge butted in with a sudden laugh.

'Of course not!' lied Freddie, blushing furiously at hearing Inge say the words out loud.

'I knew it,' said Inge. 'You must go and find him immediately and tell him how you feel.'

'I can't do that,' protested Freddie. 'I'd feel such a fool if I got it all wrong.'

'What does it matter? There's a war on and everything is topsy-turvy. Who knows what's going to happen tomorrow?' Inge jumped to her feet and pulled Freddie up to standing. 'You won't know if you don't give it a try.'

NINE

Freddie hesitated before pushing open the double doors of the general ward. To think she'd been working here only the day before, oblivious to the existence of a man she'd yet to meet. A man she was sure was about to turn her life upside down.

She had never seen the ward like this, even on its busiest days, and she found the scene distressing. As well as the usual orderly rows of beds down each side, there were also rows of trolleys with patients waiting to be allocated a bed. There were so many packed in that it was hard to get from one side of the ward to the other. Patients were moaning, screaming and calling out for attention and, although the quota of nurses rushing to and fro were trying their best to attend to everyone, it just didn't seem enough to cope with the demands of a ward at full stretch.

With a feeling of mild panic, Freddie knew she should have come looking for Will earlier. She was convinced she'd never find him in this chaos. She made a quick scan of the beds and trolleys, but couldn't see any sign of him. Was he even here? She set off down the ward and was checking each of the beds' occupants when, to her dismay, she saw the senior nurse striding towards her.

'Nurse Oversteegen. Not a moment too soon. I don't have your name on the rota, but as you're here you can get to work.'

'I'm sorry – you have it wrong. I've only just finished my shift. I'm actually looking for a patient who was admitted early this morning to the emergency department. I think he may have been transferred here.'

The nurse clicked her tongue. 'So you're not here to work?' she said in irritation.

'The doctor who saw to the patient asked me to come and check on him.' Freddie spoke in a firm voice, though the doctor had said no such thing.

'I see. What is the patient's name?'

Freddie swallowed. 'Will Cooper. He's an RAF officer and he was injured in a plane crash—'

'I didn't ask you for the details. Just his name will do,' said the nurse sharply and turned on her heel. Freddie wasn't sure whether she was expected to follow her to the nurses' station, but did so all the same, still glancing all around her in case Will was indeed in one of the beds.

'There is no one called Will Cooper on this ward,' confirmed the nurse, after she had consulted her clipboard containing patient details. She frowned over her glasses, then seemed to relent. 'There are some patient rooms on floor three for special care. I would try there.'

Freddie felt sick. When she'd seen him come round, she hadn't been overly concerned for his state of health. She'd had no prior experience of a patient losing consciousness, so hadn't considered that he might have to be transferred to the special care wing as a precaution in case he suffered a relapse.

She thanked the nurse and, relieved to leave the chaos of the general ward behind her, immediately began to run in the direction of the main staircase in the centre of the hospital, taking the stairs two at a time and up several flights until she came to the third floor. Stopping to catch her breath, she saw a sign for the special care ward that pointed down a long corridor in a part of the building she hadn't been in before. When she finally got there, she went through the double doors and was struck by how quiet it was after the cacophony of the ward on the lower floor.

A nurse on the reception desk confirmed that Will was being kept under observation and directed Freddie to a corridor with typed names beside each door. Tom Freeman, John Brown – she mouthed the names to herself as she passed each door. When she saw the name Will Cooper, she felt her heart begin to flutter like a caged bird. Taking a deep breath, she knocked and put her ear to the door, but there was no answer. She opened it a fraction and peered in. She recognised him by his short fair hair, just visible above the bedclothes. He was lying turned away from her.

'Will? It's me. Freddie,' she said, her voice catching, and moved to his bedside. When he didn't stir, she gently passed a hand over his forehead. It felt cool and she was reassured that he didn't have a temperature. After a moment or two, he sucked in a long breath.

She was comforted to see him respond. 'It's Freddie. Remember I said I'd come back?'

He rolled over and blinked open his eyes. She smiled and her heart swelled – it was just like the first time he'd gazed at her with those irresistible blue eyes. Could they have really only met that same day?

'How are you feeling?' she asked.

'Better...' he said, struggling to sit up, 'for seeing you.'

Freddie smiled and felt herself relax. He remembered her, which she took to be a good sign. She plumped up his pillows to make him more comfortable.

'Sit down beside me, so we can talk,' he said, meeting her eye.

Freddie lowered herself onto the edge of the bed, knowing

that if a nurse or doctor came in now they would wonder about her motives. It was strictly against the rules to fraternise with the patients. And yet, it didn't feel as if she was doing anything wrong – she told herself she was just being friendly.

'What do you want to talk about?' she said with a shy smile.

'I want to know everything about you – how old you are, where you live, how long you've been a nurse here...'

She giggled nervously and he gave a gentle laugh. 'OK, I'll go first,' he said. 'I'm twenty-one. I qualified as a pilot two years ago with the RAF after I was sent to train in Canada for nearly a year. I've wanted to fly planes since I was a boy, and joined up as soon as I was old enough. This latest campaign has been about getting as many of our boys over to Arnhem as humanly possible. There's always a danger of being shot at, but you have to put that out of your mind and get on with the job.'

He gave a rueful smile, and Freddie could tell he was finding it difficult to recount what had happened to him the night he came down, not just because of his concussion but because of the shock of surviving the crash when others may not have been so lucky. She reached for his hand.

'You asked about me, so here goes.' She waited till she had his attention. 'I'm nineteen and I trained as a nurse in Haarlem, where my family is and where I grew up. It's quite a big place and only a few miles from Amsterdam. Do you know it?'

'Can't say I do. I've heard of Amsterdam, but then who hasn't?'

She nodded. 'Do you live in London?'

'No,' he said with a chuckle. 'Is that the only English city you've heard of?'

'Of course not,' she said indignantly, though she knew he was only teasing. She felt herself blush as he kept his eyes on her. 'I've heard of Birming-ham.'

'That's so sweet,' he said, and suddenly his hand was in

hers. 'It's Birmingham.' He spoke the word correctly. 'But it's not a place many foreigners know of, so I am impressed.'

He was teasing her again and she liked it. She also liked the feel of his hand warm in hers. 'So where do you live?'

'At the moment near an RAF base in the middle of the country. The last time I made it home was six months ago.'

'And where are you living now?'

Withdrawing his hand, he took so long replying that she wondered if his memory was failing him again. 'You definitely won't have heard of it. I currently live in a place called Saltby near the base.'

'Will you go back?' she said almost fearfully.

'I don't have much choice,' he said. 'The RAF are desperately short of pilots and it doesn't help that I didn't make it back home. But what about you? Have you always been a nurse?'

'Only since the war began. Before then I was still at school.' She gave an embarrassed laugh, knowing how young that must make her sound. 'I trained in Haarlem, and only came to this hospital a few days ago.'

'That makes two of us.' He gave her a wry smile. 'Why here?'

'It wasn't my choice. I was told they needed more nurses. I didn't want to come, but I'm glad I did now I've met you.' The words tumbled out before she realised it and she thought she'd said too much. She was a nurse, for heaven's sake, and should be behaving with restraint; but she was unable to help herself. Her cheeks grew hot with embarrassment as she stole a glance at him. She noticed the way his nose crinkled up when he smiled.

'I'm really glad I met you, and I'm not just saying that,' he said tenderly. 'Before they moved me into this room I asked the nurse if she could tell you where I was, but she didn't seem to know who you were. I thought I'd never see you again.' He frowned.

She glanced at his hand, which lay on the sheet. It was so

close to hers that it caused a physical ache inside her just looking at it. She slid her own hand across the sheet and their fingers touched.

'I promised you I'd come, didn't I?'

There was a knock at the door and Freddie sprang up and grabbed Will's notes. The door opened and an orderly came in with a tray of food, which he put on a table that he then swung across the bed. 'Your meal, sir,' he said in Dutch, and turned to stare at Freddie before giving her a cursory nod.

'Thank you,' said Will and watched as the man left the room.

They looked at each other and burst out laughing.

'I think it's time I went,' said Freddie.

'Stay with me a little longer, Nurse,' he said in a pleading voice, then gave her a wink. 'I need you to help me eat.'

They both looked at the unappetising meal, a piece of bread and butter with a minute piece of cheese next to a few slices of apple, which were turning brown. Will pushed the table aside and reached for her hand. 'On second thoughts, I'm not really hungry. Supper can wait.'

TEN

Freddie tried to see Will whenever time allowed despite working fourteen-hour shifts, but her priority was to tend to the growing number of Allied airmen who had sustained life-threatening injuries after their planes had been shot down or their parachutes failed to open. She was often called to help the doctors in surgery with complex operations to remove bullets and shrapnel from deep internal wounds, or treat severe burns to the face and torso. The hardest case she witnessed was of a young man who'd lost both his legs below the knee in a bomb attack. Freddie couldn't allow herself to dwell on the horror or scale of what they were dealing with. Her only consolation was knowing that Will had got off relatively lightly and would be waiting for her and looking forward to seeing her. Her guiltily snatched moments were all that sustained her before she had to dash back to attend to the next casualty.

With each passing day, Freddie could see Will's health improving and that it wouldn't be long before he was ready to leave the hospital. So far, they'd avoided talking about the inevitability of his leaving and had relished getting to know each other, as if that was the only thing that mattered. She had a duty to him as a nurse too, which was to ensure that he was fit and well enough to leave the hospital; but how could he leave without the Germans noticing, and where would he go? She knew only too well that he was an Allied pilot in enemy territory and would surely be a prime target. But how could she help him escape when, other than Inge, she knew nobody in this hospital well enough to ask for help? The only other person she knew she could rely on was Frans, who might have resistance contacts in Arnhem, but what good was that when he was miles away in Haarlem? Her mind spun with all the questions. Then an idea began to form in her mind. She knew this was something that only she could do and that it was probably the only way to ensure Will's safety.

It was early evening, when, with a heavy heart, she went to discuss her plan with him.

'Hello, Will,' she said, surprised to find him standing at the window looking out.

'Freddie!' he said, turning to her with a broad smile. 'Come and look at the sunset with me.'

She went and stood beside him and he slipped an arm round her waist. They watched the sun sink in the orange-and-pink-streaked sky.

'You're looking so much better,' she said, turning to gaze up at him. She marvelled at how tall he was, something she hadn't noticed all the time he'd been lying in bed.

'I feel it, except for this ankle of mine. I hadn't realised how painful it was till I tried to put my weight on it.'

'Let me take a look at it,' she said and led him to sit down on the edge of the bed so she could examine it. 'It's swollen, but that doesn't mean anything. The important thing is, do you think you can walk on it?'

Will took a moment to think before shaking his head. 'I

don't think I'd get very far if I did. The doctor said I'm to keep off it for at least another two weeks. But I can't stay in the hospital that long.' He hesitated, then went on, 'I've been thinking that the longer I stay here the more I run the risk of discovery. The Germans are bound to come looking for Allied airmen.' A small frown appeared between his eyebrows.

'Will, I have something important to tell you.' She sat herself next to him and took his hand. He looked so vulnerable. It was all she could do to stop herself from leaning in to kiss him. 'You're right – it's not safe for you to stay here. The Dutch are in charge in this hospital, but not for long. When the Germans realise how many Allied soldiers are being brought here they'll storm the place, and they won't show any mercy. I think I can help you escape but, before I tell you how, is there anyone who can help you get back to England?'

Will looked blankly at her before replying. 'Two strangers found me next to the wreckage of the plane. I knew they were Dutch from the way they spoke, and I worked out that they were from the resistance. I suppose they must have brought me here. But I don't remember anything about my crew. There were four of us – Jack, Sam, Nick and me. Jack's my best friend. We flew every mission together. All this time I've been here I haven't thought of them...'

'That's perfectly normal. You've had a bad concussion,' she said.

He nodded, but didn't look convinced. 'If I tell you their names, can you find out if they were brought here too?'

'I'll see what I can do.' She brought out a small notepad and pencil from her pocket. 'Write them down and I'll find out for you.'

His hand shook a little as he concentrated on writing in her notebook. She waited patiently till he'd finished. She needed his full attention so she could stress the urgency of the situation.

'Listen to me, Will. There may be a way to help you, but it

means I have to leave Arnhem right away. I must go back to Haarlem. I've been working with a resistance group there who have a network of contacts across the country and will find you a safe place to go – and your friends, if they're at the hospital. But I do need to leave tonight.'

Will looked panicked. 'Must you go now? If you do, I might never see you again.'

Freddie swallowed hard, but she knew she must do the right thing. 'I'm sorry, but this can't wait. Your life is in danger, and if I don't go… I can't bear thinking about it.'

He pulled her towards him and kept looking into her eyes as he did so. 'Freddie. There's something special between us. Please tell me I'm not wrong,' he murmured.

Fighting back her feelings, she shook her head, but, seeing his pained expression, realised he thought she was rejecting him. 'No. You're not wrong,' she said faintly. 'I only wish I didn't have to go.'

She put her hand into her pocket and felt for the spare velvet ribbon for her hair that she always kept there. It seemed so insubstantial and wasn't anything much at all, but it was all she had to give him as a reminder of her. The ribbon was dark blue and a strand of her hair was caught up in the fabric. She left it there and held the ribbon out to him. 'Here. I want you to have this, so you'll have something to remember me by.' She felt foolish, and found herself blushing.

'Oh Freddie. Thank you. I only wish I had something to give you.' He lifted the ribbon to his lips and kissed it. 'Will you tie it to my wrist so I don't lose it?'

They were now so close she could feel him breathing. He parted his lips and slowly began to kiss her. It was a feeling quite unlike anything she'd experienced before, as if she was sinking, melting, and she didn't want it to stop. But when it did, she found her cheeks were wet with tears.

'What's upset you, my darling?' he said, concerned, and swept away her tears with his thumbs.

'I'm not upset, I'm scared. Because I don't want to leave you, but I know I'm the only person who can get you out of this hospital to safety.'

ELEVEN

As Freddie descended the stairs two at a time, it dawned on her how rash she'd been in making a promise she didn't know she could keep. She'd let her heart rule her head and it was madness to think she could simply leave, get back to Haarlem and expect Frans to sort things out for her. Although she'd heard him talk about the network of resistance contacts that was growing throughout the country, she had no idea if he even had any links to people he could trust in Arnhem. If Frans couldn't help, she would have wasted precious time when Will was clearly unable to help himself and facing great danger from being caught by the Germans. But there was no other option.

As she reached the ground floor, her mind moved swiftly to the more urgent problem of how to ask her manager for leave when the entire hospital staff were pulling together to help the many casualties of war. She felt a pang of guilt at leaving at such a critical time, but if she didn't help Will then who else would? Still wrestling with this dilemma, she realised her absence would be sorely missed. She intended to be gone no more than a day, but how could she justify walking away from her post when so many wounded men were in dire need of help? It was less than an hour before she was due to start her evening shift and she knew her request would be refused outright.

Think, think, she told herself frantically as she hurried along the corridors, pushing her way through numerous sets of double doors, until she ended up outside the main office. *I'll say my mother has been taken seriously ill and I've had a message to return home right now*, she thought to herself, though she felt uneasy about dragging her unsuspecting mother into all this. Her mother knew that Freddie was often sent to work in hospitals far from home at a moment's notice and Freddie often left it at that. She didn't want to worry her unnecessarily, and she would have some explaining to do if her mother were to find out about the dangerous situations her daughter found herself in. And then there was Will's request to find out what had happened to his flying crew. If she could only get some answers before she headed off, she thought. Relieved to have something else to distract her, she tried the office door handle, rattled it, but found it locked. Of course, it was after hours and there would be no one there till the morning, when she would already be gone. Frustrated, she turned on her heel and headed to the nurses' quarters. She hated letting Will down, but getting back to Haarlem must be her priority right now.

It was past seven when Freddie arrived back at her shared room. She was hoping to find Inge so she could explain where she was going, but there was nobody about. As she set about packing a small overnight bag, she decided to write Inge a note. She knew she could rely on Inge to understand her need to leave so suddenly, and was sure she wouldn't tell on her.

There was a pad of writing paper and some envelopes in her bedside drawer. She quickly scribbled the note, explaining briefly where she was going and asking Inge to tell the manager she'd been taken sick and would be unable to work that night or the following day. Praying that her absence wouldn't be missed, she sealed the note in an envelope and slipped it under Inge's pillow. She then changed out of her uniform and hung it in the wardrobe she shared with two other nurses.

Dressed in her one and only plain skirt and blouse and her old dark green woollen overcoat, she was ready to go, although the next part of her plan was the bit she'd given the least thought to: how was she to get back to Haarlem and to Frans so late in the evening? What if there were no trains running? All she could think of right now was getting away from the hospital; then she could think again.

Freddie headed through the reception hall by the main entrance, which was always busy with people arriving and leaving. It was unlikely that anyone here would recognise her and, if they did, she decided she would say she was simply leaving to visit an ill relative.

She marched purposefully towards the large oak door and had just put her hand up to push it open when she heard someone behind her call her name. Expecting that it was a member of the hospital staff about to reprimand her, she stopped and turned and to see who it was; she was relieved to see Doctor Akkerman, who had treated Will in the emergency room. He was coming towards her with a friendly smile on his face.

'I'm glad to see you, Nurse Oversteegen,' he said, catching her up. 'I was wondering if you had an update on our patient, the one with concussion. How is he now?'

Freddie stared at him, her mind whirring. She knew he was referring to Will and it suddenly occurred to her that he might be able to help. 'He's fully awake and seems much better. I hope he'll soon be well enough to leave.' She leaned closer and lowered her voice. 'But that's going to be a problem. He has nowhere to go.'

The doctor nodded, as if he'd already thought of that. 'Why don't you walk with me to the car park and we can have a chat about it?' He pushed open the door for her and they climbed the stone staircase to the pavement past a group of German soldiers who were clustered near the entrance. Once clear of the building, they followed the signs to the car park.

'Have you spoken to him?' Doctor Akkerman asked when they were out of earshot of anyone who might take an interest in their conversation.

'Yes, he's aware of his situation. I said I'd do what I can to find a place for him, but I'm not entirely sure where he can go. And there will be others in his situation, possibly his crewmates. I took down their details, and if they're also at the hospital I must arrange for them to get out too before the Germans come looking.' She glanced at the doctor, unsure whether she should confide in him and tell him about her connection to the resistance. His unkempt white hair and metal-rimmed glasses gave him a congenial appearance and the impression of a man who was trustworthy. He seemed genuinely interested in Will's situation, but she'd been taught by Frans that appearances are often deceptive. The most unlikely people could turn out to be working on the side of the Nazis.

Doctor Akkerman looked thoughtful, then began telling her about his son, who was the same age as Will. 'He's my only child and I suppose I feel protective towards him. I worry when he's away for work for days at a time.' He turned his head and caught Freddie's eye. 'It's particularly troubling when I have to treat badly injured young men. I have to stop myself thinking that something similar might happen to Jan Kees.'

They turned into the car park and kept on walking until they got to his car.

'Ah, here we are. I appear to have gone on a bit.' The doctor gazed at her through his glasses. 'And how rude of me. I should offer you a lift.'

'Dr Akkerman, there's something I should tell you,' Freddie began, torn between confiding in him why she was leaving the hospital and lying to protect herself and Will. But there was something about his easy manner that made her want to unburden herself. 'I left work this evening so that I can return home to Haarlem.'

The doctor frowned. 'It's far too late for that. Can't it wait until morning?'

'No.' Freddie's voice shook. 'I know this sounds ridiculous, but, if I don't help Will and his crew right away, their lives will be in danger.'

'Come and sit inside the car where we can talk freely.' The doctor spoke with concern. He fiddled with his car key, opened his side and climbed in, then reached over to the passenger door and unlocked it from the inside.

Freddie walked round and sat down in the passenger seat. It was such a relief to sit down; then without warning her eyes welled up with tears. She quickly felt around in her pocket for a handkerchief, but the doctor presented her with his own freshly laundered white one.

'I don't think people realise how hard this job can be,' he said sympathetically, which only made her tears flow faster. 'There are times when I come back to my car and sit here for half an hour or more before I can bring myself to drive home.'

'Do you have anyone waiting for you?' said Freddie, still with tears in her voice.

'No. Not any more. My dear wife passed away at the start of the war. At least I have my job to keep me going, even if there are times that I think about giving it up.' He looked at Freddie with sad eyes. 'Now tell me why you want to get back to Haarlem so urgently.'

Freddie took her time answering. As she blew her nose, she convinced herself that she had nothing to lose by telling him her plans. If she didn't, then how would she know what he could do for her?

She turned her head to look at him. He gave her a little nod to continue. 'Before I came to Arnhem, I worked at the hospital in Haarlem, but I also work for the resistance with my sister. We do a lot of undercover courier work and find places for people who need to hide from the Germans. I thought if I went back to Haarlem, my boss could use his influence to find somewhere for Will to stay until it's safe for him to return to England. But now I'm sitting here in your car I see it's a mad idea. The truth is, I don't know what else I can do.' She covered her face in her hands, overwhelmed by the fix she'd landed herself in.

'I may have a solution, Miss Oversteegen.'

'Please call me Freddie,' she said into her hands.

'I will, if you call me Hans.'

She dropped her hands and saw he was smiling. She blew her nose again and felt better for it.

'I can't promise anything, but Jan Kees may be able to help,' he said. 'Jan Kees works with the underground at designated drop zones to pick up English, American and Canadian parachutists. As soon as they're on the ground they're vulnerable to being captured, so he brings them to safe houses, mainly farms out in the country. You'd be surprised how many people want to do their bit for the Allies, especially with all the successes they've had in pushing back the Germans.'

'Surely he doesn't work on his own?' said Freddie, trying to comprehend the danger he must be putting himself in with so many Germans scouting for Allied men on the ground.

'There are several others in his cell, all trusted members of the same underground network. Jan Kees is also in charge of establishing new recruits and vetting them. There's no shortage of offers of help, but he can't be too careful who he takes on. One false move and the whole operation would be at risk. Jan

Kees is meticulous and hasn't run into any problems yet. If you allow me, I'll speak to him right away. If he can't help, I'm sure he knows someone who can. And you won't need to go back to Haarlem.'

Hearing the doctor describe his son's clandestine operation to save Allied soldiers sounded almost too good to be true. Freddie knew that time was of the essence and she couldn't waste any more time by going back to Haarlem on the off chance Frans could help. Relying on the doctor's son was a risk she had to take if the men were to get out of the hospital before it was seized by the Germans. She knew this was Will's only hope, and that he was far from being out of danger.

The doctor persuaded her to go back inside and work her shift as if nothing had happened. He promised to take care of everything and let her know the outcome as soon as he had word from his son.

As Freddie walked past a German soldier in position at the front door and back inside the hospital, she had mixed feelings about whether she was doing the right thing by placing her trust in this doctor she barely knew. What if his son was too busy to help? Glancing at her watch, she saw she was just in time for her shift if she got a move on. No time to go and tell Will about this plan now, she thought regretfully. Remembering how his kiss made her feel, she wanted nothing more than to sink into the safety of his arms once more.

TWELVE

Will

'Wake up!'

Will jumped at the deep man's voice bellowing in his ear. Instantly he was gripped by fear. He focused his gaze and found two men standing over his hospital bed pulling back the covers. Who were these men and where had they come from? He tried to grab hold of the sheet in a vain attempt to shield himself from them. He remembered Freddie showing him the alarm button. In his panic, he fumbled for the cord, but it wasn't there – it must have slipped to the floor.

'Quick! You must come with us now,' urged one of the men, speaking English with a thick Dutch accent.

Will's eyes darted fearfully between the men, who both had on dark clothes and caps pulled low over their foreheads. It made them look so sinister... why should he believe them?

'We will help you,' the man who'd spoken added, as if he'd read Will's mind. Before he could answer, they put their hands under his arms and heaved him to his feet.

Will sucked in his breath as a sharp pain shot from his ankle up his leg. 'I can't walk,' he gasped, shocked at how debilitated he felt. He'd always been so confident and fearless, a first-class soldier who threw himself into every fitness test and always passed with flying colours. Nothing ever fazed him and he was always convinced he could take on anything. But now, looking down at his ankle, he was dismayed at finding himself so diminished and feeling so frightened. He couldn't even remember how long he'd been in this place. Then he thought of Freddie, beautiful Freddie, the girl he'd only just met, and their kiss before she'd left. Had it all been a dream? Despair washed over him, for if she'd been real she would surely be here now.

'Listen to me,' said the man, putting his face up close to Will's. 'The Germans are outside the front door of the hospital. They are on their way, so you must come with us now. Don't worry. We'll get you out.'

Will nodded, not really understanding what was happening. Wasn't Freddie meant to be helping him? If it were true and the Germans were coming, he was in no fit state to get out of here unaided. And he was sure he wouldn't manage it on this wrecked ankle.

'Here. Put these on,' said the other man, pulling out some clothes from a knapsack and handing them to him. Will eyed them suspiciously, noting that they were the same dark colour as the men were wearing. It didn't bode well, he thought with a shiver of fear, and refused to take them. But when he didn't cooperate, they started dressing him like a child, sitting him back down on the bed, pulling on the trousers over his hospital garb – the trousers were too big – and fastening them with a belt. Then everything went black as they tugged the sweater over his head, and then his head was through, followed by his arms. A pair of shoes that were beside his bed – whose where they? – were eased onto his feet.

'Let's go,' said the first man, when he was satisfied that Will was able to walk.

'Where are we going?' said Will, bewildered by this sudden turn of events. He had so many questions but didn't know where to start.

'We'll tell you later,' said the second man, who was at the door and looking up and down the corridor. 'Come on. We need to go.'

Will stood in the doorway feeling completely disorientated. It was the first time he'd been outside this room. Where were the nursing staff? Where *was* Freddie?

It was small relief that the men seemed to know where they were going. They marched him down a long corridor, through some swing doors; then a door to their left suddenly opened and a tall man wearing a dark blue gaberdine coat stepped out in front of them.

'Ah, I was wondering when you'd get here,' he said, and Will realised he was English. He had the distinct feeling he might even know him, but had no idea where from.

'We need to leave straight away, before the Germans storm the building,' said one of the men. Will was still trying to think who the man in the blue coat was, but there was no time for questions. He finally understood – they needed to get out of the building, fast.

One of the others tugged Will by the sleeve towards a door that led onto a concrete stairwell. 'Don't make a sound,' he whispered, after checking to make sure there was no one coming up the stairs. But it was difficult to be quiet; their footsteps clattered as they descended the winding staircase. Will held on to the metal balustrade and tried his best to go as fast as the men wanted him to, but his legs were weak and he had to stop every few steps in order to take the weight off his ankle.

At last, the four men reached the bottom and were faced with a grey-painted door. Will looked at each of the men questioningly, guessing that the door led outside and towards impending danger. He held his breath as the Englishman stepped forward and opened the door. A strong breeze almost blew it shut again, but he managed to hold it firm.

In the distance came the noise of sirens, revving engines and the tat-a-tat of gunfire. Will picked up the sound of someone shouting through a loudhailer but couldn't make out what language he was hearing. He stood frozen in the doorway as he strained to hear.

Suddenly, the words reached him, loud and clear. 'The British are in control. Put down your guns immediately.'

'The British are here...' Will began to say, but he was being pulled roughly out across the empty courtyard towards a black car waiting at the side of the road. His ankle felt as if it was on fire with the pain, but he managed to ignore it and forced himself to keep up with the others. These men had come to rescue him and he mustn't hold them up.

Everything was going to be all right, he told himself. Breathing heavily, he threw himself onto the back seat. Moments later, the driver who'd been waiting for them started up the car and pulled away.

The Englishman sat in the front passenger seat and turned to Will to introduce himself. 'Flight Sergeant Villiers of the First Parachute Battalion. And you must be Flight Lieutenant Will Cooper.' He held out his hand and smiled.

Will took it, as it dawned on him where he'd last seen Flight Sergeant Villiers. It was in the officers' mess at RAF Saltby when he'd addressed the squadrons, telling them they would be responsible for parachute drops who were part of the airborne invasion of Holland. He remembered his voice now, authoritative and so confident that his men would succeed. It was a rousing speech, but he'd given no indication that he'd be flying that night as well. Will had left the mess with Jack, Nick and Sam at his side, the four of them slapping each other's backs and engaging in the usual banter prior to taking off. The positive feeling that they were on a mission that could not fail had lasted until the last of the men had jumped from the plane and they were preparing to head back over the English Channel and home. He remembered nothing more after that.

THIRTEEN

Freddie

Freddie was finishing up setting a young American parachutist's broken leg and was listening to his chatter. She learned his name was Joe, that he came from Michigan and his dream after the war was to be a pilot for commercial aircraft, following in the footsteps of his father. He said he couldn't wait to get back to his fiancée, whom he'd promised to marry as soon as the war was over. 'Which will be soon, right?' He looked hopefully into Freddie's eyes, as if she would know the answer. As a nurse, she'd come to expect questions like this from the scores of wounded parachutists and soldiers she saw, and always did her best to answer them as positively as she dared.

'I'm sure it won't be long now,' she said with a smile. 'But first, we need to get you back on your feet as soon as possible.' Her heart went out to this young man who despite his injuries could be so optimistic about his future.

She quickly glanced at the clock. She was impatient for the end of her shift so she could go and tell Will about Dr Akkerman's plan. She longed to see him, but dreaded having to tell him that she'd searched for his crewmates' names amongst the casualties brought in over the past two days but had found nothing. It wasn't the news he'd be hoping for, but she'd already decided to say it wasn't necessarily bad, that they might have been picked up by the resistance and taken somewhere safe. She knew she had to be upbeat for Will's sake, as she needed to prepare him for the difficulties that lay ahead.

But for now she needed to focus on her work, despite the challenges. She'd lost count of the number of casualties brought in overnight, and suspected something unusual was going on, but didn't allow herself to speculate on how badly the Allied military operation at Arnhem was going.

Freddie went to the store cupboard to fetch a pair of crutches for Joe. Once he'd got the hang of them, she knew she would have to discharge him, as there was a room full of patients still waiting to be seen. It had been the same all day. Those who had relatively minor injuries couldn't stay, but each time she assessed a patient to be fit to leave she dreaded having to tell them. Who would there be to care for their safety once they ventured outside where war was raging? She mulled over the possibility of asking Dr Akkerman for Jan Kees's help, but admitted to herself that it was unrealistic to go running to him every time she'd nursed a patient back to health.

'Here you are, Joe. These crutches should get you moving again,' she said kindly, and Joe's face lit up at the prospect. Since his arrival, he hadn't once complained, though she guessed his broken leg must have caused him considerable pain.

Freddie showed him how to use the crutches and helped him walk up and down the corridor. He quickly got the hang of them and soon she was running beside him to keep up. He joked that with these things he'd be able to escape from the Germans faster than if he didn't have them. She laughed and was about to say that he didn't need her help walking any more when an enormous boom came from somewhere deep inside the hospital. It wasn't close by, she thought with relief, but, if the explosion was a bomb, she knew that people would be injured or even killed. She knew she had to do all she could to save the patients she was caring for. Joe was the nearest, wobbling dangerously on his crutches; she went to stop him from falling, but he overbalanced, bumping heavily against her and causing them both to crash to the floor. His weight on top of her was considerable and he seemed unable to move himself.

'Sorry, sorry,' he kept repeating over and over.

All around them was pandemonium as more people were thrown to the floor. Others scattered in all directions and the screams of panic were deafening.

Freddie managed to disentangle her arm, which she used to drag herself free before attending to Joe. 'Are you all right?' she said, peering down at his pale face. She gently slapped his cheek.

'Yup,' he said at last, 'but I don't know if my leg would agree.' He grimaced in pain.

'Your leg is in plaster and will be fine. I'm sure of it,' she said, relieved.

She was helping him to his feet when one of the medical team came bursting into the ward. 'The Germans have launched an attack and are gathering in large numbers at the front of the hospital,' the man said. 'The British army are there too and have managed to rebuff their attacks, but we can't take anything for granted. We know the Germans are responsible for the bomb attack. The damage is minor, but it's only prudent that we evacuate all patients as quickly as possible in the event of another bomb blast. The porters will help with wheelchairs and stretchers. Everyone must leave the building by the back and make their way to the stores building behind the canteen.'

Freddie helped Joe into a chair and told him to wait for her while she went to assist the other nurses and porters who were working frantically to move patients, some lying comatose on trolleys, others attached to drips or in need of blood transfusions. No one was left behind.

Freddie was one of the last to leave, pushing a soldier with bandaged legs and his arm in a sling, and joined the long procession of staff in charge of wheelchairs and trolleys. A few patients were being carried on stretchers. She saw Joe some yards ahead of her in the corridor, walking more confidently now on his crutches, and she smiled. Then she noticed he was chatting cheerfully to a nurse who was pushing a wheelchair and saw that it was Inge.

'Inge – it's me, Freddie!' she called out.

Her friend had just twisted her head round to smile, when there was another deafening explosion up ahead that seemed to rock the very fabric of the building. Chunks of plaster came showering down from the ceiling, causing people to scream and shout out in alarm.

'Get down!' yelled the young doctor leading the group.

Freddie crouched down and put one hand protectively over her charge's head, the other over her own. Then she heard a sickening crack from above. She lifted her head and saw it all just before the lights went out – the doctor and those around him disappearing under an avalanche of falling masonry and furniture from the floor above.

And then there was total darkness.

Freddie felt her stomach plunge, for she knew that Inge had been in front of her and that she'd been close to the doctor. As had Joe.

There was a rumble and more debris and rubble came pouring down from the gaping hole where the ceiling had been.

Freddie took ragged gasps of air as she checked to make sure her patient hadn't been injured, then crawled forward to the place she thought Inge and Joe had been. She began frantically pulling aside chunks of masonry. Her hand touched something metal, and she guessed it was the side of a wheelchair. Feeling her way up onto the seat, she realised it was empty. Was it the one Inge had been pushing? Where was she?

All around her people were now crying or moaning in pain, but she kept on searching. She managed to lift the wheelchair free. At first, she didn't notice that someone was beside her and grabbing at the belt of her uniform. And then she thought she heard her name being whispered, ever so faintly.

'Inge...' Freddie hardly dared believe it was her. 'Are you hurt?'

'I think I'm fine. But I don't think my patient made it,' Inge said, her voice wobbling. 'He must have been thrown from the wheelchair by the explosion. It must have saved me.'

'And the patient on crutches... the one who was speaking to you?'

Inge made a whimpering sound. Freddie gathered her friend up in her arms and they clung to one another. All around them was devastation. She knew for certain that Joe hadn't stood a chance and that he would never make it back to the girl he loved.

FOURTEEN

The first signs that help was on its way came from the beams of light that bounced erratically off the walls, floor and the broken ceiling, and the rescuers calling out instructions to those trapped in the corridor.

'Over here!' Freddie lifted her head in their direction. She was working tirelessly alongside Inge, who had miraculously escaped without injury, to free people from the rubble. Each rescued person felt like a minor victory. Her hands hurt so hard from the scraping and scrabbling, but she refused to give up hope in case others were alive.

More rescuers arrived and the beams from at least a dozen torches bobbed over the scene of utter devastation. Freddie raised her hand to indicate where she was and two men from the hospital staff crunched their way towards her.

'We can take over here. You should make your way back where it's safe,' said one of the men, his eyes darting from Freddie to Inge. The other man went straight in and began lifting away lumps of plaster and masonry.

'No. Not while there are still people who need our help,' Freddie said firmly. She dragged a hand through her hair. It felt heavy and greasy with dust, but that was the least of her worries.

Inge touched her sleeve. 'I'm so tired. I'm going back,' she said. Her face looked ghostly pale in the half-light and Freddie realised the toll this whole affair must have taken on her friend.

'Do you want me to come?' she asked. She felt torn between making sure Inge received support and continuing with the rescue effort.

'No, I'll be fine.' Inge smiled weakly.

They hugged for a long moment, then Freddie watched Inge move away, carefully lifting her feet as she picked her way back towards the main hospital building.

'Can we have more assistance over here?' called a man's voice.

Freddie's heart leapt as she realised he was close to where Joe had been when the bomb had gone off. 'Coming!' she shouted. She had to step cautiously over a precarious mound of bricks and plasterwork to reach the man, who was pulling something free. She gasped when she saw a crutch emerge from the rubble.

'I think I know who it belongs to,' she said. 'Did you find anyone close by?'

'Not yet, but we're working on it,' he said, and tossed a wooden chair that had lost two of its legs to one side.

Freddie stood nervously and watched the man extract a second crutch. He continued to dig down. Nothing happened for several minutes. And then he straightened up. 'He's young. Right leg in plaster. Fair hair,' he said matter-of-factly.

Freddie felt her chest constrict as she forced herself to take a step forward to see. She looked upon the body of a man who lay with his head twisted away from her. She knew straight away that it was Joe. She dropped to her knees and laid a hand on his cooling forehead. 'Poor Joe. You didn't deserve this. Rest in peace,' she whispered.

.   .   .

When the living had all been taken back to the main hospital, the rescuers thanked everyone who had helped and told them to go back inside.

Freddie slowly got to her feet and carefully rubbed the dirt from her bloodied hands. Every inch of her body ached. She could barely think straight as she watched the line of weary helpers slowly make their way back.

The doors to the emergency room had been propped open and a table had been put up serving tea and biscuits. Freddie joined the queue and shuffled forward, waiting her turn. She was surprised to see Dr Akkerman pouring cups of hot tea from a large metal teapot and handing them out with a few words of encouragement and a smile. Despite the horrors of everything she'd witnessed that night, to see him here made her heart lift.

'Hello, Dr Akkerman,' she said when it was her turn in the queue.

He was concentrating on not spilling the hot liquid and took a moment to look up.

'Freddie, it's you,' he said, and pushed his glasses up his nose to get a better look at her. She liked that he called her by her first name and felt grateful for this small gesture. He went on, 'I hoped to see you here. I'm so glad to see you made it out.' He didn't say 'alive', but she knew that was what he meant.

It's good to see you too,' she said, adding, 'Sadly, the patient I'd been attending to didn't make it.'

He nodded and handed her a cup and a biscuit. 'Drink up. You'll feel better for it.' He looked over her head and saw that she was the last person in the queue. 'Were there any others behind you?'

'No, I don't think so,' she said, glancing over her shoulder.

'We knew that the doctor and patient he was escorting bore the brunt of the explosion. There were five more casualties. I suspect many more will have injuries.' His face seemed to sag with sadness.

Freddie quickly checked again that no one was listening. She leaned in. 'Dr Akkerman, I'm so worried for Will's safety. He'll never escape now this has happened. What can we do?'

'I've got some news on that. I spoke to Jan Kees, who said he'd arrange to get Will out but needed to brief the staff about the plan—'

Freddie interrupted him. 'When was this? Where is Will?'

'Please, let me finish. After the first bomb went off, I was on the other side of the hospital and ran straight up to the third floor to see if he was still there, but his room was empty. I can only believe Jan Kees managed to get him out before all hell let loose, but I haven't been able to confirm it yet. Then as I was coming back down the central staircase, the second bomb went off. My instinct told me to get to where I'd be needed most, so I came straight here.' He took his glasses off so he could wipe his eyes.

'So you don't actually know whether Will escaped?' She was now shaking with worry.

'There's nothing to suggest he didn't. I saw his room was empty before the second bomb went off.'

Freddie took deep breaths and nodded several times to convince herself that all would be well. She kept staring at the doctor, desperate for his reassurance.

'I wish I had more positive news, but I'm afraid this is all I know,' he said. 'We can only hope that Jan Kees has managed to get him out.'

FIFTEEN

Will

The car in which Will was travelling was already on the main road heading north when the bomb hit the St Elisabeth Hospital in Arnhem. Will was none the wiser, and it was probably for the best, otherwise he would have wanted to turn back and find Freddie. There were a lot of things Will didn't understand at that moment. What had happened to his crew members, where he was being driven, who the other three men in the car were and why his flight sergeant was with them. It was all a mystery and he wondered if it was the concussion that was causing him so much confusion. The only thing that was crystal clear to him was Freddie, her wonderful reassuring presence as he'd held and kissed her for the first – and possibly – last time.

Will had no time to dwell on his sudden rescue, if that was what it was, for the British sergeant was talkative and eager to fill him in on the details of the mission that had taken place five nights ago. Out of the ten planes that had left the base, two had failed to return. The sergeant only learned this after his own plane had developed engine trouble and the pilot had managed to land it safely.

'I happened to be on the tenth sortie, but of course we had no idea you hadn't made it back at that point. We didn't find out till later.' Flight Sergeant Villiers spoke in a matter-of-fact tone of voice.

'When you addressed us in the mess hall, why didn't you mention you'd be coming with us?' Will was feeling better now they were on the move, relieved that the sergeant's account of that night's events was helping with his own memory of the crash.

'You're quite right. I wasn't down to fly that night. I'd had a long day on maintenance and was inspecting the planes. I was hoping for an evening back at base when I was given a message that one of my men had suddenly been taken ill and wasn't able to fly. They urgently needed an experienced co-pilot and asked me to step in.'

'Wasn't there anyone else who could have taken your place?' asked Will.

'No. We were down several men that night because of two losses the night before.' He glanced at Will, who nodded in understanding, even though he hadn't known about it before he'd set off with his own crew.

The sergeant went on, 'Of course I agreed, and everything was going smoothly. Twenty-four men on board all jumped safely. We were on the way back when one of the engines juddered and cut out and we began rapidly losing height. It didn't make any sense as it had passed the inspection tests that day. Fortunately, we were flying above a vast flat landscape, so Sid was able to land her in a field without a problem. But we knew we were vulnerable. Our next worry was that the Jerries would have heard the engine giving out and come looking for us. So we all got out as quick as we could and ran for cover under some trees.'

'We were in the area searching for paratroopers blown off course,' explained Jan Kees. 'We saw the plane come down and ran over to help.'

The sergeant gave him an appreciative smile. 'None of us was injured, but as they were taking others to the hospital we went along too. Once there, I immediately set to work helping the Brits running the place to keep it out of the hands of the Jerries. It was a tense time. The Jerries were massing at the door and I knew I wouldn't stand a chance if they found me there. When you all turned up I saw my chance to get out.'

Jan Kees tapped the driver on the shoulder, gave him an instruction in Dutch and pointed to a turning off the main road. They were soon bumping along a narrow potholed track.

'When are you going to tell me where we're going?' Will asked Jan Kees. He felt his anxiety returning in a rush. Even the presence of his superior in the car wasn't enough to calm him.

'Didn't they tell you?' said the sergeant, sounding surprised. 'I thought you knew.'

'No. Nobody's told me anything. I was lying in a hospital bed recovering from concussion when these two burst in and demanded I leave immediately. It all happened so fast and now I'm here. I still don't have a clue what's going on.'

'This is where you'll be staying,' said Jan Kees, as the car slowed to turn in to a large farmyard surrounded by a series of barns and outbuildings, a tractor and an old pickup truck. In the centre stood the farmhouse, whose steep thatched roof hung so low it almost touched the ground. 'Come inside and you can meet the others.'

Jan Kees jumped out of the car before Will could ask him anything further. Will got out at the same time as the sergeant and together they walked to the house.

'You'll be wondering why I've come along,' said the sergeant, glancing at Will.

The truth was, Will wasn't wondering that at all; he was

thinking more about these other people he was about to meet. And whether, by some miracle, Jack, Sam and Nick would be amongst them.

'I'm here to organise getting you all out in the next couple of days,' the sergeant went on. 'It shouldn't take any longer than that. You'll be back home before you know it. A quick debrief and then it'll be back to work.' He chuckled to himself, then gave Will a slap on the back and went ahead through the open door.

Will felt oddly deflated at the prospect of going home. Once he was airborne again, he wondered if he'd ever see Freddie again.

'Wait here a minute,' said the sergeant and followed Jan Kees into the large kitchen, where Will heard the two of them fall into conversation with the farmer and his wife. He wasn't sure what he was meant to do. He glanced around and noticed how neat and tidy the place was, with just a couple of old coats hanging next to the door and two pairs of dirty clogs on a shoe rack. There were no signs of anyone else staying at the farmhouse. He guessed this must be a deliberate ploy in case the Germans came snooping for people in hiding.

The farmer came out of the kitchen, smiling broadly, and held his hand out to Will. He was a stocky man of about forty with thinning grey-blond hair. 'I'm Karel,' he said in English, 'and this is my wife Tineke.'

A small fair-haired woman with a kind face appeared at his side and shook Will's hand.

'I'm Will. Thank you for letting me stay,' he said.

'It's no problem,' the farmer said. 'You boys are doing a difficult and dangerous job saving our country from the Germans. Without you, things would be so much worse than they are already. We are very grateful, so it's the least we can do. Come into the kitchen and eat some supper, then we'll show you where you'll be sleeping.'

The five men sat round the kitchen table while Tineke served them bowls of vegetable soup with bread. Will hadn't realised how hungry he was, but found himself wolfing down his food. He listened to the farmer explain that he had been taking in *onderduikers*, as he described the people he was sheltering, since the onset of hostilities leading up to Arnhem. 'I got involved as soon as I heard about the operation to drop airmen over Arnhem. The resistance groups came asking for local people to put them up.'

Jan Kees nodded, and said, 'We're picking up British, Americans and Poles who've missed their target and are in danger of getting caught. They need places to wait it out until they can return home. We needed people fast and Karel offered to help.'

'Because I have a large farmhouse that's in the middle of nowhere. The Germans never think to come looking here,' Karel added, exchanging a glance with his wife. 'But we're not the only ones. Most farmers round here are doing their bit.'

Will was only half listening to the conversation, which kept lapsing into Dutch when Jan Kees's men joined in. He was finding it hard to keep his eyes open. His ankle throbbed and he longed to put it up. He suppressed a yawn. He was aware he still wasn't back to his normal self. A moment later, or so it seemed, he felt a tap on his shoulder and realised he'd been dozing. Tineke, standing over him, said she would take him up and show him where he would be sleeping.

It wasn't until Will woke up early the next morning that he appreciated how large the attic room was. He counted eight camp beds, including his own, and they were all occupied by men who were fast asleep. Will sat up and stretched his arms above his head. He felt surprisingly well rested; almost normal, he thought, until he swung his legs over the side of the bed and remembered his sprained ankle. He gazed down at it and saw it had swelled overnight – he was sure he wouldn't be able to get his shoe on, and hoped he wouldn't be made to run anywhere soon.

'Hello,' said a man with an American drawl. He had propped himself up onto his elbows to get a better look at Will. 'You must be the new guy. I heard you come in last night. I'm George, by the way. I'm from Kansas.'

'Pleased to meet you, George. I'm Will and I'm stationed at a place you won't have heard of in England.' He gave him a wry grin.

'Try me,' said George.

Will laughed. 'No one knows it. It's a tiny village called Saltby.'

'Uh... no,' said George with a shake of his head.

'Did you say Saltby?' came a sleepy voice from across the room.

Will's heart gave a thump of recognition. 'Nick! I can't believe it.' He heaved himself up and managed to hobble over, sitting down heavily on his bed. 'How long have you been here?'

Propping himself up on his elbows, Nick gave Will a broad grin. 'Since the night we crashed. They brought me straight here. They told me you'd been taken to hospital. Are you all right, mate?' He looked down at Will's swollen ankle.

'So-so,' said Will. 'I didn't know I'd hurt my ankle until I came round. From concussion. I don't remember hitting my head, or how I got there. How did you get out of the plane?'

'I was lucky and got out moments before it went up,' Nick pursed his lips. 'But Jack... and Sam...' He took a sharp intake of breath. 'They didn't make it.'

'Oh God, no. Can you be so sure?' He searched Nick's face, hoping he'd made a mistake.

'I'm afraid so. I saw them... you don't want to know. I know how close you and Jack were,' said Nick, dropping his gaze to the floor.

Will tried to hold it together, but his cheeks felt wet with tears. He swiped a hand across his face and took a deep breath. 'It's just you and me then,' he said in a shaky voice.

'Yeah. It's just you and me,' said Nick and gave him a wobbly smile.

Will sighed and looked around. 'Except you'll never guess who came with me last night.'

Nick shook his head and shrugged.

'Old Villiers. He said he was going to get us home.'

Nick's eyes widened. 'Never! What the hell's he doing here?'

'Same as us, apparently. He was called to fly at the last minute when one of the crew called in sick. Says he was at the hospital helping the British.' Will raised an eyebrow.

'Well, good luck to him. He's not the first person to have some grand plan to evacuate us. The Americans are better organised at getting their people home.'

Will nodded, but his mind had wandered back to Freddie and he thought that if he couldn't get back home he would definitely go and find her. 'Nick, I met someone at the hospital.'

'Don't tell me. He promised you a flight home.' Nick hit his forehead in mock exasperation.

Will laughed. 'No, nothing like that. She's a nurse, Dutch, and we immediately hit it off. And then I had to leave. Honestly, Nick, it's like the whole thing was a dream.'

'You met a girl you like?'

'Yeah. More than like. And she feels the same way about me... I think.'

'Did you say you had concussion?' Nick gave him a playful punch.

'I did. I don't care if you don't believe me. I know it was real and I have to do whatever it takes to get back to her.'

SIXTEEN

The number of men hiding at the farmhouse fluctuated, but as far as Will could work out the farmer always made room for new arrivals. Shortly after he had arrived, another four American soldiers turned up in the middle of the night, and by morning two more had left. Despite assurances from the flight sergeant to the British contingent that it wouldn't be long till they got home, he was unable to give them a date for their departure, which was, he said, dependent upon the resistance operatives providing safe escape routes. Not just that. Operation Market Garden wasn't going according to plan and there were too many downed men waiting to be rescued.

For the most part, the men were unconcerned and bided their time, knowing their fate lay in the hands of strangers who had the power to get them out. Because there were so many of them, the farmer had drawn up rules to stop the men from wandering around the farmhouse or walking outside where they might be seen, if not by Germans, then by anyone who couldn't be trusted to keep quiet. They were allowed downstairs during the day to eat and help Karel and Tineke with chores. As a security measure, there would always be two of them on guard at the

front and back of the house. The rest of the time they were
confined to the attic, where they occupied themselves with card
games, chatted, or else lay on their beds, bored, as they waited
for something to change. Will quickly realised it wasn't just
their safety the farmer was concerned about, but his own.
Hiding such a large number of Allied soldiers was exceptionally
risky, even in a place as remote as this. If caught, he would
almost certainly be arrested and probably be sent to a German
concentration camp, where the conditions were said to be
brutal.

Will was on guard duty with George at the back door. Will sat
on the step resting his ankle while George stood surveying the
margins of the fields for any movements. After a few minutes,
George took a packet of Camel cigarettes out of his shirt pocket
and held it up. Will shook his head and watched George light
his cigarette using his metal lighter. He listened as George told
him how he'd been stationed at one of the bases in England. A
pilot like himself, George had taken part in a successful mission
to capture a strategic area from the Germans in the south of the
country at Eindhoven. No sooner was he back at base than he'd
been sent to drop paratroopers close to key bridge-crossing
points at Arnhem.

'The first of our guys was about to jump when we were
attacked,' said George, sucking on his cigarette and exhaling the
smoke with a sigh. 'The bastards well and truly got us and the
plane came down fast. It was a miracle we got out before it went
up in flames. Nobody was badly injured, so we ran. I'm a fast
runner and made straight for a copse of trees a couple of
hundred yards away. Then I realised the others weren't behind
me. They'd been ambushed by a bunch of Krauts who'd sprung
out of nowhere. I was terrified they'd seen me and kept myself
well hidden. I had to watch the rest of my crew being rounded

up and marched away. I waited I don't know how long – it could have been hours – and it was well after dark when I saw the outline of two men running towards the wreckage of the plane. "Hello. Is anyone in there?" they called in English. I thought they could have been German and I didn't know whether to trust them. Anyway, what alternative did I have? So I called out. Turns out they were Dutch. Called Piet and Dirk. They brought me here.' He took another drag on his cigarette and Will watched him blow out a row of perfect smoke rings.

'Piet... I was rescued by someone called Piet,' Will said as the name of the Dutchman who had found him came to him. 'Do you think it could be the same person?'

George grinned. 'Yeah, I bet it is. Goes by the name of Piet van Arnhem. He's a hero in these parts and leads one of the resistance cells. Is that who brought you here?'

'No, it was someone else, called Jan Kees. I got the impression he's also big in the resistance.'

'That's right. The two of them are in charge of the operation to get us out of the way of the Germans. But it's a slow business with no guarantee of success. There are just too many of us and not enough of them, and the chances of getting caught are high. I guess we just have to play a waiting game till we get home.'

Will nodded, but he hadn't given any thought to how he'd return to England. He knew it was unlikely to be straightforward, not while there was still a war on. He'd heard of colleagues trapped in enemy territory and that it could take weeks to cross into the liberated south, and even then there were obstacles to getting home. It wasn't something he wanted to dwell on right now. 'My friend Nick says the Americans are better organised at getting their people out. How long have you been here?' he asked instead.

George scoffed. 'Dunno where he heard that. I've been here over a week. It's frustrating, but it's out of our hands. Piet said his men are in touch with ours and they're preparing to get us out, but the plans keep changing. Let's hope your guys do a better job than ours have.' He blew out a final plume of smoke and stubbed out his cigarette. 'Hey, did you hear what happened at the hospital in Arnhem?'

Will was brought up short. He took in a sharp breath. 'No. Tell me.' He felt his chest constrict, dreading that it was bad news concerning Freddie.

'It was bombed a couple of days ago. Isn't that where you were? You were lucky to get out.'

Will was suddenly gripped by a fear that Freddie had been there when the bomb went off.

George gave him a sympathetic look. 'Hey, buddy, you've gone quite pale. What's up?'

'Who told you this?' Will refused to believe it was true.

'Karel. I think he heard it from one the guys he's in touch with. I'm sorry. It must be a shock seeing as you were there.'

'No, it's fine. It's just that someone dear to me works there. Do you have any more details?'

'That's too bad, you knowing someone. Honest, I don't know any more than I told you. Do you want to tell me about them?'

Will couldn't help but smile as his thoughts were pulled back to Freddie again, the beautiful Dutch girl with the dimpled smile who had put a charm on him. He touched the ribbon, still tied to his wrist, his only tangible connection to her. If only he'd had something of his own to give her, he thought regretfully. Then he remembered their conversation. She said she would help him escape from the hospital and that she was going to Haarlem to arrange it. Briefly, he closed his eyes in relief. Surely she must have left before the bomb. But what if she hadn't? All he wanted was to go back and find out, but he knew it would be impossible. Men had risked their lives to help him escape and it was his duty as an RAF pilot to get back home and report for duty.

He opened his eyes to find George studying his face, waiting for an answer. 'Her name's Freddie and she's a nurse. I've never met anyone like her before.'

He suddenly stood up, his mind made up. 'I'm sorry, but I must write to her straight away. Do you mind...?'

'Course not. She sounds like one helluva special girl,' said George with a wink.

SEVENTEEN

Freddie

The Germans took swift control of the hospital and ordered all British military staff to be removed. No one knew where they'd gone, but there were rumours that the officers were being transported to the concentration camps. German medical staff were brought in to help the Dutch teams left behind, and allowed them to continue their work tending to the influx of wounded Allied men.

The mood on the wards was still one of shock when Freddie returned to work the day after the bombing. Everyone had known the doctor and nurses who had lost their lives; some were personal friends. Their absence was keenly felt and made worse by the fact that everywhere they turned there were signs of bomb damage. The rubble had been cleared away and the corridor leading from the emergency department where the roof had caved in was out of bounds, but somehow the staff managed to keep going and provide the best possible care to the never-ending number of wounded arrivals.

There were German soldiers everywhere, patrolling the

hospital corridors, stationed outside the wards and operating theatres and generally making life difficult for everyone working there. They wanted to know details about every patient; their nationality, the nature of their injuries and how likely they were to recover. Everyone did their best to stall them by delaying handing over the information, but there was only so much they could do. They all knew the Germans' intentions were dishonourable. Freddie feared that if the Germans held on to control it wouldn't be long before they sent every one of the patients to the concentration camps. But she couldn't allow herself to think that way. She vowed to continue working as normal, treating her patients to the best of her ability and trying to prevent them from falling into the wrong hands.

The day after the bombing, Dr Akkerman sought Freddie out and reassured her with the news that Jan Kees had managed to steal inside the hospital with two of his men and smuggle Will out of the back, where a car was waiting to take him to a safe hiding place in nearby woods. It was the best Freddie could hope for under the circumstances, and she had to believe he was in safe hands. But for how long? She worried about just how protected this remote place was from the Germans and whether she'd ever see him again.

That night, she wrote him a letter by torchlight under her bedcovers.

My darling Will

I can't believe it was only last night that I saw you for the last time. I will never forget our kiss and wish we'd had more time together. Today the doctor who treated you told me you're safe and that makes me very happy.

Let me tell you about last night. I didn't return to Haarlem. When I was leaving I met the doctor and he talked me out of going. He said his son would rescue you, so I went back to work my evening shift. At about ten o'clock there was a big explosion and we were told to evacuate. Then there was another bomb and it was terrible – the roof collapsed and killed five people. It was such chaos and I did what I could to help the patients. It's a miracle that more didn't die, but I was spared, and so was my best friend Inge.

I'm so relieved to know you were rescued just before the bomb went off. We've both had a lucky escape and I'm feeling more hopeful now, even though there are dangerous times ahead. We just have to get through the rest of the war. I'm determined we will see each other again.

Now I know where you are, I'll write often. Please promise you'll write back soon. I'll be waiting every day for your letter.

Veel liefs (that's Dutch for much love!)

She signed off with her name and slipped the sheet of paper into an envelope on which she simply wrote, 'Will'. The act of writing down her thoughts had soothed her mind and given her a feeling of closeness to him. She sealed the envelope and intended to pass it to Dr Akkerman so he could hand it over to Jan Kees. She hoped it wouldn't be too long till she got a reply.

A letter from Will came two days later, but when she read it she realised he couldn't have seen her own.

My sweet Freddie

I've just heard about the bomb at the hospital and have been going out of my mind with worry. Please, please write to me and tell me you weren't there. I can only hope you left for Haarlem as you said you would. I'll give this letter to the man who brought me here and hope he gets it to you.

It's been a strange few days, but I'm getting used to it here. I'm in hiding at a farm but I have no idea where it is. Probably for the best. There are eight of us here, all crammed into the attic on camp beds. It's not that bad, especially since I discovered Nick is here. I couldn't believe he'd made it out of the plane alive. Frankly, it's the best bit of news I've had since I got here. All I need is a letter from you to make my happiness complete.

It sounds like I'll be here for a few more days because the people behind our move are overwhelmed with finding places for Allied airmen who failed to reach Arnhem. People come and go all the time and I never know who I'll wake up next to! Thank goodness for Nick!

I'd better sign off now as the farmer wants us to do some work and earn our keep.

Please write and tell me you're safe!

Much love

Will

Freddie was overjoyed and relieved to hear he was safe. She wrote straight back and kept the letter in her apron pocket to give to the doctor the next time she saw him.

She was on duty in the emergency department, attending to a patient who'd been brought in with cuts to his hands and face, when she was told to go to the matron's office on an urgent matter. She finished off the dressing as quickly as she could and asked one of the other nurses to cover for her until she came back. She went with a certain amount of trepidation, wondering what could be that important. The emergency department was no busier than normal and she would have been among the first to know if there'd been an influx of war casualties.

Matron was sitting behind her desk, writing in a ledger. She was a formidable woman who inspired fear and respect in equal measure amongst her staff. But Freddie had learned that behind her stern expression was a woman who only wanted the best from the nurses and understood they worked under difficult circumstances.

'You called for me,' she said, putting her head round the door.

'Ah, Nurse Oversteegen. Thank goodness you're here.' Matron put down her pen and gave her a brief smile. 'Dr Akkerman has asked for you to go and assist straight away in the operating theatre. A patient has been admitted with serious abdominal injuries. Dr Akkerman has persuaded the German officer in charge to let him conduct the operation. It's a delicate matter, because the Germans insist on having one of their own medical staff present.'

Freddie frowned. This wasn't normal procedure. She suspected something more sinister was involved. 'Can you tell me anything about the patient?' she asked, wondering if he was a special case.

'The patient is John Hackett, a brigadier in the British army,' Matron said solemnly. 'He was leading his men into battle to gain control of the bridge in Arnhem when they were ambushed. He was caught in crossfire and suffered gunshot wounds to the abdomen. The Germans captured him and brought him under armed guard to the hospital this morning. He's one of the most senior men in the British army and the Germans will no doubt be wanting to interrogate him. We've been told they want their man present while Dr Akkerman operates. The doctor wants as many eyes and ears present as possible as he doesn't trust their motives. He asked for you personally.' She paused and gave Freddie an appraising look. 'Do what you can. And hurry.'

Freddie didn't need Matron to spell it out. The Germans

only had their own people supervising surgery when the patient was important enough. They weren't going to allow someone as important as a brigadier with the British army to slip through their hands, however badly wounded he was.

Outside the operating theatre, she hurriedly scrubbed up, before slipping inside the door and taking her place with the rest of the medical team preparing the patient for surgery. Dr Akkerman didn't look up, nor did he introduce the man in a white coat – the German doctor, Freddie assumed – who was watching the proceedings intently. A German soldier stood guard at the door.

'I need to determine the extent of the patient's injury, but he's lost a lot of blood. He'll need a blood transfusion,' Dr Akkerman said to his team, pointedly ignoring the German, who was leaning over the patient and shaking his head in irritation.

'Is there any point operating? It is obvious the patient won't survive,' the German said in passable Dutch. 'I think it's best to administer an injection to speed up the process.'

Freddie was horrified. In all her years of nursing, she'd never encountered a medical person who was prepared to end a patient's life, and so callously. Everything she'd ever been taught had been about treating patients to the best of her ability and to use every available method to save their life. But she knew it wasn't her place to object. This man would never listen to her. She waited for Dr Akkerman to reply, but he carried on working on the patient as if he hadn't heard, issuing instructions to his team to stabilise the patient and prepare him for surgery.

'This is outrageous,' the German piped up. 'Did you not hear what I said? This man is as good as dead. Why are you wasting your time?' His face had turned an alarming shade of puce.

'Dr Brandt,' said Dr Akkerman, scalpel in hand, pausing just for a moment to address him. 'This man has a right to the best medical care that we can offer. I will continue to operate on him. I believe there is a strong chance that he will pull through. Allow me to carry on, and if I fail I will know that I did everything to facilitate his recovery.'

Freddie stared at them in dismay, knowing that if the brigadier did recover he would be arrested and removed from the hospital to be interrogated, maybe even tortured. But what choice did Dr Akkerman have? He had to do all he could to save the brigadier's life, knowing that in doing so the patient might be interrogated, maybe even tortured, ending in his death. She watched Dr Brandt, who looked as if he was about to start shouting again; but he didn't. He spoke in a low voice, though the menace behind his words was all too clear.

'Very well. You may carry on for the time being. If there is any change to the patient's condition then you must keep me informed. We will need to keep a close eye on him.' He walked to the door and whispered a few words to his guard, who nodded. After he'd left, everyone exchanged looks of relief, but no one dared speak another word as long as the guard remained in the room.

The surgery was lengthy, as it appeared that the brigadier had sustained injuries not only to his stomach but to his surrounding internal organs. When he had finished, Dr Akkerman spoke a few quiet words to his team, telling them he was satisfied with the way it had gone, and the brigadier was wheeled out to the recovery room. From there, he would be taken to a private room to convalesce, though it was apparent that he would remain under German armed guard.

Before the team left, Dr Akkerman took his medical team to a quiet room where they wouldn't be overheard to discuss what would happen next. 'We can take nothing for granted. The brigadier is a major catch for the Germans. As soon as they believe he is likely to pull through they will want to find out everything he knows about the Arnhem campaign. But he's very ill and needs a period of recovery if he is to survive. They will put their guards outside his room, but there's nothing they can do to stop us mounting our own bedside vigil.'

'I'll sit with him. Let me speak to the nurses and set up a rota so one of us is there at all times,' said Freddie, still reeling from the German doctor's callous remarks.

'Count me in,' said Wilma, one of the other nurses. 'How long will we need to keep this up?'

The doctor sighed heavily. 'Ideally just for a few days, but, as you know, abdominal injuries can take a long time to heal. In the meantime, I will make arrangements to get him out of the hospital unseen as soon as he is strong enough to do so. I'm banking on you all to help me execute the plan.'

EIGHTEEN

Freddie soon discovered which Germans took it in turns to stand guard outside the brigadier's room. Noting that it was the same men who turned up each day, she put herself down for a late evening shift for the following three nights. She needed to understand their movements if the plan was to have any chance of succeeding.

The first evening a young German soldier, no more than twenty, was on the door when she arrived, and she gave him a cheery greeting.

'Hello, I'm Freddie and I'll be sitting with the patient for the next two hours.' She knew she spoke passable German and hoped he'd be impressed. For good measure, she flashed him a smile and smoothed down her blond locks as she passed by him into the room.

'How is the patient?' she said to Wilma, who stood up to show Freddie the brigadier's most recent readings. Satisfied that he was stable, Freddie murmured to Wilma that she'd take over; she went to check on her patient, who was sleeping. When she'd finished, she turned to the guard. He was standing to the side of the closed door.

'What's your name?' she asked innocently.

He didn't answer at first, but she saw him slightly shift his position so he could look at her. 'Gunther,' he said.

Freddie nodded and smiled. 'My cousin is called Gunther. He's German too, but I haven't seen him since the beginning of the war. He's only ten.' It was a lie, but she could tell from the look of interest on Gunther's face that her words were having an effect. What she'd learned during her time working for Frans was that the Germans never suspected women of scheming, especially ones who were friendly and flirty.

He cleared his throat. 'You speak good German.'

'Thank you. No one's ever said that to me before.' She let out a giggle, and her hand flew up to her mouth in a pretence of being shy.

He was staring at her now and she felt her insides cringe, but she kept on chatting in this vein, asking him about himself and where he came from, until she could be sure she'd got him on her side. She learned he'd only been in the army for six months and was homesick for Darmstadt, where he'd lived all his life. She didn't want to make it too obvious what she was up to, so she took out a book from her bag, and sat reading for the remainder of her shift.

When she came the following evening, he was there again, and his eyes lit up when he saw her. He was more chatty this time and asked her about herself, how long she'd been a nurse and if she lived locally. Freddie was careful to keep the conversation just friendly enough without giving the impression she was flirting openly with him. Then halfway through her allotted time, Gunther's replacement turned up, an older burly guard with a sour expression on his face. He gave Freddie a long stare and Gunther whispered something to him that made them both laugh. It was annoying to see them chat so obviously about her, so she ignored them. She knew she must be careful not to rile them.

Freddie was banking on Gunther being on duty the following evening. The plan had been meticulously worked out between herself, the doctor and Inge, who would play a key role in all this. All Freddie had to focus on was her own part, and she knew she must carry it out without a hitch.

At half past six, she went back to her quarters to get herself ready and wait for Inge. Standing in front of the mirror, she put her white cap in place, fixing it to her hair with pins, and examined her reflection. 'You can do this,' she whispered to herself, though her heart was beating dangerously fast and seemed to contradict her words. She was aware that what she was about to do was the most daring thing she'd ever done, even more daring than being a courier of highly confidential information that could bring down the Nazis. She heaved in a breath and turned to see if there was any sign of Inge. She'd promised to come promptly at half past six, and if she didn't turn up—

Freddie heard quick footsteps from the corridor and Inge appeared in the doorway.

'Sorry, I got held up. There was a queue at the pharmacy. I came as quickly as I could,' she said.

'Thank goodness you're here. Did you manage to get the tablets?'

Inge held up a small brown bottle and shook it. 'Only just. I had to beg the pharmacist to give me them. Apparently, there's a shortage because so many patients need them. I hope I've brought enough.'

'Two should be fine,' said Freddie, taking the bottle and shaking the pills out into her hand. 'On second thoughts, I'll take three. I'll have to crush them first. Do you think he'll notice?' she asked anxiously.

'No. Not if you make his tea good and sweet. I'll give you a hand.'

.   .   .

At seven o'clock on the dot, Freddie arrived at the door of the brigadier's room holding a tray with two cups and saucers and a plate of biscuits. Gunther widened his eyes, then became wary as he narrowed them. Freddie's heart skipped a beat. Did he suspect her? Her mouth went dry. She pictured her plan falling apart, but managed to pull herself together.

'You do drink tea, don't you, Gunther? I was in the canteen and thought I'd get an extra cup for you.' She walked past him and put the tray on a low table.

'Didn't you get me one?' said Wilma with a disappointed frown as she got up to go.

'Sorry. I didn't think to,' said Freddie, and realised she hadn't let Wilma in on this part of the plan. She quickly changed the subject. 'How's the patient?' She glanced over at the sleeping brigadier.

'He's fine. He's been asleep the whole time I've been here. He shouldn't be any trouble. I'll leave you to it.' She gave Freddie's arm a squeeze on her way out.

Freddie silently let out her breath. She picked up a cup and took a sip. 'Come and join me. Will you?' she said to Gunther.

He seemed unsure, as he quickly glanced up and down the corridor, before coming over and taking the cup she was holding out to him.

'I put two sugars in it. I hope that's how you like it,' she said and offered him a biscuit. Her heart pounded. He accepted both and took a small sip of the tea she and Inge had prepared.

'It's very sweet,' he said, making a face. 'Like you, Freddie. I've been watching you and... I think you're very pretty.'

He licked his lips and she wasn't sure if it was from the sugar in the tea or something else. She gave him a thin smile and watched him take another sip, willing him to drink the whole cup.

At that moment, the brigadier groaned, and she turned to see what the matter was.

He caught her eye and called out. 'Nurse! I need a drink of water. I can't get comfortable.'

Freddie stood rooted to the spot. She wanted to make sure that Gunther drank the tea, but she couldn't ignore the brigadier's pleas. Of course he wouldn't have any idea what was going on and it would be impossible to say anything with Gunther standing by her side.

'Excuse me,' she said politely to Gunther, and put her cup down on the tray. By the time she'd made the brigadier comfortable and given him a drink of water, Gunther was back standing at the door. She quickly glanced at the tray and saw both cups there – one was empty, but the other had hardly been touched. Her heart gave a lurch. Was the empty cup the one she'd drunk from? She was unable to remember whether she'd taken more than a sip of hers.

'Nurse, can you give me something for the pain?' The brigadier's voice was insistent.

Freddie blinked and remembered she was here to look after her patient. 'Let me check when your next dose is due.' She fetched his notes from the end of the bed and scanned through them, though her mind wasn't on it. 'Yes, it's almost time for your next dose.' She moved to the cabinet in the corner of the room, unlocked it and measured out the medicine. She kept turning over the possibility that Gunther had not drunk from the right cup, and that it might be her empty cup on the tray.

It took time before the brigadier was settled. Freddie kept checking the time on her fob watch. Twenty past seven.

Next, the brigadier asked her to adjust the position of his pillow. Twenty-two past. It was twenty-nine minutes past by the time he closed his eyes and appeared to be sleeping. Only then did she dare check on Gunther, who was standing with his back to the door, facing her.

He can't have drunk the sedative, she thought in dismay. She opened her mouth to say something, but then she saw him blink rapidly, as if he were trying to keep his eyes open. And then very slowly he slid to the floor, where he lay without moving.

There was a soft knock on the door. Realising that Gunther was blocking it, she risked calling softly, 'Who is it?'

'Hospital porters come to move the patient. May we come in?'

Freddie hovered over the motionless body of Gunther. 'I can't open the door,' she whispered, and glanced down. 'The guard is blocking it – he's on the floor.'

'No problem. Just stand aside.' The man's voice was reassuring.

Freddie moved back and watched the door being slowly pushed open. A man dressed in hospital uniform stepped over the prone body of Gunther.

'Hello. I'm Jan Kees. And you must be Freddie,' he said with a grin. 'You're exactly like Will described. He keeps asking after you, you know.'

'Does he?' she said in surprise, feeling immense relief to have news of Will. She smiled at this man who had saved him. But she had no time to reflect on it as she stared down at Gunther, worried he'd wake at any minute. Quickly standing aside, she let Jan Kees and his partner take over.

They easily moved the guard out of the way and brought in a trolley. Jan Kees asked Freddie to keep an eye on Gunther in case he woke up. Then, working quickly, they transferred the brigadier onto it. Freddie wondered if they'd done this before. The brigadier briefly opened his eyes, but didn't protest.

It was over in a couple of minutes.

'We can't just leave him lying here,' said Freddie with an anxious glance at Gunther, who remained slumped on the floor. 'What shall we do?'

'Nothing if we're to get the patient out before anyone notices,' said Jan Kees.

Freddie nodded uncertainly. 'Yes of course,' she said, then remembered the tray with the two cups. She could at least get rid of the evidence before Gunther came round and realised what was going on. 'You carry on and I'll catch you up,' she said, and reluctantly watched the men race down the corridor pushing the trolley to the service lift, where Jan Kees had said a colleague was waiting to help.

Freddie picked up the tray from the floor and hurried to a nearby toilet to swill the teacups out. She hoped it would be enough to cover her traces.

She caught up with the others as the lift doors were about to close and slipped inside, her breath coming hard and fast. Glancing down at the brigadier, she thought how vulnerable he looked. Her nurse's instincts kicked in. 'I should have given you his medication to take with you.'

'There's no need. The doctor has all of that in hand, but you probably know that already,' said Jan Kees.

She nodded, reassured that the brigadier would be in safe hands and well looked after until he was well enough to return to his unit. She went with them as far as the back entrance.

'We'll take over from here,' said Jan Kees. 'We've got an ambulance waiting outside. And thank you for all your help.'

He was turning to go when she suddenly remembered the letter for Will she'd been carrying with her these past few days. 'Wait a moment,' she called out and fumbled in the pocket of her apron for it. She'd been careful not to address the envelope, but had forgotten to stick it down. She quickly licked the seal and pressed it with her fingers. 'This is for Will. Can you please get it to him?'

Jan Kees pocketed the letter without looking at it. 'Just in time. The airmen are due to be moved any day now.' He gave her a sympathetic smile and, before she could answer, he pushed the patient through the double doors and out into the night.

NINETEEN

Freddie jerked awake to find Inge shaking her arm. She'd slept badly and been plagued with vivid dreams that seemed all too real – the brigadier crying for help as German soldiers burst screaming into the room and roughly dragged him from his bed. In her dream, she tried desperately to stop them, but Gunther loomed over her, restraining her by holding her hands behind her back. Her relief at waking and realising it wasn't real was brief: with a feeling of deep dread, she knew she'd be blamed for the brigadier's disappearance and for drugging their guard. And at the heart of it was her fear that however hard she tried to outsmart the Germans she would never win.

'It's gone eight o'clock. You have to get up.' Inge stood over her, her voice urgent.

Freddie instantly knew that Inge was about to confirm her worst fears. She sat up and rubbed the feeling of grittiness from her eyes. 'What's going on?'

'Matron sent me here with a message. You're to report to the German commandant's office immediately. It looks like he's put two and two together and realised you must have been the last person to see the brigadier. Is that true?'

'I'm afraid so,' said Freddie. 'I was so consumed with getting him to safety that I didn't give a thought to what would happen when the guard came round. At least I washed the teacups before I left.' She gave Inge a weak smile.

'Are you sure there's nothing else to prove you had anything to do with it?'

'I don't think so.' Freddie dropped back onto her pillow. She should have thought things through more carefully – how stupid of her to imagine she'd get away with it. 'Oh God. What am I going to say?'

Inge sank down on the bed and looked Freddie in the eye. 'They're looking for a scapegoat because they refuse to believe their guard was stupid enough to let the brigadier slip through his fingers. You'll be fine as long as you act innocent and don't get riled. I've every faith in you.'

Freddie gave her another feeble smile and hauled herself up to sit on the side of the bed. How could she be positive when she was certain that the commandant would see straight through her lies?

Ten minutes later, she was dressed and climbing the stairs to the third floor, which had been taken over by the Germans as their headquarters. Why did they need a complete floor to themselves when the hospital was so short on space, she thought irritably as she passed door after door displaying the names of various German officials typed up in bold. She wished that Inge had come too, but what good would that have done? She would still have to defend herself. If not Inge, then Dr Akkerman, who she was sure would be able to argue his way out of any awkward situation. But she hadn't had time to go and see him that morning, and he probably also had his hands full making sure the brigadier was safe and well cared for.

She approached the commandant's office, which was at the end of the corridor, took a deep breath and knocked three times.

'*Kommen Sie herein!*' The harsh, clipped voice of the commandant sent a chill though her.

She stepped inside and the first person she saw was Gunther, standing ramrod straight next to the big oak desk that faced the door. He stared coldly at her with an unreadable expression on his face. The commandant, a balding man with grey strands of hair neatly combed across his scalp, sat behind the desk. He was wearing a dark grey uniform embellished with insignia and medals, all polished to a high shine. He was writing with a gold fountain pen in a large black book.

Freddie nervously cleared her throat. 'You asked to see me, sir.' She spoke in German. 'I'm Nurse Oversteegen.'

The commandant lifted his pen from the page and looked up at her. His face was expressionless, but Freddie wasn't fooled. Behind his cold grey eyes lay a steeliness that made her heart thump.

'You speak passable German. That makes things easier for me,' he said, and his thin lips stretched into something that resembled a smile. It faded as soon as he started on about the graveness of the situation regarding the disappearance of the brigadier.

'The patient was in no fit state to walk out of the room of his own accord. And you were the last nurse on duty before he disappeared. Can you confirm it?' He fixed her with a hard stare.

Freddie's mouth went dry. She swallowed painfully as she tried frantically to think of a plausible answer, but was only able to stutter, 'Yes, that's correct.'

'And that you gave the guard here a cup of tea – that you had doctored.'

Freddie's heart thumped as she said, 'I did bring him a cup of tea but I know nothing about it being doctored.'

'Let me tell you that if it turns out you are lying the consequences for you will be severe. But I'm not an unreasonable
man, so I will ask you one more time – did you doctor the cup of
tea with a sleeping draught in order to remove the patient from
the room without the guard noticing?'

Freddie told herself that he wouldn't be able to prove it.
'No. It wasn't me.'

The commandant frowned in irritation as he turned to
Gunther. 'Herr Schmidt. Why don't you take over from here
and explain exactly what happened?' He gave him a warm
smile, though Freddie wasn't taken in.

'Of course,' Gunther said, and kept his eyes on her as he
spoke. 'I tasted the tea and told her it was very sweet, but I was
thirsty and drank it down. It was only then I suspected that
she'd added something to it. The next thing I knew I woke up
on the floor. The room was empty. Both the nurse and the
patient had gone.'

'Thank you, Herr Schmidt,' said the commandant and
turned his head to address Freddie with a satisfied smile. 'As a
nurse you have easy access to sedatives, so it was simple enough
for you to add them to his tea, ensuring he was unconscious
when the patient was taken from the room. I have no doubt you
were helped by others in doing so.'

'No. You've got it all wrong,' protested Freddie, thinking on
her feet. 'All I was doing was looking after my patient. When I'd
finished, I admit I saw Gunther lying on the floor. I went over to
him to help and took his pulse. He came round then. I told him
he must have fainted.' She met Gunther's eye and smiled coyly,
hoping he wouldn't contradict her. 'I helped him up, but he was
still dizzy, so I sat him on a chair and went to fetch a doctor.'

'Why did you do that? You're a nurse, aren't you?' The
commandant sat back in his chair and steepled his fingers.

'Yes I am, but I wanted a second opinion.' She swallowed

again, her mind frantically working to come up with a reason he'd accept. 'It was late and the only doctor on duty was in the emergency room, which is at the other end of the building on the ground floor.' She took in a deep breath to steady her nerves, and to give herself a moment to reflect on what she'd said. Did he believe her? She couldn't tell from his expression, which had remained blank throughout her explanation. She kept on. 'The doctor was busy seeing to patients and when I got back I found the patient had gone. I was shocked because I was meant to be looking after him. I could only think he'd been taken to another room. It's not uncommon for patients to be moved if a room is needed.' She made herself meet his gaze, hoping he'd believe her lie. 'The guard had evidently fainted again. I didn't know what to do.'

The commandant gave her a disbelieving look. 'Did you go and find out what had happened to the patient?'

Freddie could detect simmering anger in his voice. She shook her head. 'It was late. There was no one around to ask.'

The commandant stood up, and Freddie was surprised to see he was a small man, no taller than her. But what he lacked in stature he made up for in his demeanour. When he brought his hand down on the desk with a loud thump it was obvious that he was boiling with rage. 'It's outrageous for such a thing to happen with two people in attendance. Not to say totally incompetent.'

Freddie stared at her hands, her mind grappling with a way to defend herself before he punished her. 'Please believe me when I tell you it's the truth. Do I look as if I'm capable of losing a very sick patient?' she pleaded.

The commandant stared at her for a moment, then burst out, 'I've heard enough from you. Now, get out of my sight!'

Without another word, she hurried to open the door before he could change his mind. As she closed it behind her she heard the commandant's angry voice start up again as he turned on Gunther. She didn't wait to hear anything more; she fled before he had a change of heart and called her back.

TWENTY

Freddie almost collided with a German SS officer coming out of one of the other offices. She was forced to stop as he was blocking her way.

'What's the hurry?' he said, holding his hands up in surprise. His eyes slid over to the door of the commandant's office, the door she'd just come out of. 'What are you doing up here? This is the German headquarters. Surely you know that?' He towered over her and stood with his arms folded and legs apart.

'The commandant wanted to see me about the patient who disappeared last night, but I wasn't able to help. If you'd excuse me, I need to report for work.'

'Of course, but not before you tell me your name.' He smiled then. It wasn't an unpleasant smile, but Freddie shuddered at the realisation that there was some sinister motive behind it. Wary of whatever evil intention he had, she was desperate to get away before Gunther or the commandant appeared and found her still standing there.

'Nurse Oversteegen,' she said, knowing the officer could easily check up if she were lying.

'Nurse Oversteegen,' he repeated slowly, as if he were committing her name to memory. 'And I am Obersturmführer Hauptman. But you may call me Manfred. I would like very much to meet you when you're off duty. You know where to find me.' He tilted his head towards the door he'd just come out of.

She disliked the way he smiled then, and wasn't sure what he meant by it. The idea that he might be chatting her up repelled her. 'Yes,' she said, but she had absolutely no intention of coming back and discovering what he had in mind for her. She couldn't wait to get away. One thing she had learned from these two encounters was that the Germans were clever at saying one thing while meaning another in order to trip her up. She might have extricated herself this time, but wasn't so sure that she'd be able to if she were called back for a more thorough interrogation.

Freddie descended the stairs two at a time to the ground floor and made her way to Dr Akkerman's office. He'd been forced to move to temporary accommodation when the Germans had requisitioned the third floor. It was a long walk to the back of the building, giving her time to reflect on recent events, which had shaken her to the core and made her realise how hazardous her position in the hospital had become. The incident with the brigadier would firmly link Freddie to any other patients who mysteriously disappeared from the hospital. She couldn't afford to make another false move, for it could endanger the lives of those she'd been trying to help.

Before she knew it, she had arrived outside Dr Akkerman's office. She hesitated before knocking because she knew she would have to tell him of her decision. 'It's for the best', she said out loud.

Whether the doctor heard her or was about to come out anyway, he opened the door just as she raised her hand to knock.

'Freddie! I was so worried something had happened to you. Do come in.' He ushered her in and shut the door. 'I heard the commandant had sent for you. What did he say?'

She walked to the small window that overlooked a concrete yard and noticed a German soldier patrolling the perimeter. Seeing yet another German in charge only confirmed her decision, that with so many of them swarming around the hospital it was too dangerous for her to continue in her job.

She turned to face Dr Akkerman. 'He knows I was on duty last night, though I did my best to pretend I was innocent. The guard I'd sedated was there too, which was incredibly unnerving. I managed to stand my ground, but I don't think for a moment the commandant believed me when I said I had nothing to do with it.'

'What makes you think that?' The doctor pushed his glasses up his nose to get a better look at her.

'He was so angry when he couldn't pin the blame on me, but I wouldn't put it past him to keep watch on me. It frightens me what the *moffen* are capable of, especially after the bombing. Their lack of regard for human life is horrific. I can't help think what would have happened if you hadn't stopped that German doctor killing the brigadier by lethal injection. Dr Akkerman, as much as I want to keep helping smuggle out patients, I think it's too dangerous for me to continue. In fact, I think I should go back to Haarlem.'

He fiddled with his glasses again, taking his time to answer. 'You're right,' he said eventually. 'You must go, but it may only be for a short while until things blow over. I have a suspicion it won't be long before the British are back in control, leaving us to get on with our work without interference from the Germans. But I want you to know how much I appreciate your support and everything you've done.'

'Thank you, but I wasn't the only one involved in his

escape. But now it seems the whole of the German cohort on the third floor know about me. I've become a liability.'

The doctor shook his head. 'If it hadn't been for you, the Germans would almost certainly have transferred the brigadier to a prisoner of war camp. He would have been interrogated and then probably shot for his role in the assault on Arnhem. He's a very senior figure in the British army.' He let out a long sigh. 'I should have realised the burden I've put you under.'

Freddie hated seeing him so dejected after everything he'd done to help save Will's life. 'There are others who can still help with the smuggling. People who the Germans won't suspect, like Inge and Wilma.'

'But no one who has your commitment and clear-headedness in such difficult situations. But I respect your reasons for wanting to leave and I wouldn't dream of pushing you to change your mind.'

'I appreciate it,' she said, and turned away to look out of the window before he could see the tears filling her eyes. The German soldier in the yard stopped and stared at her. Shocked by his insolence, she stepped away from the window.

'What's the matter? You've gone quite pale.' The doctor went to her side and put an arm round her.

'I'm just feeling a bit overwhelmed,' she said with a sniff. 'I knew the commandant would try to pin the blame on me, but I thought I'd got away with it.'

'Why don't you sit down for a moment. I have something that might cheer you up.'

Grateful for his kindness, she took a seat and watched as he went to fetch something from the inside pocket of his jacket, which was hanging from the back of a chair. 'A letter for you.' He smiled and held it out.

Her heart lifted as she took the brown envelope with only her first name written in the top left-hand corner. Even without opening it she knew that it was from Will, but why so soon?

She'd only just given Jan Kees her letter to take to him last night. Surely Will couldn't have written a reply so quickly? Puzzled, she looked up at the doctor. 'I wasn't expecting to hear from Will. How long have you had this letter?'

'Only a couple of days. I meant to give it to you sooner, but I forgot. I'm sorry. I've been so busy.' He looked sheepish. 'Erm... why don't you read it while I sort through these patient files.' He gestured to a pile off folders on his desk.

'Thank you. I will.' Freddie barely registered what he was saying as she gazed at Will's letter and wondered what news it contained. Slipping it out of the envelope, she read:

My dear sweet Freddie

I'm writing to you again in case you didn't receive my last letter. I've heard from JK that you survived the bombing and I'm so relieved. It gives me hope that we'll be able to see each other before too long.

There's talk that I'm going to be moved with the other British pilots within the next few days. It's what I must do, but I have terrible mixed feelings about leaving you behind and wish there was some way you could come too. We haven't been told exactly when it will happen as it depends on the top brass in London who are organising the routes. I wish they'd tell us more, but they won't for security reasons. There's so much speculation and uncertainty amongst the men that it's nerve-racking, but I don't want you to worry. The underground do a marvellous job in communications, so I'll write to you whenever I can.

Please keep writing. JK has promised he'll get letters to me. You're all that keeps me sane. I'm thinking of you every day and in my dreams.

Your Will

TWENTY-ONE

Will

The farm housed several large barns and outbuildings used for the storage of crops and farm equipment. And now they also provided an additional safe shelter for *onderduikers* who were fleeing from the Germans. By the time Will arrived, he was one of the last few downed airmen to be afforded the relative luxury of staying in the farmhouse. Others who came after him were accommodated up in the rafters of these outbuildings, sleeping on bare boards with only a covering of straw in lieu of a bed.

It wasn't just an act of kindness that Karel, the farmer, was prepared to take in fugitives – he had another reason. He had lost most of his farm workers when the Germans introduced *arbeidsdienst*. All Dutch men over the age of eighteen had to report to the authorities for work in German factories building bombs for use against their own people. In reality, very few men put themselves forward and many were dragged from their homes against their will.

Most of Karel's workers fled to go into hiding rather than be forced to work for the Germans. It was a devastating blow. As much as he tried to keep the farm going by himself, he was forced to watch his livelihood slip away. When Jan Kees approached him, he leapt at the chance but made it a condition that the *onderduikers* helped him on the farm. He swept aside any concerns Jan Kees had that they could be caught working in plain sight. He'd heard from other farmers in the area that if he was cautious, the men in hiding would never be spotted, either by visiting Germans or locals turned collaborators. His plan was for the men to start work before dawn until sunrise, when the Germans were most likely to be patrolling the area. The fugitives would then go inside and wait until dusk when they would go out again to work till it was too dark to see what they were doing in the fields. They would also take it in turns guarding the entrance to the farm and report any sighting of suspicious vehicles or anyone approaching the property.

Will had been on the farm for over a week and still there was only patchy news on when he'd be moved on. There was so much uncertainty and Will worried whether his superiors back home even knew how many of their men were missing or in hiding. And as for Flight Sergeant Villiers, who had been so certain he'd be able to get the downed Brits out within a couple of days... nothing had happened. He'd left the farmhouse before Will had a chance to ask him what was going on. No one knew anything about him or where he'd gone.

Will's mind often turned to Freddie and whether there was anything she could do to help him get out of this place. But he didn't want to burden her, knowing she was working flat out at the hospital – who knew what terrible situations she was having to deal with? The thought of another bomb hitting the hospital when Freddie was inside terrified him.

Will managed to put his worries aside as he got ready for a day working out in the fields. At least it meant being outdoors and away from the cramped conditions in the attic, which were beginning to get him down.

In the semi-darkness, he felt his way down the stairs and into the scullery, where Karel was fitting the men out with wooden clogs that had seen better days.

'How are we expected to walk in these?' said one of the Americans, taking a few tottering clattering steps amid roars of laughter.

Karel looked on, amused. 'You'll get used to them and find they're ideal for walking in the fields, which are always muddy.'

Will was given the last pair of clogs, which were clearly too small for his large feet. He swapped with Nick, who had the opposite problem, and they exchanged a smile.

Karel handed out the tools they would need and they were ready to step out into the chilly grey dawn. He led the way to the edge of the field where the mist hung in wisps close to the ground.

'See those fences over there?' Karel pointed to a line of wooden posts, just visible through the grey mist. 'I haven't had time to repair them, but they need to be made secure to keep animals and people out.'

'What people?' asked Will innocently.

'Some of the neighbouring farms have had Germans sneak onto their land and steal food. They come at the dead of night to dig up potatoes, beets and turnips to send home to feed their families. It's a bad problem and it's only going to get worse when the cold weather comes.'

Karel sniffed deeply and set off across the lumpy soil to the far corner of the field while the men tried to keep up in their cumbersome clogs. He stopped in front of an area of fence where the wood was rotting at the base. 'These all need replacing with the posts from the pile over there.' He indicated with a tilt of his head. 'I'll bring over some barbed wire for you to fix all the way down this side. There are plenty of you, so I'm hoping the job will be done before the sun comes up. Then it's back inside.' He rubbed his calloused hands together. 'I'll be in the barn if you need me.'

The men worked solidly as a team and were determined to finish the work by sunrise. They quickly removed the old rotting wood and replaced it with sturdy posts. 'Anything to keep those bastard Jerries out. Here's one for you, Fritz... and you,' said Will with each blow of his mallet. Soon sweat was beading on his brow and he could feel it trickle down his back. It felt good to be doing something worthwhile and to repay the farmer for all he was doing for them.

It needed four men to carefully roll out the barbed wire and secure it to the top of the fence. By the time they were on the last stretch, an orange glow had appeared on the horizon.

'We should stop here and go back in,' said Will, aware that it would soon be broad daylight.

'What's the point when we're so close to finishing up?' said George, surveying the small area left to complete. 'Come on, guys. Let's put our backs into it.'

They carried on and were hammering in the last nails when Will heard a low rumble from the road that led to the farm. They all stopped what they were doing and remained rooted to the spot. The rumble increased and Will realised he was hearing more than one vehicle and that they were slowing down to enter the farmyard. A cry of alarm went up from one of the men guarding the front entrance. Realising what it was, he panicked.

'It's a raid! Quick, get back inside!' he shouted to the others.

They dropped their tools to the ground and tried to move as fast as they could across the rutted field back to the farmhouse. But Will found running in the unfamiliar clogs impossible, and then the pain in his ankle started up. He stumbled and almost lost his balance. In frustration, he tossed his clogs aside, and was able to move more quickly. He could hear voices from the front of the house and was sure he could get inside before they came for him. But just as he reached the edge of the field, he ran headlong into a man in uniform, who grabbed him violently by the arms.

'Go back into the field,' Will yelled over his shoulder, but it was too late. There were German soldiers swarming everywhere and it was clear that none of the men stood a chance. Wildly, he looked around him, and saw that every one of the men he'd been working with had been caught. He tried to writhe free, but his captor tightened his grip. An image of Freddie's sweet dimpled smile flashed into his head, making him resist even more as he panicked that he might never see her again. A sharp kick to the backs of his legs made them buckle and he was forced to give up his struggle.

Together with several others he was manhandled back to the house, and they were all ordered to put on their shoes and coats while the soldiers stood shouting at them to get a move on.

Will's hands shook as he fumbled to tie his shoelaces. Then, one by one, they were led out in a line, with their hands on their heads, to the front of the house, where a lorry was waiting to take them away.

TWENTY-TWO

Freddie

'Is everything all right?' Dr Akkerman frowned over his glasses at Freddie, who was rereading Will's letter. There was something about Will's casual tone that she suspected masked the reason for the delay in moving the airmen across enemy lines. She was unable to shake off her feeling of dread that things weren't quite going according to plan.

'I'm not altogether sure,' she said, putting the letter down. 'Will says the men should be moved on soon, but doesn't sound terribly convinced about the matter. In fact, he sounds quite anxious and I wonder if enough is being done to help them. I hate to ask you after everything Jan Kees has already done for him, but would you mind asking him if there's anything more he can do to help?'

'I'm sure the reason is the sheer number of airmen needing to escape. Jan Kees will know more about it. Why don't you come home with me this evening? We can have a bite to eat. It's quieter there and I can make a telephone call to Jan Kees and ask his opinion. What do you think?'

'I'd like that very much,' she said. There was nothing more she wanted than to get away from the hospital and clear her head while she processed her involvement in the brigadier's escape, even if it were only for a few hours. Briefly, she consoled herself with the idea of Jan Kees coming to Will's rescue.

'I can't promise much of a supper, but my housekeeper always makes enough for two meals, so we won't go hungry.' The doctor gave her an apologetic smile.

'That sounds wonderful and I'm sure it'll be a lot better than hospital food.' She returned his smile, and her heart felt lighter as she let herself believe that things would work out.

'Good. Then I'll meet you at the main entrance at six o'clock. Just ignore the *moffen* milling around there. They won't stop you from leaving if you're with me.' He winked, and she felt herself relax knowing he was on her side.

No sooner had she settled into his car for the short journey to his home than she fell asleep. She woke only when he turned off the engine. 'I'm so sorry,' she said, stifling a yawn.

'Don't be, you've had a tough time. And in our line of work it's important to grab a few minutes' rest whenever we can.'

Dr Akkerman lived in Velp, a village a few miles from Arnhem on the edge of the Veluwe woods. Freddie wasn't sure what she'd been expecting, but was surprised to see he lived in such a modest house with a neatly tended garden out front. She put her assumptions to one side as she followed him into the hallway, bare except for a mahogany table with a black telephone on top, below a Frisian wall clock that struck the half-hour as they walked through the door. He took her through to the small kitchen and went straight over to the stove to check what his housekeeper had left for his supper. He lifted the lid of the black pot and stirred the contents with a wooden spoon.

'It's bean soup and I think Gesina may even put a little

bacon in it for flavour,' he said, with an approving sniff. He lit the gas under it and went to fetch two glasses and a bottle of beer from a cupboard.

'I know you'll be anxious to know what Jan Kees says, but we'll both feel better with something inside us.' He lifted his glass to hers. '*Proost!*'

'*Proost!*' she said, grateful for his attempt to lighten her mood. The truth was she would rather have got the call over and done with before settling down to the meal, but she was too polite to say so. 'Have you been here long?' she asked, taking a long sip of the cool beer.

'A couple of years. My wife and I lived in a large townhouse in Harderwijk old town, which is much prettier than Velp. After she passed away, the house was too big for me on my own. Then my job brought me to Arnhem, so I decided it was time to make the change. That was in the early days of the war, before the Germans made it too difficult to move house.' He poured the rest of the beer, which frothed from the bottle into the two glasses. 'What about you, Freddie? How did you get into nursing?'

'My friend Inge persuaded me. We've known each other since school but lost touch after we left. You know how it is. If I hadn't bumped into her when I did, I would probably never have considered nursing. My sister Trudi and I were working for a local resistance group – Trudi still is. We were taught how to use guns, though I've never had to use one. My role was to get around town on my bike and get as much information as I could about the people we were targeting so I could pass it on to others who would move in and shoot. Not pleasant, but necessary. Before I got involved, I had no idea how many people were prepared to betray their neighbours. It's become a serious problem.'

'Do you have any regrets about leaving the resistance?'

His comment brought her up short. 'I've never thought I've

left. I learned a lot from the people I worked with and it tough-
ened me up for dealing with difficult situations. In my head, I'll
always be that person fighting for freedom. And in many ways,
working as a resistance operative and nursing are similar. When
I was helping catch traitors, my motivation was to stop them
from collaborating with the Germans and harming innocent
people. As a nurse, I care for vulnerable people who are unable
to help themselves. In both cases it's about protecting the innocent. Does that make sense?'

'It does, though it takes a certain degree of courage taking on
an enemy as brutal as the one we're facing. I've seen that
courage in my own son – and now you.'

They were scraping up the last of the soup from their bowls
when the telephone gave a shrill ring. Their eyes met. Carefully, the doctor put down his spoon, and, without saying a
word, got up to take the call.

Freddie sat back in her chair, still thinking about what he'd
said. If she was as courageous as the doctor suggested, then
surely it should be within her capabilities to prevent Will from
falling into the wrong hands. She just had to find a way.

The doctor was still talking on the phone, so she cleared
their plates from the table and took them over to the sink.

'Was it all of them?' she heard him say. There was a pause.
'Are you absolutely sure?' Another pause. 'I see. Yes, of course.
I'll make sure I tell her.'

She heard the click as he replaced the receiver, and waited
for him to come back into the kitchen. She turned to see him
standing in the doorway. His face had gone very pale, with
shadows she hadn't noticed before smudging the skin underneath his eyes.

'I'm afraid it's bad news.'

'Is it about Jan Kees?' she made herself say, though of course
she was thinking of Will.

The doctor slowly shook his head. 'The farmhouse was

raided today at dawn. The men were out in the fields when the Germans arrived. They didn't stand a chance.'

It didn't make sense. 'What on earth were they doing in the fields?'

'Working for the farmer. He thought they'd be safe. Apparently, it's never happened before.'

'Well, it has now,' said Freddie bitterly, unable to understand the stupidity of exposing *onderduikers* to such danger. 'Does Jan Kees know what happened to them?' she asked fearfully.

'All of them were taken away. The Germans must have received a tip-off because they swooped on the place before anyone knew what was happening.'

Freddie felt herself drowning in panic. She was convinced she was about to lose Will and would never see him again. 'Where have they been taken? Where's Will?'

'It's too soon to know. Jan Kees says he's going back to the farmhouse to see if he can find any clues.'

'Then I must go too. I have to find out what's happened to Will. Dr Akkerman, please, I beg you – take me there now.'

TWENTY-THREE

Will

The foul stench of exhaust fumes hung thickly in the still early morning air. They emanated from a grey-green German army lorry with a canvas roof, belching out black clouds of exhaust as it stood idling in the yard. Soldiers were positioned at each corner with rifles at their shoulders. When the men approached the yard, two of the soldiers stepped forward, let the back of the lorry down and turned round to face them.

Will was flanked by two soldiers and saw it all. As each man drew level he was roughly blindfolded and his hands forcefully tied behind his back, before being dumped into the dark gaping maw of the lorry. Several men refused to be cowed by the brutal actions of their captors, but their howls of protest were ignored as they were lifted up bodily and flung inside.

It was now Will's turn, and he swallowed down his panic at the thought of all those men squeezed inside, and how cramped and airless it must be. He blinked, then everything went black as a blindfold was tightly knotted round his head. His arms were wrenched backwards and bound with rope that dug painfully into his wrists. Biting down hard on his lip, he suddenly felt himself being lifted up, and tried hard not to cry out. But it was useless even to try, for he fell awkwardly with his bad ankle onto the unforgiving metal floor of the lorry, and let out a yelp of pain. He struggled to find a comfortable position as he was squashed on all sides by the others, like sardines in a tin.

The doors banged shut and the driver struggled to engage the engine into first gear. The lorry jerked forward and the men were thrown even closer together amid gasps and much swearing. It was matched by an outburst of German curses and loud thumping on metal from the front of the lorry. Instantly, everyone fell into stunned silence, not daring to speak for fear of further punishment.

Will refused to allow himself to speculate on what might be about to happen, and managed to calm himself down by imagining that Freddie would find a way to get him out of this situation. He knew it was unlikely, but thinking of her sweet gentle face and the feel of her in his arms was the only thing that kept him from crying out in fear.

The journey was endless and Will's anxiety returned. He knew that Arnhem wasn't far from the German border, so it wasn't inconceivable that they were heading in that direction. And then what? Were they heading east towards one of the terrible concentration camps he'd heard about? No sooner had this thought occurred to him than the lorry slowed down and appeared to turn off the main road. He knew this because he was shoved uncomfortably onto the next person, who swore under his breath at him.

'Get the hell out of it, will you?' came an irritated whisper close to his ear.

'Nick? Is it you?' Will exclaimed in surprise.

'Yeah, it's me. And you can get off me now.' Nick jabbed Will in the ribs, almost making him yelp.

'I can't,' gasped Will, but he was closer to laughter than

tears. It was such a relief to be next to someone he knew and trusted.

There was a loud thumping on the partition that separated them from the driver's cabin. Everyone fell silent again.

Will had just gone back to mapping out their route in his head, when the lorry came to an abrupt halt. The engine went off, the soldiers jumped down from the cab and slammed shut their doors. The clicking of boots moved away. Minutes passed but nothing happened.

'Surely they won't leave us in here?' came a panicked voice.

'They wouldn't do that,' said another, incredulous with fear.

Suddenly, the back of the lorry fell open and a welcome rush of fresh air filled the space.

'*Schnell! Alle raus!*' chorused a number of German voices.

The men scrambled out as best they could without being able to see or hold onto the side of the lorry. Will felt his knees buckle as his feet hit the ground.

Where were they?

They were roughly manhandled into a line and ordered to walk into a building that smelled strongly of disinfectant. It reminded him of the hospital in Arnhem, and he was briefly consoled by the thought that this was where they'd been taken. But why were they blindfolded and tied up? He didn't have time to think further about it as the troop were ordered to keep moving. Some of the men still wore clogs, which made a fearful clatter on the tiled floor as they were marched down a long corridor.

'*Halt!*' screamed a German, and the sprawling line of men bumped into one another as they stumbled to a halt. The German shouted out a command and no one moved.

Aware from the muttering that more Germans were now surrounding them, Will felt someone hoick him up by his arm and propel him towards a staircase. As he went up, he counted the steps and number of turnings and guessed they were climbing all the way to the top of the building. A few more steps along a landing, or maybe it was a corridor, before they were pushed into some kind of room. He heard a door closing shut behind him. Only then were their blindfolds and arm ties removed.

Will opened his eyes. Blinking, he took in his surroundings. A small window high up on the wall let in a sliver of sunlight. It was the only cheery aspect of the white-painted room, which looked as if it might once have been a hospital ward. He took in beds with mattresses, but no sheets. He counted six beds and seven men.

Stan, one of the English airmen Will had got to know in the farmhouse, found his voice and addressed one of the Germans in his own language. The German looked surprised but did answer him.

'What's he saying?' piped up an Englishman with a cockney accent.

Stan turned to address the men and sighed heavily. 'This place is a mental asylum. The Germans have taken it over and they're keeping us here for the time being.'

The men began complaining amongst themselves, until their captor yelled at them to shut up. Shortly after, he and his collaborators left the room and locked it from the outside.

'Are they just going to leave us here?' said Will, looking round at everyone's dazed faces.

'Looks like it,' said George, who was walking between the beds. He suddenly turned. He had a coin in his hand, which he tossed up in the air, then caught it. 'I'm flipping this coin to see who gets to share one of these beds.' He gave a brittle laugh, but it was no laughing matter. They were trapped and there was no means of escape.

TWENTY-FOUR

Freddie

Dr Akkerman obliged Freddie by driving her to the farmhouse to meet Jan Kees. He warned her that there was little Jan Kees could do until he found out where the men had been taken, but she wasn't to be deterred and insisted on going and seeing for herself.

They drew up into the yard, where a small light was visible from what seemed to be the kitchen.

'I'm going in,' said Freddie, then jumped out of the car and ran over to the back door, half expecting to find the farmer and his wife. But it was Jan Kees who greeted her. He was looking around at the mess. Bowls of half-eaten porridge lay on the kitchen table, the chairs had been shoved back, and the stove had long gone out.

'Oh, hello, Freddie. I just got here myself. It looks like they all left in a hurry,' he said in a flat voice.

'Are you sure no one was left behind?' Freddie asked hopefully, and realised she'd half been expecting to find Will here.

But there was no one, and the emptiness of the place filled her with sadness.

'It doesn't look like it, but I haven't checked upstairs or in the barns. There's always a chance someone got missed and is hiding.'

The doctor came in and went straight over to his son and gave him a hug. 'I'm so glad you're safe. Have you any idea if the *moffen* knew what was going on here?'

Jan Kees shook his head. 'I spoke to a neighbour, someone I've spoken to before and have always found trustworthy. It was early when he heard the vehicles in the lane. He went to investigate and looked through the hedge and saw several men in the field. He watched as German soldiers ran into the field and started grabbing the men, who were shouting and resisting them. The neighbour took fright and didn't stick around to see in case they came after him too. He said the whole operation was over within minutes.'

'You don't think the neighbour was lying and could have betrayed the farmer?' said Freddie.

'Anything's possible,' said Jan Kees with a resigned sigh. 'But what's done is done and my priority is to find out where the men have been taken.'

'If you need me to follow up any contacts, just let me know,' said Dr Akkerman.

'Thanks, Pa,' said Jan Kees, slapping him on the shoulder. 'But first, let's take a look round for any clues and make sure no one's been missed.'

Anxious to help, Freddie said, 'Let me go upstairs and see for myself.' She wanted to get an idea of where Will had been staying.

'Shall I come too?' asked the doctor.

'No need. I can do this,' she said with more confidence than she felt.

She went into the hall, found the light switch and turned it on. Light illuminated the stairs. which rose steeply. She climbed to the first-floor landing and walked across it to vertical stairs leading to the attic. It was darker here and she couldn't find a switch, so had to feel her way up to the top and through a door.

At first, it was hard to make out what she was looking at. When her eyes had adjusted to the gloom, she was surprised to see a number of camp beds lined up under the eaves. There were so many that there was barely any space to move between them. And yet they were so uniform and orderly, with items of clothing neatly folded on the end of each bed. She was disappointed; she had been hoping to find something of Will's that would show her which bed had been his.

She moved down the line of beds and softly called out in English in case anyone was still there. 'Hello,' she said repeatedly, lifting a cover here and there and crouching to peer under each bed, even though she knew it would have been impossible for anyone to hide in such a small space. She moved back to the door and surveyed the room one last time, just to make sure. At least she now knew where Will had been staying. She was satisfied there was no one hiding up here and had no reason to stay. But as she was turning to go, she noticed something small lying on the floor beside one of the beds. At first she thought it was a couple of coins, but as she bent down to pick them up she saw they each had a hole punched through them and were attached together by a piece of frayed string. Squinting at the engraved letters and numbers, she tried to make out what they meant, but it was too dark up here to see the detail. She was convinced they meant something, so pocketed them and went downstairs.

'What's that you have there?' said Jan Kees, coming back into the kitchen at the same time as Freddie, who took the discs out of her pocket and laid them on the table. One was pale red and round, the other a green oval shape.

'I found these next to one of the beds. I'm not sure what they are,' She held them up to show him. She turned one of them over and slowly read out the inscription: 'W. Cooper. Offr. CE. 137499.' She glanced up, feeling heat rise to her cheeks. 'They must belong to Will. His name is Will Cooper. He must have dropped them by mistake.'

Jan Kees took them from her for a closer look. 'I think you're right. These are called dog tags. Offr means Officer and CE is his religion – Church of England. The number holds more information – his rank and where he comes from. All the airmen have them and they're meant to wear them round their neck at all times. He'll be without his now.'

'Do they have two in case they lose one?' she asked innocently.

Jan Kees pursed his lips. 'No. If they die, one of the discs is kept with the body and the other is returned home to confirm their death.'

Freddie felt the blood drain from her face as it dawned on her that Will could die at the hands of the Germans. If he wasn't wearing his dog tags, then no one would be able to identify him.

Jan Kees was watching her. 'Do you want to hold on to them? Then you can give them back to him when you see him again.'

'Do you really believe I will?' she said despondently, taking the tags and squeezing them tightly into the palm of her hand.

'Yes, I do. It'll mean outwitting the Germans and it won't be easy. I won't leave a stone unturned until I find where they've been taken. But you have to trust me.'

TWENTY-FIVE

Freddie had mixed feelings when she went to see Inge on her return to the hospital later that evening. Although aware she needed to keep a low profile in case she ran into Gunther, Manfred, or indeed any of the Germans who knew of her connection to the brigadier, she felt she owed it to Inge to return and explain all that had happened in the meantime. She was creeping quietly along the corridor towards their dormitory when she ran into Inge coming out of the bathroom.

'Where have you been? I was beginning to think something had happened to you,' Inge said, flinging her arms round her friend.

'I'm fine,' Freddie said with a laugh. 'But I do need to talk to you in private,' she added as a couple of nurses walked by on their way to the dormitory.

It was a warm evening, so Freddie suggested they went outside to the hospital garden. She'd never seen any Germans out there and suspected they didn't know about its existence.

'It's too dangerous for me to stay,' she said, after they'd found a secluded bench and she'd told Inge about her difficult encounter with the commandant that morning. 'There'll be no second chances if he discovers I'm working against them. At least Dr Akkerman will cover for me. He said he'd tell Matron I've been recalled to Haarlem on an urgent matter.'

'I see. With any luck, it won't be for long. There are rumblings that the British could already be about to take back control,' said Inge encouragingly.

'I hope you're right.' Freddie sighed. 'And there's something else.' She lowered her voice. 'The farmhouse where Will and all the airmen were staying was raided this morning. The Germans took them away but that's all we know. The doctor and I went straight away and met Jan Kees there, but he's had no further news. I'm so scared, Inge. I feel it's the wrong thing to do, leaving right now, but what choice do I have?'

Inge lifted Freddie's chin and made her look her in the eye. 'You must go. There's nothing you can do for Will by staying. It's not as if you're going far.'

'I know,' Freddie agreed doubtfully, and shuddered as a sudden image of Will being driven away to an unknown destination came into her head. 'I have a bad feeling about all this.'

'It's only a feeling. Try not to worry.'

Inge's words were a comfort and she was grateful for her friendship and support, but she felt guilty leaving her at such a dangerous time. 'What will you do... is it really safe for you to stay?' she whispered.

'Don't worry about me. I can look after myself.'

Freddie opened her mouth to ask if she was sure, but thought better of it when she saw the determined look on Inge's face. She had to believe it was true.

Two days later, Freddie was back in Haarlem. Despite everything, she was pleased to be back in familiar surroundings with her sister Trudi. She hadn't realised how much she'd missed her till they were sitting together in Trudi's rented room, chatting companionably till late in the evening over cups of tea, just like old times. It felt good being able to talk freely without the worry of constantly being alert to the possibility of being interrupted or overheard.

Trudi filled her in on her work with the resistance and how things had changed in the weeks Freddie had been away. Since Dolle Dinsdag, the day of celebration when everyone believed they were close to liberation, only to be shocked by the subsequent realisation that the war was far from over, the Haarlem group had doubled in numbers. Frans was swamped by applications – all were from men who wanted to play a part in pushing the Germans out after the failure of the Allies to defeat them.

'It's weird, but Hannie and me are still the only women in the group and we're often put together on assignments. And of course you, dear Freddie, when you're home.' Trudi took Freddie's hand in hers and gave it an affectionate squeeze. 'Not that I mind, but there must be other women who think the way we do. I don't understand why more don't want to get involved. Frans is keen to recruit more women and says it's not for want of trying. He's always reminding us that we're the group's best asset, not least because the Germans never suspect us when we go into action. And it's not just our willingness to use guns – I've lost count of the number of times I've smuggled classified information and weapons to our contacts right under the *moffen*'s noses.' She gave a brittle laugh.

'Perhaps women are put off by the kind of men who like to boast about how they don't feel the need to be part of a group,' said Freddie. 'Women can be just as courageous in standing up to the Germans in lots of other ways. As we both know.'

Freddie went on to tell Trudi about her run-in with the commandant and how it hadn't taken much to persuade him that she had nothing to do with the brigadier's disappearance. 'If I'd been a man, I don't think I'd have got out of his office alive,' she said, only half joking. 'But seriously, the reason I came back to Haarlem is that it wasn't safe for me to stay as long as the *moffen* are in charge. My name will forever be associated with the brigadier and they're smarting that they let him slip through their hands. At least here I can lie low for a while.' She dropped her eyes and fiddled with her hands in her lap.

'That's not all that's going on, is it? Tell me what's troubling you,' said Trudi.

Freddie raised her eyes to meet Trudi's. There was nothing she could hide from her sister. 'It's about someone I treated at the hospital... he's a British pilot whose plane was shot down. He was brought in suffering from concussion. I was there when he woke up.'

'Go on,' said Trudi.

'The moment he opened his eyes, it was like a thunderbolt had hit me. I can't explain it.' Freddie pressed the backs of her hands to her cheeks which had suddenly grown hot.

Trudi grinned at her. 'Freddie, I'm so happy for you. It sounds like you're in love.'

Freddie shook her head vigorously, but was unable to keep the smile off her face. 'It was wonderful while it lasted. He made me laugh and I felt as if we'd always known one another. I wish our time together hadn't been so short. I suppose I should be grateful for the time we had together.'

'What happened to him?' asked Trudi gently.

'The resistance managed to get him out to a farm in the countryside, where he was in hiding with other Allied men. The plan was to help them escape from Holland so they could rejoin their units, but there were so many delays. We wrote to each other and it was bitter-sweet – joy at hearing that he was safe, but I was so worried that things might go wrong. And it did go wrong. Before I could reply to him, there was news that Germans had stormed the farm and rounded everyone up and driven them away in a lorry. I dread to think where to – probably a concentration camp.' As soon as she spoke the words, tears began to spill down her cheeks. It was unbearable to think of Will being interrogated, tortured – or worse.

'I'm so sorry. Are you in touch with the resistance people behind their escape?' asked Trudi.

Freddie nodded. 'I got friendly with a doctor whose son is one of the leaders. Dr Akkerman promised to let me know if there was any news and told me to be patient, but I haven't heard a thing, which makes me think that something is seriously amiss. How can so many Allied airmen vanish into thin air and no one know anything about it? Now I'm here I feel so helpless for not doing anything.'

'Then you must ask Frans to take the matter up. He's always going on about all his connections with resistance groups across the country. He must be able to do something.'

Freddie agreed, but was doubtful that Frans would be able to help. By the sounds of it, he had his hands full running his local operation and wouldn't have time to deal with a situation that was outside his control. Arnhem was over seventy miles from Haarlem, and there was a strong likelihood that the Germans had taken the men even further afield. Perhaps even to Germany and to one of those horrific concentration camps. And who knew what their intentions were for them after that. She'd heard how brutal the conditions were in the camps, and feared for Will's health, knowing he wasn't fully recovered from his injuries. She knew that concussion was a serious medical condition and that some people went on to suffer a relapse. What would the Germans do if they found they had a very sick man on their hands? It was hard, but she forced herself to stop imagining all the things that could possibly go wrong.

When she first broached the subject with Frans, he admitted there wasn't a lot he could do to influence the situation. 'Until we have firm information about where they were heading, it's all speculation. The problem is that there are hundreds of downed airmen in the Arnhem area who the resistance are trying to deal with. It's inevitable some of these men will fall into the wrong hands.'

'But the men I'm talking about weren't just wandering around after their plane came down. They were picked up and taken to a farm for shelter in the Veluwe woods. They were meant to be safe,' argued Freddie in frustration.

'Perhaps so, but the resistance there is overstretched. They haven't the resources to check up on everyone who offers a hiding place. And that's when problems occur. I'm afraid not everyone who says they'll help is trustworthy.'

It wasn't the reply Freddie wanted to hear, but she wasn't prepared to let it lie. 'There must be something you can do. I mean, you've always said you have good contacts with other resistance groups.'

Frans sighed. 'That's true, but in this situation I have to leave it to those who are best placed to know what is happening in their own area. If it would put your mind at rest, I will put out some feelers and see what comes back.'

Freddie was left feeling frustrated at his vagueness. Was there really no one he could turn to for help? So she was surprised when a few days later Frans called round to tell her he had information that could possibly lead to the missing airmen.

'There's a mental asylum close to Apeldoorn that has been taken over by the Germans. It's a big place. Someone I know locally has been keeping a watch on it and has seen lorries arriving – he doesn't think they're bringing in more patients. He's seen their uniforms and suspects that some of them are airmen who have been picked up close to Arnhem.'

'Why would they take them there?' asked Freddie, briefly consoled by the thought that Apeldoorn wasn't too far from Arnhem.

'I wonder about that too. My scout believes it may be only temporary before they're transported to concentration camps. The Germans are emptying other mental institutions across the country. You see, they look on people who are invalids or have a physical or mental defect as inferior, and therefore think they don't deserve to live. So they bring them all together in one place, before deporting them to the camps.' He paused when he noticed her stricken face. 'I'm sorry, but it's probably best you know.'

'And you think they'll send the airmen to the camps as well?' The very thought of it filled her with cold dread.

'I can't be certain, but I wouldn't put it past them. Hitler is looking for revenge after the Allies came so close to victory. Look, I don't mean to shock you, though the situation is serious. But I do think there's something you can do in your role as a nurse. The Germans aren't that smart and I suspect they won't even notice if there's an extra nurse in their midst. And I'm sure the nursing staff would welcome an extra pair of hands to deal with all the patients they have to move. The Germans won't get involved as they don't want anything to do with patients they consider infectious. From what I understand, there are hundreds of patients at the institution. And possibly a few dozen airmen. I think there's a good chance you could get those airmen out undetected. What do you think?'

If there was even the smallest chance that one of the airmen there was Will, she would go. Without hesitation, she said, 'I'll do it, but I will need help, especially once we get out. Where will we go?' She let the enormity of the task sink in.

'Rest assured, you won't have to do this alone. I'll make sure of it.'

'But rescuing the men is only the start. I'll need maps, contacts, hiding places for us all, not to mention details of a safe escape route if such a thing exists. It's a huge undertaking. Do you really think you can organise it?'

Frans briefly frowned. Freddie could tell he didn't like to have his authority tested, but this was important – she had to know.

'Freddie, I wouldn't suggest it if I didn't think I could. Please bear with me while I fine-tune the details. I'll need to speak to a number of contacts about secure escape routes out of occupied Holland. It'll mean travelling south. I have a plan in mind for you to reach the river border into liberated Holland. It's a well-tested crossing route that the British often use. The local resistance in the area will organise for the men to get across the river by boat. And then your job will be done.'

He gave her a smile and she found herself returning it, amazed at how easy he made it all sound. She knew then that Frans was the only person who could make this perilous escape happen. For that reason she had to put her trust in him.

TWENTY-SIX

Freddie set foot on the long drive edged with pine trees that she was told led to the front door of the mental institution. The gravel crunched beneath her feet and her heart lifted at the sound of sweet birdsong. She was thinking how peaceful the setting was when she caught a glimpse of the place through the trees – it made her catch her breath. The building that came into view was enormous. It had three storeys and was flanked by wings that were twice the length of the building itself. Compared to the places she'd worked in, this was vast. It was sobering to imagine the hundreds of patients inside and the awful fate that awaited them.

She was interrupted in her thoughts by a German soldier who came marching towards her and demanded to know what business she had. His voice was unfriendly and she sensed waves of hostility coming off him. Fully expecting to be questioned, she had prepared a reply in German, but was unnerved by his manner – she had to remind herself that she was a bona fide nurse.

'I've been sent by the hospital in Arnhem to help with the

evacuation of patients,' she said firmly. She hoped she sounded convincing enough for him to allow her entry.

'Arnhem. I see. That's one of our hospitals, isn't it?' He looked her up and down, taking in her uniform. He seemed to be calculating whether she could be trusted.

'That's right. I was working there when the Germans took over. The commandant in charge asked for me to be sent here. Commandant Huber.' She knew it was risky mentioning the commandant by name, but she wanted to get inside the building and disappear as quickly as possible.

He nodded with what seemed to be approval. 'Well, you're just in time. The evacuation starts today.' He watched her face closely.

Freddie managed to keep her voice steady, even though she was alarmed to hear that the removal of patients was to start so soon. 'Of course. That's why I've come,' she said evenly.

'Good. Then I will show you where to go.' He turned on his heel and walked to the front entrance, greeting a guard as they passed through the heavy oak door. Freddie looked down at her feet, unwilling to draw attention to herself.

Inside, he led her along a corridor she guessed would take them to the patients' wards. There were uniformed Germans everywhere, striding in and out of the rooms they passed, and all seemed to be in a hurry. Freddie was relieved that they barely gave her a glance.

When they came to a set of double doors with a sign stating *General Ward*, the soldier stood aside.

'I won't come any further. Go through here and ask for the nurse in charge. She will show you where to go.' He gave her a brief nod and quickly retreated the way they'd come – it was as if he couldn't wait to get away. Suppressing a smile, Freddie watched him depart, then pushed open the door.

The ward was the longest she'd ever seen and packed with

beds. Some of the patients were moaning to themselves, others were calling out for attention, or simply shouted to some unseen person or being. It was a disturbing sight; Freddie was used to seeing patients in distress, but never this many.

A young nurse with rosy cheeks came by pushing a trolley and stopped to accost her. 'Hello. You look lost,' she said, sounding flustered. 'I'm Lottie,' she added with a smile.

'I'm Freddie. And yes, I am lost. I'm here to help with the evacuation that I was told is happening today.'

The nurse's smile faded and she gave Freddie a sympathetic look. She leaned in and lowered her voice. 'I'll be glad of the help. We've been told to prepare five hundred patients for evacuation. They said it's to make way for German soldiers, but when we asked where the patients were to be taken they refused to say. It doesn't look good.'

Freddie desperately wanted to ask if she knew anything about the group of airmen, but this definitely wasn't the time or place. At that moment, a cry went up from a man with wild-looking grey hair, who was sitting on the side of his bed and rocking back and forth. 'Help me, Nurse. Please help me,' he wailed pitifully.

'I can see you're overstretched. Would you like me to go and see to him?' said Freddie.

'Would you mind? There's a cubicle down the end where you can leave your things. I'll catch up with you later. Lunch is at twelve.'

'Thank you. I'd appreciate knowing what's going to happen as I haven't been given any instructions.'

No sooner had Freddie managed to settle the patient than she was called over to help a woman who wanted to be taken to the toilet. When she returned, another patient attracted her attention, and so it went on. There were clearly not enough nurses on duty and Freddie began to wonder how on earth they would be able to get so many people ready for the evacuation, let alone how she would find out where Will and the men were being held captive. She began having serious doubts that she would ever find them in this chaotic place.

At twelve o'clock she went to look for Lottie, but she was nowhere to be found. Rather than approach one of the other nurses, she decided to go and explore on her own. She felt agitated about the mammoth task facing her, knowing she would need to hurry if she was to get them out without anyone suspecting her.

Freddie walked back through the ward and retraced her steps to the main building. Walking swiftly and purposefully, she looked quickly around to make sure no one saw her climb the main staircase to the first-floor landing. There was no one around as she glanced nervously at each of the doors leading to what looked like administrative offices. She decided to keep on climbing the stairs till she reached the third floor. This was the top of the building, and where she imagined the men were most likely being held captive.

The first door she came to was locked. She rattled the handle and listened, but there was silence from inside. She kept on down the corridor, trying each door until she came to the last one. To her surprise, it moved ajar with a squeak. She looked behind her to make sure she was alone, then put her hand against the door to open it and stepped inside.

It looked like a storeroom, stacked with tables, chairs and cardboard boxes. High up on the opposite wall was a window that let in a little light. Dust motes danced in the musty-smelling air, giving the impression that no one much bothered with this place. It was obvious nobody had been in for a while.

She was about to leave when she was sure she heard the low murmur of voices from across the wall. Moving closer, she put her ear against it and listened. The voices were hard to make out, but she could tell they were speaking English. She kept still while deciding her next move, then saw the outline of what looked like an interconnecting door behind a tower of cardboard boxes. She moved a couple to one side and saw she was right. She lifted her hand to rap softly on the door. The voices immediately fell silent. She knocked again and called softly in English, 'Hello. Can you hear me?'

She heard footsteps move closer to the wall and an American voice replied, 'Yeah. We can hear you. You sound Dutch. Are you staff?'

Freddie couldn't help but smile. 'Sort of. I'm a nurse. This place is being evacuated tonight and I've come to help you get away before the Germans suspect anything.'

A familiar voice broke in. A voice she would know anywhere. 'Freddie, is it you?'

A surge of emotion washed over her as she leaned her head against the door and whispered, 'Will... thank goodness you're here.' Her voice trembled. 'I need to get to you, but this room is filled with junk and it's blocking the door. Let me try and move it.'

She heard murmuring from across the wall and then the American said, 'I'm afraid you're wasting your time. We've tried and the door is locked.'

Freddie was undeterred. 'Let me at least try,' she said. She shifted items aside as fast as she could until she could get to the door handle. She jiggled it but it held fast. Then she saw a key lying on the floor, poking out from underneath a chair. Her hand shook as she picked it up and tried it in the lock. It fitted. Pulling the door handle towards her, she turned the key with a grating sound, and it eased open.

She stood rooted to the spot as her eyes roamed over the men who had crowded round to see. But she only had eyes for one man, who stood in the centre, taller than the rest, his clear blue eyes fixed on hers. He was just as she remembered him.

'Will,' she gasped, tears pricking her eyes. She threw herself into his warm strong arms and breathed in the scent of his skin as she buried her face in his neck. He held her so tightly she wasn't sure if it was his heart or hers she could feel pounding against her chest. She didn't want to let go. It felt like coming home.

TWENTY-SEVEN

She wasn't sure how long they stood locked in a tight embrace before she became aware of the murmur of voices. Will broke away first with an embarrassed grin. 'Give us a moment, chaps, will you? I haven't seen my girl for weeks.'

'Lucky you,' piped up the American, and laughter rippled amongst the others.

Freddie felt herself redden with embarrassment, but also with pleasure that Will had called her his 'girl'. Not that it meant anything under the present circumstances. She wasn't just 'his girl'; she had a dangerous job to do and not much time in which to achieve it.

She smoothed down her apron with both hands and gazed around the room. It was grubby, with paint peeling off the white walls and no carpet on the floor. Just metal bedsteads, with mattresses and hardly any bedding to speak of. It looked as if it had been used as a ward at some point, but was clearly unsuitable for the number of men locked up here. Their faces were grey and drawn, as if they hadn't slept for days. Freddie felt a pang of pity as she looked around at their expectant expressions.

She cleared her throat and explained why she was here. 'My name's Freddie. I'm an undercover nurse and work for the resistance. I'm here to help you escape.'

'There are seven of us. Will it just be you?' said one of the men, folding his arms.

Freddie chose not to address his remark directly. 'I'll be working inside the building and others will help with your escape route once we get out of here. But I need your coopera-tion. You're in a great deal of danger and there isn't much time before the Germans start emptying out this place and trans-porting the inmates to concentration camps. They're starting tonight and there's only one chance to get you all out without them noticing.'

They started whispering amongst themselves.

Will spoke up. 'We haven't been told a thing since we were brought here. We were blindfolded and this room was the first thing we saw. It's a hospital, isn't it?'

Freddie nodded. 'It's an asylum, and there are hundreds of mentally disturbed patients being treated here. The Germans have taken it over to accommodate their own soldiers. They want to get rid of all the inmates and staff – they haven't any time for sick people.'

'How are you going to get us all out by yourself without anyone noticing?' said the man who had challenged her.

He had touched a nerve – Freddie had been wondering the same thing herself – but she needed them to believe in her. She formulated a plan as she spoke. 'That's what I'm about to tell you. I'll get hold of clothing for you so you'll look the same as the other patients. It's important you play your part, just as I'm playing mine. Do you understand?'

'No, I don't understand,' he said defiantly. 'We've been let down by those fellows who were meant to help us. Just look at the mess they've landed us in. Then you come in and make out you're going to save us from the Jerries.' He gave a dismissive scoff. 'Why should we believe you?' He looked around the others for support; some murmured their agreement.

'Nick, stop this,' interrupted Will. 'There's a very real chance we'll suffer the same fate as everyone else here if we don't go along with Freddie's plan. Unless you've got a better one, I suggest you listen to what she has to say.'

Nick grudgingly fell silent.

'Thank you,' she said with a quick grateful look at Will. 'But you're right, Nick, to question me. I think I'd do the same if a stranger turned up saying they could get me out of trouble. I'm offering you a lifeline, but if you don't choose to take it, that's fine. It won't stop me from helping anyone else who is prepared to put their trust in me.' She held her breath as she looked from one to the other – one or two wouldn't meet her gaze, but most did.

She began to outline her plan and hoped she could win them all over. When she'd finished she was relieved that there were no objections.

'Good. I'll be back later.' She gave what she hoped was an encouraging smile.

Will walked her to the interconnecting door, his hand in the small of her back. He spoke to her quietly. 'It's been tough these past days not knowing what's going to happen to us, so please don't let Nick get to you. The men might not show it, but we appreciate what you're doing.'

She glanced at him, wishing she could have had more time to tell him her fears that it could all go horribly wrong. Even so, it was a relief to know he was on her side. She hoped that when she'd gone he'd be able to reassure the men that she was up to the job.

Lottie was sitting with a bewildered-looking woman who was in floods of tears. 'I don't want to leave,' she wailed, as she gripped Lottie by the hand.

'There's nothing to worry about, Mevrouw Steen. The nurses will look after you, just like they always do.'

'Where are we going? What if I don't like it there?' The woman was inconsolable.

Lottie handed the woman two tablets and a glass of water. 'Now swallow these down. You'll feel better for it.'

Freddie waited for the woman to take her medicine before attracting Lottie's attention. Lottie stood up and came over.

'I'm so sorry. You must have thought I abandoned you, but I've been run off my feet. Did you find the canteen?'

'No, I didn't have time. Lottie, there's something I need to speak to you about urgently.'

'Let's go and grab a bite to eat before the canteen closes.' She steered Freddie out of the busy ward, ignoring the pleas that went up from patients as they hurried past.

The canteen was empty, except for a table of Germans in one corner. They were engrossed in conversation as they studied some papers that covered the entire tabletop. Freddie exchanged a worried glance with Lottie, who indicated a table as far away from the Germans as possible, where they settled down with a cup of weak tea and a cheese sandwich.

'How long have you been working here?' said Freddie as quietly as possible.

'Two years. It was a very different place then,' Lottie said wistfully. 'We've always prided ourselves on the level of care we were able to offer patients. Many have severe psychiatric problems and all are so vulnerable.' Leaning a little closer, she whispered, 'What's happening today is a tragedy.' Then she seemed to compose herself. 'I'm so glad you've come to help out.'

Freddie nodded, feeling more than a little guilty that she

hadn't been entirely honest in telling her why she was here, but relieved that Lottie wasn't on the side of the Germans. 'Did you know there are Allied airmen in hiding on the third floor?' she whispered.

Lottie's eyes widened as she shook her head. 'How do you know this?'

Freddie lowered her voice even further. 'The resistance. I've come here to free them.'

Lottie hesitated as she took this in. 'So – you're not a nurse then?'

'Yes I am, but I also work for... you know. The men were all picked up near Arnhem during the Allied invasion and were safe until the Germans discovered where they were hiding. We heard about the Germans taking over this place and that it was likely the men would be brought here. And from here to the concentration camps.'

Lottie responded in shock. 'That's terrible. But that's not what we've been told. We thought the patients were being taken to an institution at Franeker in Friesland.' She cast an anxious glance at the Germans, but they didn't look up.

'It's possible I got it wrong. But because of the evacuation tonight it's essential I get the men out of here before the Germans realise they're not part of the group of patients. Can I rely on your help?'

Lottie looked uncertain. 'We're going to have our hands full moving the patients. You've seen how vulnerable some of them are. My priority is to help them. I'm sorry I can't give you what you want.'

Freddie nodded and thought quickly. She needed Lottie's support, otherwise her plan would fail disastrously. 'I understand. I was wrong to suggest it. I think I can manage it alone, but they'll stick out like a sore thumb if they're not dressed like the patients. Can you provide me with hospital garments for them to wear?'

Lottie smiled and looked relieved. 'Of course. I can get you everything from supplies. It's the least I can do.'

'Thank you,' said Freddie, glad to have at least one of the nursing staff on her side.

TWENTY-EIGHT

All afternoon the place was in turmoil. Freddie blended in with the other nurses, who were rushed off their feet getting the patients dressed and sorting out enough medication to see them through the next few days. She helped out as best she could, though she found it painful knowing they were unlikely to end up in Friesland and in safety.

Lottie took Freddie to the laundry room and joined the queue for clean clothes, laundry bags and bedding. When it was their turn, Lottie spoke for both of them and asked the male orderly for enough for seven patients. As he handed over the items, Freddie remembered seeing that several of the men had still been wearing clogs and worried that this would give them away.

'Can I have some pairs of men's shoes as well? I think five should be enough.'

'What do you think we are – a clothing store?' the orderly said sullenly, but he went over to the shelves and brought back a few pairs of slippers. 'That's all I can spare,' he said, slapping them down on the table between them.

Freddie gave her thanks, though she wasn't sure what use

slippers would be when they were running away from the Germans.

'It's too much for you to carry. Let me come with you,' said Lottie, and moments later Freddie realised why. Two German soldiers were standing on either side of the central staircase, blocking their way.

'Follow me,' said Lottie, walking straight past them. They carried on till they reached a service lift. The doors opened and another German stepped out. He stared straight at them. 'Where are you going with those?' he asked suspiciously.

'Second floor. Isolation ward,' said Lottie over her pile of garments.

He frowned and quickly stood aside. The two women stepped into the lift and Lottie pressed the button for the third floor.

'Don't tell me. There's no isolation ward on the second floor,' said Freddie wryly.

'No, but he doesn't need to know that, does he? Works every time,' said Lottie as the lift arrived at their floor. 'Now it's your turn. Show me which room the men are in.'

After a long day preparing the patients for their journey, the evacuation began. It was a slow operation that involved moving many people, not only because of the large numbers but because many were frail and clearly upset by the chaos all around them. Under trying circumstances, the nurses did their best to keep order.

Outside the main entrance buses stood ready to receive the patients and their nurses. Each bus could take up to thirty-six passengers and as soon as one was full it set off rumbling down the long drive in a thick black cloud of diesel fumes.

Inside the building, German soldiers swarmed everywhere, not standing to attention as they normally would but helping to carry out bedding and pushing patients in wheelchairs to the waiting buses. It seemed like they were in a hurry to empty the place as quickly as possible.

At the bottom of the main staircase stood a line of nurses dressed in white who guided the stream of patients towards the front entrance. The weakest were being supported. Freddie positioned herself at one end, trying hard to hide her anxiety while her eyes kept darting to the staircase for any sign of the airmen.

She almost jumped when a German soldier came marching through the front door and blocked the way of those about to leave. '*Halt!*' he boomed. 'Nobody is to go outside until more buses arrive.'

'Why can't we wait outside? You can see there are too many of us in here,' pleaded a nurse who was at the front of the queue.

'These are my orders. You must stay here until I say you may go.' He spoke the words harshly and several patients nearby began to cry, but he refused to budge and stood watching the unfolding chaos, his face set hard.

Something was up, perhaps some hitch in the organisation, thought Freddie anxiously, and exchanged a worried look with Lottie. All she could do was wait and hope her plan wasn't about to unravel.

As the minutes crept past, the hallway kept filling up with patients and their carers. Freddie sensed the rising tension could erupt at any moment.

She flicked her eyes back to the staircase, just as Will appeared on the landing. He was dressed in loose-fitting pyjamas and was clutching a laundry bag to his chest. Her heart leapt as he caught her eye and she dared give him a tiny nod of recognition. He began to descend the first few steps and the others followed him in single file, just as they had been told to.

Suddenly, two German soldiers came pushing past,

carrying a patient on a stretcher. They shouted to be let through, almost knocking one of the men flying. At the bottom of the stairs, the nurses rushed forward to move patients who were blocking the way.

Freddie knew it was now or never. She glanced over to the German at the front door, but he hadn't moved and wasn't looking in her direction. She glanced at Will and gestured to him with a small jerk of her head, then walked purposefully away from the throng. Not daring to see if the others were following her, she prayed that none of the Germans had noticed her group of men.

She swiftly turned down a corridor, checked to see the men were behind her and headed for a set of double doors at the far end. Once they were all through, the doors swung shut, deadening the noise from the foyer.

They were in a large room, a salon of sorts, which had seen better days. It smelt musty and was furnished with an assortment of dusty sofas and tables and a set of French doors at the far end. Earlier, Lottie had told her these doors were their best chance of escape.

Freddie turned to address the group and did a mental head count. 'Is everyone here?' Her eyes landed on Nick and he dropped his gaze to the floor.

'Yes. We're all here,' confirmed Will, with a look that told her he'd managed to persuade Nick to accept her lead.

'Good. Then this is what we're going to do. Those doors are our escape route. See those trees at the far end of the lawn? That's where we're heading, but we have to keep running once we get there. We won't be out of danger till we reach our refuge, a woodland house about a mile away. But let's not worry about that yet. First, we have to cross the lawn without being seen.'

She went over to the French doors and tried the handle, but it didn't budge. She rattled it and began to panic. Lottie had been so sure it would be unlocked... if she couldn't open the door what other means of escape was there?

'Let me,' said Nick, shooting her a scornful look. He put his shoulder against the door and it immediately flew open, letting in a cacophony of noise from the busy foyer directly opposite. A mass of people with German soldiers in their midst were clearly visible through the far windows. Freddie was relieved to see it was still bedlam in there.

She took in a breath and thanked Nick for his help. She was first out on the patio, and waited till everyone had come through. But now they were outside, she could see that the green manicured lawn was much bigger than she had first thought.

Fear shot through her. 'Let's go,' she said to the group, and ran.

They were not even halfway across when her worst fears were realised. A figure came running round the side of the building, yelling in German at them to stop.

'Keep going!' she shrieked to the men and kept sprinting towards the trees. Some of the men were faster runners and overtook her. Then Will was next to her. 'Stay with me,' he cried, and grabbed her hand, pulling her along with him.

The crackle of gunfire was terrifying as it tore through the air. There was a piercing scream, but Freddie knew she would be a target if she turned to see who had been shot. She had to keep going. She held on tight to Will's hand as they raced for the safety of the pine forest.

TWENTY-NINE

It wasn't over yet. Even though they could no longer hear any more shouts, Freddie insisted everyone kept running until they could be sure the Germans weren't on their tail. She had memorised the layout of the grounds from a map Frans had supplied her and knew exactly which way they should be heading. 'Look out for a wooden fence that marks the boundary. Beyond that the forest will offer us protection.'

At first, they made good progress. The ground was soft underfoot with fallen pine needles, before the path petered out into heavy undergrowth. This part of the grounds looked as if it hadn't been tended for some time.

Forced to stop and take stock, Freddie was waiting until everyone had caught up when someone at the back called out, 'Where's Nick? Did anyone see him?'

'I'm sure I saw him after we'd made it into the trees.'

'Well, he's not here now.'

Freddie froze. She quickly went round counting heads. There were seven of them, including herself, and no Nick. This was serious. What should she do? Go back and risk them all being caught, or carry on regardless, knowing she'd left a man she was entrusted with saving to his fate?

'I'll go back and look for him,' said Will, running his hand over his short hair.

Freddie thought he looked exhausted, but didn't they all after what they'd just been through? Even so, she wished he hadn't been the one to volunteer. 'And run straight into the arms of the Germans? Please don't go,' she begged. 'Let's at least get to the safety of the house and then we can decide what to do.'

'I'll go with you,' said the American, ignoring Freddie's suggestion. 'Nick's one of us and he might be badly hurt. We can't just leave him. Why don't y'all carry on and we'll catch you up?'

Freddie could feel her authority slipping away. It was hard enough keeping seven – now six – men on her side, but the thought that she could be sending Will back into danger after everything he'd already endured was unbearable.

'I think George is right,' Will said before she had a chance to answer. 'I'd hate myself if I didn't go. Apart from me, Nick's the only one of my crew who made it out of the plane alive.'

Freddie understood then that these men were a band of brothers who would do anything for each other – they would stop at nothing to save their own from the enemy. She felt she had no choice but to agree. 'Of course you must go. We'll meet you at the house. It's not far once you get over the boundary.'

Freddie and the rest of the group carried on and, once they'd found the wooden fence and the path leading away from it on the other side, the mood was calmer.

When they came to a clearing in the trees, Freddie had to stop to consult her map. Daylight was failing and it was hard to make out where exactly they were, for there were no distinguishing features to speak of – just dense forest and pine trees stretching as far as the eye could see. It made no sense to her.

'Can I help?' A young man wearing metal-rimmed glasses came over to take a look. 'I'm Ed, by the way. I'm a navigator, so I should be able to work it out.' He gave a self-deprecating laugh as he brought out a small compass from his pocket and took a moment to set it, then he used it together with the map to work out the direction they needed to be heading.

'It's this way,' he said confidently, and pointed to a faint path that Freddie hadn't noticed before. 'Come on, chaps,' he said cheerfully, and led the way through the trees.

Freddie hurried to catch him up and they soon fell into easy conversation. Ed told her his plane had come down on the day that the bomb hit the Arnhem hospital. 'It was a miracle that any of us survived. It was a right dogfight up in the sky. We were outnumbered by the Jerries, who surrounded our planes and wouldn't let off shooting at us. As far as we knew, most of the damage to our plane was superficial. We were convinced we'd made it. Then suddenly a load of them swooped in out of nowhere and took out our engine, sending us into a tailspin—' Ed broke off to bring a man walking behind them into the conversation. 'Thanks to our pilot – Alan here – we managed to land the plane in a field without crashing it. Naturally there were more Germans waiting for us. If it hadn't been for the men on the ground – good resistance chaps they were – we'd have been done for.'

'Did you lose any men?' asked Freddie, humbled by the easy way in which he spoke about something so devastating.

'We were the lucky ones.' Alan smiled. He was older than the others and had flecks of grey in his dark hair. 'We all know it could have been any of us.'

They all walked on in silence until Alan said, 'You mustn't worry about Nick or the others. We're used to difficult situations like this one. You have to remember we've all had combat training and been tested under extreme pressure.'

'I can't even begin to imagine it,' murmured Freddie, and found herself wanting to confide in this kind man. 'I'm afraid I'm not making a very good job of all this and I should have noticed that Nick wasn't with us. I promise things will improve when I hand over to someone with more experience in helping evadees.'

Alan looked sideways at her. 'I have to admit a lot of us weren't convinced about you when you said you'd come to save us. We're all used to dealing with men and I don't think any of us have ever had a woman in charge. But you've proved us wrong.'

'It's kind of you to say so,' she said, trying hard to accept what she saw to be a backhanded compliment. 'But I only do what I believe is right. Anyway, it's not over until I can be sure you are all safely home.'

It was almost pitch black under the trees and hard to see where they were going. Suddenly, there was a shout from somewhere to their right. Freddie guessed it must be Ed, who had walked on ahead.

'Come on, boys, I've found the house,' he called out excitedly.

The forest was even denser here and the tall trees seemed to crowd in on them. Freddie had to strain her eyes to the direction of Ed's voice. She spotted a faint light shining through the branches. It came from a wooden cabin that was almost entirely shrouded by thick pine trees.

'I'll go on ahead,' she said, not quite trusting that they had reached the right place. She walked up the narrow path and a dog started barking frantically from inside the cabin. Moments later, the door was flung open, and she recognised Jan Kees silhouetted against the light.

'Thank goodness you made it,' he said, stepping forward to shake her by the hand.

'You sound surprised,' she said, overjoyed with sheer relief at it being him, forgetting for a moment that not everyone was accounted for.

'I never doubted it.' Jan Kees smiled and ushered them all into the cabin, which was filled with the inviting aroma of cooking.

An older man appeared, holding the collar of his large dog. 'I hope nobody minds dogs. Max is a good guard dog, but he's really very friendly.' The dog gave a small, less aggressive bark, as if agreeing with his master's remark.

With a smile, Jan Kees turned to the group and said, 'Gijs and Hendrika are very good friends of the Allies. They've put up many men over the past few weeks before they continue their journey southwards. The plan is for you to rest and then we'll split you into several groups, led by me and Piet, who will be with us in the morning.'

'I bet that's Piet van Arnhem,' said Alan. 'Good chap. He got us out of a sticky patch when the Jerries were after us.'

'That's him,' said Jan Kees with a nod, then handed over to Gijs.

'We are very pleased to meet you,' said Gijs in good English. 'You must come in and make yourselves comfortable. I'm sure you will be hungry. My wife is in the kitchen and has prepared a meal for you.'

While he showed the men through, Freddie took Jan Kees to one side. 'Not everyone is here yet. We're waiting for Will and George, who went back to look for Nick. We think he may have been shot when we were escaping through the grounds of the asylum.'

'Do they know which way to come?'

'In theory, yes, but it's dark now and we struggled even to find this place.'

'Then I should go and search for them. I know these woods better than they will and can also give first aid if Nick is injured.'

'It was my fault. I should come too. After all, I'm a nurse,' said Freddie.

'No one's blaming you. Go and join the others and eat. You've been through more than enough today.'

THIRTY

Freddie settled into an armchair in the couple's sitting room after Gijs had shown the men to the building out the back where they would be sleeping. Hendrika sat down opposite with her knitting and began gently probing Freddie about her experiences at the hospital.

'Jan Kees tells me that you were there when the bomb exploded. I can't imagine how terrible that must have been. We heard there were casualties and that a young doctor died in the blast.' She glanced up over her glasses at Freddie, while continuing to knit without looking at her work.

Freddie sighed. 'We'd been told to expect an attack on the hospital, but what occurred was an evil barbaric act. The *moffen* bombed the emergency department with no regard for all those vulnerable patients. I'd just finished bandaging a young airman when we were ordered to evacuate. Then a second bomb went off while dozens of us were squeezed into the corridor going towards the exit. It's a miracle more didn't die.'

Hendrika nodded sympathetically. 'A young American airman came to us from there and he told us how terrified he'd been when the place was plunged into darkness. He was such a nice young man and wasn't badly injured, but it must have deeply affected him. And it all came on top of his own troubles. He lost his best friend when the two of them were dropped over Arnhem. His friend's parachute failed to open and there was nothing he could do but watch him struggle to gain control while plummeting down to earth. Can you imagine how awful it must be, seeing your friend die in front of your eyes?'

Freddie shook her head as she thought of Will's distress at losing his best friend in similar harrowing circumstances. She wondered if he'd ever get over it. 'I'm afraid these stories are all far too common. These men are so brave taking on what they do for us,' she replied. 'They keep on because they really do believe Hitler will be defeated and that the war will be over soon, but I'm not so sure. What do you think?'

Hendrika let out a sharp sigh and placed her knitting down in her lap. 'I haven't given up hope yet, though it was hard after Arnhem. We had so many airmen sent to us by the resistance. We would have had to turn some away if Gijs hadn't made space in the barn. Gijs and I will keep doing what we're doing to provide a safe haven for these young lads.' She yawned and folded her knitting away. 'I should really go to bed. We're early risers,' she said with an apologetic smile.

'Of course, and I hope I didn't keep you up. If it's all right, I'll stay here a while until the men return. I can let them in.'

Hendrika stood up. 'There's a key on the rack to the side of the door, if you wouldn't mind locking up after they arrive. And try not to worry. The chances are they'll have found the young man and will be back soon.' She patted Freddie's hand, then went out of the room.

Left alone, Freddie didn't feel particularly hopeful about Nick's chances, for it was more than two hours since Jan Kees had left. The longer it took for them to return, the more convinced she was Nick must have been gunned down in cold blood.

She sat back in her armchair and shut her eyes; she managed to block out her turbulent thoughts by listening to the peaceful ticking of the clock on the mantelpiece. She realised she must have been dozing when she was awakened by the soft scrape of a key in the lock.

Jumping up, she came into the hallway to see Jan Kees walking through the door, then had a moment's panic when she couldn't see the others behind him. 'Did you find them?'

'I'm afraid we didn't find Nick,' he said as Will and George materialised out of the darkness. They had dark smudges on their tired faces and their clothing was dirty and ripped in places – she'd forgotten they would still be wearing the pyjamas she'd made them put on earlier.

'I'm so sorry,' she said, ushering them in and locking up. 'Hendrika's left some food for you in the kitchen. You must be famished.'

Jan Kees let the pair eat, while he filled Freddie in on why it had taken so long for them to return to the cabin. He'd come across the pair deep in the woods, having strayed far from the path they should have been on, after searching for Nick up to and beyond the boundary fence.

Will pushed his plate to one side. 'It was dark by then and we didn't have a torch, but I'm pretty sure Nick would have responded if he'd heard us call his name.'

George nodded in agreement. 'He could of course have been caught, but I personally think the Germans wouldn't bother pursuing him, even if they had shot him. Their priorities are to get rid of the inmates, not run after the odd person who manages to escape.'

'Even so, I wanted to keep searching for Nick, but we underestimated how big the forest was,' said Will. 'We got lost pretty quickly. I can't tell you what a relief it was when Jan Kees appeared.'

'So Nick's still out there somewhere. What do we do now?' asked Freddie.

Jan Kees gave her a serious look. 'There's nothing more we can do, except hope he's not badly injured and somehow finds his way here.'

Freddie looked across at Will and read the anguish in his eyes. What must he be going through, she thought, having already lost two of his friends in the crash? It seemed so callous to abandon the search for Nick when he might be lying injured and lost in the forest.

'Look, these things happen and we have to carry on,' said Jan Kees, as if he could read her mind. 'It's always hard to lose people, but unfortunately it's the reality of war. We'll carry on with the plan because it depends on our contacts who are waiting to take the group south to the Biesbosch. It's tricky terrain, but they're experienced in getting Allied men across the river into liberated Holland. I'll be able to tell you more tomorrow when Piet arrives. Who knows, Nick might even have turned up by then.'

'You're right. Never say never,' said Will with a slight scoff that suggested he'd resigned himself to never seeing Nick again.

Sighing, Jan Kees stood up from the table and made his excuses. 'We've got some long and difficult days ahead. I suggest we all get a good night's sleep.'

THIRTY-ONE

Will brought his chair round so he could sit beside Freddie. He lifted her hand and kissed it. 'How are you feeling?'

It was the first time they'd been alone since they'd declared their feelings for each other, which already seemed like a lifetime ago. Freddie felt shy at the memory, and wondered how much she really knew about him. It seemed incredible, considering how often she thought about him. Gazing into the blueness of his eyes, she let herself imagine a time when they would be together without war raging, a time when they would properly get to know each other and talk of a future together.

She shook her head to bring herself back to the present. His gentle touch made her want to sink into his warm embrace and forget about her part in Nick's disappearance. 'I was just thinking how relieved and grateful I am you made it here.'

Will kissed her hand again, and she lost herself in his trusting blue eyes. This time, he leaned in and kissed her mouth.

'This all seems so unreal, especially knowing that Nick didn't make it,' she said, moving away, but he drew her back and kissed her again. 'And fragile,' she breathed after a long moment.

'So, maybe we should make the most of it.' He gazed at her, then sat back and rubbed a hand through his hair. He looked troubled as he went on, 'All this running and hiding... Freddie, the only thing that kept me going is you, and it's about to end. I have no choice but to return to England and report back to my unit. The RAF have lost so many men that I know they'll expect me to get into a plane as soon as I'm back.' He seemed to shudder at the thought. 'What will you do when I'm gone?' he asked bleakly.

Freddie looked away, unsure how to reply. 'I'll carry on working with the resistance for the remainder of the war. And then? To be honest, I haven't thought about it. I suppose I'll go back home to Haarlem to my family and friends and work at the hospital,' she said with a sigh.

He held her gaze for a long moment and she lifted her hand to his face so she could trace its contours with her fingers. 'Don't be sad,' she murmured, and smiled in an attempt to be cheerful. 'Tell me about England and where you come from. Would I like it?'

He laughed. 'I grew up on the south coast of England in a town called Plymouth. Have you heard of it?'

She shrugged, remembering her faux pas when she'd pronounced Birmingham. 'You know I'm not very good with English place names,' she said blushing. 'But I thought you lived in a village called Saltby.'

'That's where I'm stationed, but Plymouth is my home-town.' He straightened up and grew animated as he said, 'You know, I should take you to Plymouth and we could go out on my dad's sailing boat. He taught me to sail and whenever I'm home I try to go out with him. It's time I paid him a visit. I've been stuck over at the RAF base, which is miles from the coast. I miss it. I haven't been home for more than a year.'

'I'd love to sail with you. When I was younger, my family used to visit my aunt and uncle in Sneek, up in Friesland. The lakes are so beautiful there and I know you'd love it. Before the war, my uncle always entered the annual sailing competition. People came from all over Holland to compete and the atmosphere was so exciting. One year, my uncle came second in his race. It was thrilling.' Her heart filled up with the memory.

'Let's make a promise to each other. I'll take you sailing in Plymouth if you take me to meet this famous uncle of yours.' He chuckled.

'After the war, whenever that is,' she said, jolted back to the present.

'Whenever that is, I will come and find you.' Will seemed more cheerful as he took her hand and covered it in kisses.

Freddie couldn't help but smile. 'And if you don't turn up, I'll come and find you,' she said repeating his words, badly wanting to believe him.

They kissed, and Freddie suddenly remembered she had something of his.

'Will, have you lost something?' she said, searching his eyes. She put her hand into the pocket of her apron and kept it there till he answered.

'Have I?' he said, looking puzzled.

She brought out the two dog tags on the piece of frayed string that she'd kept close to her ever since she found them at the farmhouse.

He took in a sharp breath. 'How did you get those? I've looked for them everywhere. I could have sworn I'd lost them.'

'I saw them lying on the floor of the attic under one of the beds. Jan Kees helped me work out the engraving, though of course I knew it was your name.' She held them out in the palm of her hand, reluctant to hand over the one memento she had of him, but she knew she must.

He took them and loosened the string, then removed one

and pressed it into her palm, his eyes locked on hers. 'This one is for you.'

Freddie shook her head as she tried to push it back to him. 'I can't possibly take this. I know what they're for and… if you die, how will anyone ever know what's happened to you?'

Will shrugged but his expression was serious. 'I'll still have one, which will help identify my body in the event of my death. Freddie, it's the only thing I've got that I can give you. And I've kept your ribbon with the strand of your hair, which is so precious to me. Please take it.'

She didn't reply, but watched as he threaded the disc back onto the string and tied it round her neck, then kissed her where it nestled against her skin. 'Will, I'm beginning to think you're crazy.'

'Crazy is as crazy does,' he said with a half-smile.

'What does that mean?' she said with a little laugh.

'Never mind. All you need to know is I'm crazy about you.'

THIRTY-TWO

The following day Piet van Arnhem, the man Freddie had heard so much about, arrived. It was clear from the offset that Piet was in charge. Although not especially tall, he was a muscular man with closely cropped black hair and an intriguing scar slashed down one cheek, which gave him the air of someone who was not afraid of combat. He was also clad from top to toe in black, giving him a commanding, somewhat menacing presence. Freddie wasn't surprised to hear that he had organised for dozens of airmen to escape occupied Holland by crossing the dangerous Biesbosch region to safety. For the first time in weeks, she felt herself unwind a little.

'First things first. We need to get you out of those rags and into decent clothing that will give protection and help to conceal you when we're running from the enemy. I've brought enough clothes for all of you, so kit yourselves out and then I'll talk plans for the next three days.'

Relief was etched on everyone's faces as Piet handed out the clothes, which included black turtleneck sweaters, trousers and boots. At last they had something proper to wear.

Piet came over to Freddie and looked her up and down. 'We

can't have you standing out in that nurse's uniform of yours. You need to wear the same as the men. Here, these clothes should fit you.' He held up a couple of garments against her for size, before handing them over.

'Thank you,' she said, eyeing the sweater and trousers a little uncertainly. Will was pulling his sweater over his head and gave her a secret wink that made her blush. She could tell he approved of the fact that she would now be one of the men.

'Now, on to the serious stuff,' said Piet. 'Gather round and I'll show you our route.'

He unrolled a map, which covered the kitchen table. Freddie moved closer to see. She'd heard about the Biesbosch region but hadn't appreciated just how vast it was. The map showed marshy terrain criss-crossed with a myriad of rivers and streams, some narrow, some wide, with little discernible dry land in between. Piet roughly traced the route they would take but warned that it could change or become flooded at any time depending on the rise and fall of the tides.

'The place is a wilderness, but that makes it ideal for anyone looking to escape the Germans. They avoid it if they can help it, but that doesn't make it any safer for us. They will use search-lights and missiles if they suspect anyone of trying to reach the river crossings. Not just men like you, but their own deserters.' He looked up, examining each person in the group. 'Is anyone good at reading maps?'

Ed's hand shot up. 'I'm a navigator and I've got a compass.'

'Most of us know our way around a map. It's our job to do so,' drawled George.

Piet nodded, then narrowed his eyes. 'We shouldn't have any problems then,' he said, and proceeded to divide them into two groups. Freddie stood beside Will and was glad when they were selected to be together, along with Jan Kees, Ed and an American called Woody. The other group went with Piet and were made up of the rest of the Englishmen, Alan, Stan and Derek.

Piet went back to the map to indicate their route. 'We set off on foot to this farmhouse, which is about three miles away. You'll be assigned to your groups there. The Brits will go with Jan Kees and me. George, Woody – you'll meet your American contact and the other Americans at the farmhouse. It may take a while to drive everyone to Biesbosch, but this is where you'll be dropped.' He pointed to a village that seemed to be surrounded on all sides by water. 'You'll have twenty-four hours to reach the Merwede river. Our contacts will be with you all the way up to when you reach the shoreline. All being well, the boats will be ready to take you across. Now, there's a lot of us, so it's really important that we don't make it obvious we're together – it'll only arouse suspicions. Stay in your own group and listen to your leader. We have all travelled this route many times.'

He then handed round maps and from another bag took out several guns in holsters. 'I'm afraid the resistance is always short of guns and ammunition. I've got three guns. Decide amongst yourselves who should take one.'

Will volunteered. After examining one of the guns, he slipped it into his trouser pocket. He moved back next to Freddie and she felt his fingers intertwine with hers. Her heart faltered, knowing that they were about to embark on their most dangerous mission yet, and that at the end of it she must let him go.

THIRTY-THREE

Standing in front of the bathroom mirror, Freddie gazed at her reflection. If she was to blend in with the men, she had to do more to disguise herself. Hendrika helped by giving her a length of blue-and-white checked ribbon to tie back her long hair, which she then tucked away into the neck of the sweater. Unsure of the effect, she studied herself in the mirror, turning her head from side to side, but it made no difference: from whichever angle she presented herself she still looked like a girl. How suddenly her life had changed, she realised, thinking back to her first days at Arnhem when her ability as a nurse had been put under severe scrutiny. And little did she know she'd been about to meet the love of her life, let alone set out on her most dangerous mission to date, which could so easily result in her losing him. Drawing in a long breath, she forced herself to remember the positives.

When it was time to go, Hendrika passed round some provisions to see the group through the following days. As she and Gijs waved them off from the door of their cabin, Freddie noticed how Hendrika's eyes shone with tears and wondered how hard this was for her, even though she must have done it many times before. It never ceased to amaze Freddie how many kind generous people she'd met who thought nothing of putting the safety of others before their own.

Perhaps it was because Piet was now in charge at the front of the group, but the forest seemed a far less threatening place than when they'd first entered it. The trees, which had seemed so forbidding at night, stood proud on either side of the path, their sunlit branches in full leaf and alive with the sweet sound of birdsong. In normal times, Freddie might have strolled happily through the woodland, but she couldn't forget that this walk was a means to an end. They needed to get to the farmhouse where Piet's contacts were waiting to accompany them on the next, far more hazardous, part of their journey.

The path narrowed as it wound through the trees, and they were forced to walk in single file. After it broadened out, Freddie moved beside Will.

'Hello, you,' he said quietly with a smile in his voice, and gently brushed his fingers against hers. Warmth flooded through her as she smiled up at him. He intertwined his fingers with hers and they walked without speaking, enjoying the simple pleasure of being in each other's company.

'There's something I want to ask you,' she said after a while. She hadn't had a chance to speak to him alone since the night before. 'You seemed keen to take one of Piet's guns yesterday. Are you used to using guns?'

He stopped to look at her and traced a finger across her cheek. 'Don't look so worried. We were taught about guns as part of our pilot training. I never thought I'd be called on to use them, but we were told to be prepared at all times. It's what I'm trained to do.'

Freddie briefly studied his face, but his expression gave nothing away. 'I've been taught about guns too,' she replied, 'but I've never fired one. My role was always to gather intelligence.

But since we've been on the run, I feel uncomfortable not having a gun to defend myself.'

'Guns aren't always the be all and end all. You have a clear head and can run fast, both important qualities.'

Freddie knew he was trying to reassure her as she said, 'I only hope you're right,' and held on more tightly to his hand.

They kept on walking through the forest till they came to the others, who had stopped in a clearing. Jan Kees was deep in conversation with a tall blond man holding a bicycle. Two others turned up, also riding bicycles.

'Listen, everyone,' said Jan Kees. 'Piet's gone ahead, but we have to wait a few minutes, because the road ahead is full of Germans. They seem to be on some kind of exercise, but we'll arouse their suspicion if they notice so many of us. Our friends here have brought bikes for some of you to cycle to the farmhouse, which is about a mile down this road. The rest of you will walk with Marieke, who has come from the village. The Germans know her and she's quite used to these situations.' He gestured to a woman who looked about Freddie's age and had a cheerful smile. Jan Kees went on, 'The Germans won't bother us if we look like friends out enjoying ourselves.'

'We don't speak Dutch. Where will you be?' said Woody, who was nervously smoking a cigarette. The thought had also occurred to Freddie, who didn't much fancy being interrogated.

'I'll accompany the cyclists.' Jan Kees sounded unconcerned. 'Leave any questions to Marieke. With any luck, they won't bother you. The Germans usually have other things on their minds than stopping people out walking.'

He put Freddie in the walking group with Ed and Woody, then went over to the blond man, who was adjusting the seats of the bikes. She noticed that none of the bikes had tyres and that the men would be forced to ride on the wheel rims, which would surely slow them down. When he'd finished, she grew apprehensive as she watched Will tried to gain his balance on a rusty bike, then wobble alarmingly down the road.

With a sigh, she went over to Woody and offered to partner him, saying she would pretend to be his girlfriend if the Germans accosted them. Marieke, who was talking to Ed, glanced critically at Freddie and gestured to her black sweater.

'We can't have you looking like the men,' she said to her in Dutch, then took off her own jacket. 'Here, put this on.'

Freddie accepted the jacket with a word of thanks, grateful that she and Marieke were roughly the same size. She then removed the ribbon from her hair, letting her dark-blond locks fall around her shoulders. Blending in with the men would have to wait.

Woody was good company and chatted to her about the wheat farm his father owned in Kansas. 'My two little brothers are too young to fight, so they stayed behind and are working on the farm. It's huge and I love nothing more than to drive the tractors all day with my little dog Missie up beside me.'

It was all so going well as they walked in twos, arm in arm, but as soon as they joined the road they encountered four Germans with rifles at their shoulders marching straight towards them. Marieke feigned not to notice and, shrieking with laughter, she turned to Ed and teasingly poked him in the ribs. One of the Germans muttered something as he went past and was so busy looking at her that he collided with Freddie. He let out a string of German expletives, then demanded to know where they were going.

'We're not going anywhere. We're just friends out for a stroll.' As soon as she spoke, Freddie realised the words had come out more sharply than she'd intended. She knew the first rule was never to rile a German soldier, for it would only lead to awkward questions. But it was too late for that. She kept silent as his eyes moved suspiciously from Woody to Ed, his mouth set in a cruel sneer. Then he spoke rapidly in German to his colleague and Freddie understood they were asking to see the men's *Sperre*.

Sperre. An exemption for work, authorised by the Germans and the only way men aged between eighteen and forty-five could legitimately avoid forced labour. *Why had no one thought of this?* Freddie thought in frustration.

Then Woody shrugged and looked at Ed, who did the same.

Freddie let out a quiet breath. Thank goodness they had the sense to keep quiet.

Only one thing was worse than being a Dutch man without a *Sperre*, and that was being a foreigner with no reason to be in the country. She listened quietly as Marieke took over in fluent German.

'They don't speak German,' she explained. 'Of course they have a *Sperre*, but why would they have it on them when we're only out for a quick stroll? Surely you know that, Helmut.' She gave him a conciliatory smile.

One of the other Germans was growing impatient. 'Helmut, *hör auf damit. Wir müssen uns beeilen.*'

Freddie silently translated to herself: Leave off. We have to hurry.

Helmut didn't look pleased at being undermined, but he reluctantly agreed, although not before saying, 'Don't let me come across you again. Next time you're out without a *Sperre* there will be trouble.'

Woody took hold of Freddie's arm and marched her away. When they were out of earshot, he slid her an appreciative look. 'Well done,' he murmured.

Freddie pulled a face, feeling undeserving of his compliment. She had caused this confrontation and she vowed to herself to do better next time.

Just then, there was a commotion up ahead. Will and Jan Kees were standing at the side of the road, holding on to their bikes, while George stood staring in disbelief at a uniformed German who had mounted his bike and was riding it away.

'Stay back,' warned Marieke. 'Let them deal with it. It looks like they've only stolen one bike.'

'The bastards! Is there nothing they won't stoop to?' Woody spat on the ground with a look of disgust.

'I'm afraid not. The Germans steal our bikes all the time. It's like a joke to them,' said Marieke. 'Fortunately, there are more where those come from, but we keep our best bikes out of sight. Oh, I forgot to say – we're very good at getting stolen bikes back.' She spoke with the hint of a smile, which dropped when a convoy of motorbikes came speeding down the road with a deafening roar, followed by a black limousine with darkened windows. On its front and back, small swastika flags fluttered in the breeze.

'Who in God's name is in there? Hitler?' said Woody, incredulous, as he turned to watch the procession.

'No, he wouldn't bother coming to a backwater like this,' said Ed. 'It's probably just some trumped-up officer drunk on power who's passing through.'

Marieke laughed. She explained that the Germans had their regional headquarters a few miles from here and the high command were often ferried around in smart cars.

'I don't wanna stick around here any longer. Can we get going now?' said Woody, now looking thoroughly disgusted.

Marieke nodded. 'Of course. I'll take you a different route across the fields. It's longer, but safer.' She crossed the road and led them down an alley between some houses, which ended up at a large field with a couple of sheep that lifted their heads to gaze at them.

Marieke strode ahead and Freddie hurried to keep up with her. 'You do this often, don't you? Moving airmen from place to place.'

Marieke nodded. 'That's right, but I'm not the only one.

The whole village is involved. We keep a close watch on the Germans and we've never been caught yet. They must be stupid or something.' She giggled, her hand flying up to cover her mouth, then gave Freddie a quick glance. 'How did you get into the resistance?'

'I worked in a group in Haarlem as a courier and scouted for collaborators. When the bombing started at Arnhem, I was transferred to the hospital – I'm a nurse by training. I saw how much danger these airmen were in and the risk of them being caught. Then I met a doctor whose son, Jan Kees, was helping evadees and I knew that was what I wanted to do too. I never planned it, but once you're involved it takes over your life.'

'Is it your first time doing the Biesbosch run?' asked Marieke, turning her head to look Freddie in the eye. Freddie nodded.

'Well, good luck with that,' Marieke said sympathetically. 'I've heard the terrain is treacherous. The place is a swamp and difficult to navigate and the *moffen* are getting smarter at tracking down evadees. I hope you're well prepared. Not everyone makes it across.'

Freddie felt a chill trickle through her, but she couldn't allow herself any doubts. 'Our contacts have done this many times before. We have no choice but to put our trust in them,' she heard herself say, letting the enormous reality of what they were about to face sink in.

THIRTY-FOUR

All Freddie wanted was to spend her last few hours with Will before leaving for the Biesbosch. She no longer had any illusions about what lay ahead, but did he? She'd noticed how Piet hadn't actually given them much information on what to expect once they got there – was it because the terrain and consequences of getting caught were so terrible, and he was trying to keep up morale? The conversation with Marieke left her in no doubt. She needed to speak to Will about it, but also about other more important things regarding their future. She knew that today would be her last opportunity to do so.

Marieke came as far as the end of the dirt track that led to the farmhouse, and said she had to leave them as she needed to escort more Allied airmen to another safe address.

'Hell's bells!' exclaimed Ed. 'How many more of us are there?'

'I can't answer that, but I do know you're the last group to go via Biesbosch.' Marieke hesitated, and Freddie suspected she hadn't meant to let slip that last piece of information.

'That sounds ominous. What's going to happen to all the others?' said Ed, sounding concerned.

'They'll be going via Belgium. The resistance has decided to use another route over the Pyrenees into Spain and Portugal. It'll be dangerous, whichever way you go.' She didn't quite meet his gaze. 'Well, I must go. I'll say goodbye to you here. And I wish you all luck.'

'I don't like the sound of that,' said Woody, staring after her as she hurried away. 'I've been trying not to think about this swampy hellhole we're about to enter, but, sure as anything, she's not helping.'

'Let's not dwell on that now,' said Freddie, trying to calm things down. 'We all know it's going to be tough. Let's just concentrate on getting across that river to freedom.'

The farmhouse was crowded with airmen, mostly British and American, as well as some Canadians, who were awaiting for instructions to leave. All had been rescued by the resistance after botched landings and parachute drops over Arnhem. They had spent weeks in hiding until their regiments were able to organise personnel to come to Tilburg, which lay over the border in liberated territory. From there, they would be transferred back home by road, rail or plane. There were joyful reunions between the men, as well as tears when one man saw his missing crew member, presumed dead, walk through the door, alive and well.

Will stood apart from the rest, talking quietly to Jan Kees. Freddie went over to him and lightly touched his hand, knowing how hard this must be for him. As far as Will was concerned, he was the sole survivor of his crash now that Nick had gone missing. Freddie's heart twisted as she remembered their futile attempts at finding Nick. She still blamed herself. There was no celebration to be had here.

Hans Dekker was the owner of the farmhouse and obviously relished having so many people around. He stood at the kitchen table, pouring wine and gin into glasses and handing out cigars to anyone who wanted one. 'Drink up. There's plenty more where this comes from.' He chuckled. 'We had some German officers staying here until a couple of weeks ago. When they left, they gave us all this as a thank-you.'

Freddie was surprised by his remark and didn't like the sound of it. 'Aren't you worried they might come back and find a load of airmen here?' she said.

He looked at her and grinned. 'No, not at all. They were so grateful to have a comfortable place to stay and said they'd make sure that none of their people would bother us in future.' He offered her a glass of wine, but she declined. His comment made her uneasy. It seemed wrong to be celebrating with wine, knowing how he'd come by it.

Jan Kees was standing close by in conversation with Piet; he gestured for Freddie to follow them to a quiet corner of the kitchen.

'It's not safe here. What does the farmer think he's doing handing out alcohol as if this is a cause for celebration?' she said in an urgent whisper.

Piet looked unconcerned as he replied. 'We don't have much choice but to trust him. His farmhouse is the biggest around for miles and we've been using it as a stopover for some weeks. The Germans are far too busy entertaining their people at their HQ in town to worry about whether the farmer is helping airmen. It's worked so far.' He let his gaze dart around the room at the clusters of men drinking and laughing. 'I don't have a problem with it. It's their last chance to let their hair down before things get tough.'

'It won't be long till we leave,' said Jan Kees quietly to Freddie. 'Our driver has already gone with the first group and will be back before nightfall.'

'I'll say goodbye to you here, Freddie,' said Piet, holding out his large hand and gripping hers in a firm handshake. 'To be honest, I was surprised when I saw you at Gijs and Hendrika's with all those men. I haven't come across women doing this kind of work before.'

'Well, you have now,' said Freddie, pulling her hand away, 'and I hope you'll be seeing more of us in the future. I'll see you later,' she said, turning to Jan Kees.

She turned on her heel and went to Will, whispering that she didn't want to stick around all these men who were behaving as if this were some kind of celebration. She led him round behind the farmhouse, where the sun was just starting to sink behind the trees. They sat on the step holding hands, half listening to the hum of voices interspersed with laughter from inside. Cigar smoke clung to her clothes, a reminder of times past and the parties her parents used to throw before the war. She couldn't imagine things ever returning to how they were back then.

Leaning her head against Will's shoulder, she sighed. 'I was talking to Marieke, the Dutch girl I was walking with today. She was telling me the Biesbosch is more dangerous than people realise and that the Germans are getting better at catching evadees. Sometimes the men don't even get as far as the river crossing. I'm scared you might be one of them.'

Will lifted her chin and gave her a long look. 'Not if I can help it. I've been through hell these past few weeks, but you've helped me get through them. So why should it be any different now? Before we know it the war will be over and then we can be together.'

Freddie felt a rush of warmth as she searched his eyes, wishing she could share his optimism. The Germans were still very much in control and, if anything, the failure of the Allies to capture Arnhem had made them even more determined to win.

'Have you even thought what happens when you get back to England... how will I know you're safe? I don't even know your address,' she said at last.

'Don't be sad,' Will said, letting his eyes roam over her face. 'You forget you have my details on your dog tag,' he murmured, fingering the disc that lay nestled in her throat. 'I've still got mine, so if you contact the RAF in London they'll be able to tell you where I am. But I'm sure it won't come to that. I intend to let you know as soon as I'm back on British soil. And as soon as it's safe to do so, I'll come back for you.'

She so wanted to believe him, but there were still too many obstacles to overcome before that could happen.

'We'll get through this,' he said, as if reading her mind. Then he slid his hand into his pocket and drew out the ribbon she'd given him all those weeks ago. It still had a strand of her hair wound round it. She laid her hand over his, the ribbon clasped tight between them, and gave him a lingering kiss on the lips.

'Will you go back to the hospital in Arnhem?' he murmured, bringing her back to the present.

She had to think. She hadn't actually allowed herself to plan anything beyond Biesbosch but knew her nursing skills would be sorely needed wherever she went. After everything that had happened at Arnhem, she instinctively felt that was where she should be, working alongside Dr Akkerman and Inge. She belonged there, treating casualties, saving lives and making a difference. 'Yes, I'll go back to Arnhem. And you should ask for Dr Akkerman – he'll know how to get hold of me.'

Then, from behind her, she heard a click, the sound of the back door opening. She turned her head and saw it was Jan Kees. His face was covered in dark streaks.

'Ah, I'm glad I found you,' he said, crouching down to their level. 'The van's arrived and it'll be ready to leave in ten minutes.' He took a cork from his pocket, and a lighter, lit one end of the cork till it smouldered, then blew on it. He handed it to Freddie. 'Rub this over your face and hands. We need to be as well camouflaged as possible. In that way, there'll be no reflections and the Germans won't be able to see you.'

Freddie waited till the cork was cool enough to touch, then made a dark stripe across the back of her hand. 'Not bad,' she said, exchanging a smile with Will.

'Right,' said Jan Kees, getting up. 'I'll see you in the front in a few minutes.'

After they'd applied their camouflage, Freddie started to get up, but Will prevented her by grasping her hand and pulling her back down. 'Wait a minute.'

'What is it?' she said, searching his eyes.

'Nothing. I just want to hold you before we go.'

She nodded quickly, understanding, and melted into his arms for one last urgent kiss. She wondered if it might be the last one they ever had.

THIRTY-FIVE

The small delivery van didn't look capable of holding so many of them, but somehow they all managed to squeeze in. Freddie wedged herself between Jan Kees and the driver on the unforgiving hard bench, but knew it was nothing compared to the discomfort of the British airmen hidden in the back, squashed together under sacking. Every time the van rounded a bend with a lurch, there was much grumbling and swearing, and Freddie smiled at their choice of words she'd never encountered before. Eventually, they quietened down and their swearing was replaced with snores.

Jan Kees studied his map by the light of his torch, and showed her each landmark she needed to be aware of. He would guide them to a village called Drimmelen, where they would meet Anton and Erik, local men who risked their lives every night to ferry people across the river into liberated Holland. Jan Kees mentioned others who might or might not be working the area depending on who else was trying to cross the border. Freddie listened carefully, familiarising herself with their names, and concentrated hard as Jan Kees traced their route along a confusing web of streams and tributaries of the main river, interspersed with marsh, bog and mudflats. The landscape was like nothing she'd ever come across before, but Jan Kees assured her that it was the job of the local resistance to navigate them across. She hoped this was true, and committed everything he told her to memory, knowing that at some point he would be relying on her to be the eyes and ears of the group.

The van slowed and came to a halt at the side of a road. Freddie peered out of the window into pitch darkness. She guessed it was too dangerous to go any further in case they were seen.

Jan Kees opened his door and jumped onto the road.

Fighting the desire to stay put, Freddie made herself follow him. She looked around but found it impossible to make out anything other than the road immediately in front of her. Jan Kees had given her one of two torches he had, but had warned her against using it unless absolutely necessary. Any light could give them away.

Leaving the engine running, the driver went round to open up the back and one by one the men climbed out, stretching their arms, pulling dark woollen hats over their ears and swinging their duffle bags onto their shoulders. Jan Kees thanked the driver, who got in the van and seemed in a hurry to turn it round and drive back the way they'd come. As he disappeared down the road, Freddie could feel herself tense up; she had to push aside her fear that they'd just been abandoned in a place where the enemy could spring a sudden attack at any time. At that very moment she started at the distant thump of a bomb exploding and the stutter of machine-gun fire from afar. A flash of white light illuminated the night sky, repeating several more times before it fell dark again.

'That'll be the Jerries,' said Ed, his worried-looking face briefly visible each time there was a flare. 'Isn't that where we're heading?'

'It's hard to say, but hopefully they'll stop soon,' said Jan

Kees. 'Not too far from here is a barn that's used by the resistance where we can stop and take stock for an hour or two. It's across the field to our right. Freddie, can you stay at the back? And make sure we all keep close together. We don't want to lose anyone before we've even started.'

It was an attempt at a joke, but no one laughed as they set off after him. No sooner had they stepped onto the field than their boots became heavy with mud that sucked at their feet with every squelching step they took. It wasn't long before Freddie had the cold sensation of mud oozing over the top of her boots and seeping through her socks.

'Bloody hell! I can barely move. Isn't there an easier way than this?' one of the men grumbled.

'Shut up and stop whining,' someone else retorted.

They carried on. The only sound was the squelch-squelch of their boots and the occasional word of encouragement from Jan Kees.

Freddie concentrated on putting one foot in front of the other and looked forward to removing her boots and drying out inside a warm barn. She had no illusions that the reality would probably be nothing like it, but imagining a safe place to stop helped blot out her misery.

Eventually they reached a stony path at the far edge of the field, where they stamped their boots to remove the worst of the caked mud. Jan Kees flicked on his torch and the beam picked out the dark shape of a building not far from where they stood. There were sighs of relief all round. When they got there, they found it wasn't a barn but a stone building with creeper growing up the uneven walls and the bare bones of broken rafters, open to the sky. To top it all, there was a gaping hole for a door.

'This can't be right, can it?' said Ed.

'It's the only building around for miles, so I think it must be,' said Jan Kees. 'I'll go inside and take a look.'

'What a shithole,' said Ed while they waited, and kicked his boot against the wall.

'Language. There's a lady present,' said Alan.

'Don't mind me,' said Freddie, too tired even to raise a smile.

Jan Kees appeared in the doorway. 'It will have to do. It's not for long, so we're going to have to make the best of it.' He briefly turned on his torch to show them the way. 'You can leave your boots at the entrance.'

'In case we tramp mud over the clean floor,' said a disgruntled Ed, but he was the first to take off his boots and go inside.

From far off came the dull thud of another bomb exploding. Freddie moved next to Will so she could clasp his hand; together they went inside.

Shining her torch around, she saw it was every bit as dismal as she'd feared. The place looked as if it had been long abandoned, and there was nothing to suggest it had once been a barn. Just piles of rubble where the roof had fallen in and the depressing sight of rodent droppings scattered on the cold dirt floor. But someone had obviously been here, possibly even slept overnight, for there was a stack of blankets, some empty tin cans and bottles piled up in one corner.

A couple of the men found old wooden pallets and arranged makeshift seating in a semicircle. Jan Kees discovered a small heap of some candle stubs that still had usable wicks. He lit them and placed them in the centre of the floor, where they flickered, sending wavering shapes that shifted eerily across the walls.

'I've got jenever and some food we can share,' Jan Kees said and opened his duffle bag. He took out a parcel containing slices of bread and unwrapped another of chunks of dried sausage. When he dug in the bag again and produced a bottle of the strong spirit, everyone cheered.

'Good man,' said Ed, accepting the bottle and taking the first swig. 'Just what I need.' He sighed and wiped his mouth on his sleeve. The bottle was passed from person to person and once everyone had taken their fill of the potent drink the mood lightened considerably.

Freddie joined in but her heart wasn't in it. She kept listening out for any let-up in the bombing, counting every muffled explosion that came from deep within the Biesbosch. She knew this meant it would be too dangerous for them to continue, but neither could they stay here. Not just because of the dilapidated building, which was only suitable for a brief stopover, but because it was essential they stick to their timetable. If they didn't meet the line-crossers, who were waiting for them to turn up at the appointed time, then they would assume they weren't coming and leave without them. And if that happened, she knew the evacuation was as good as off.

THIRTY-SIX

Freddie hurried to find her boots, which were lying in a heap with the others by the entrance. Her socks were uncomfortably damp, but without them she knew she would get blisters. She dragged them half-heartedly onto her feet, eased on her boots and tied the laces.

Jan Kees came over and spoke in an urgent whisper. 'Freddie, at least take the map, will you? Even the locals get lost finding their way through the swampy terrain and you've never even been here before.'

She knew he was right, but was determined to do things her way. 'I never use maps and I'm not going to start now. It'll only slow me down and I haven't got time for that. I took mental notes when you showed me how to get to Drimmelen. If I get lost, I'll rely on my instincts.' She let out a sigh. 'I appreciate you're worried about me going alone. If I run into anyone I'll be able to talk my way out of it, which is more than any of the men here would able to do. Besides, I know I'm good at scouting for information, even if I haven't done anything quite like this before.' She gave him her best smile, remembering Piet's comment about women working for the resistance. She still felt she had something to prove. 'You do think I can do this, don't you?'

'Of course I do. I'm just making sure that you're absolutely prepared before you set out.' He brought out his pocket compass. 'Please take this. If you get lost it'll help you work out which direction you should be going.'

'Thank you,' she said, taking it.

'Are you sure you have your torch?' he added.

She was anxious to get going and always worked better without interference, especially when she was scouting out a new area – it nearly always saved valuable time. 'Yes, I've got my torch. Once I've worked out the route I promise I'll come back and fetch you. Make sure you're all ready to leave.'

'Will do. I know I can rely on you.' Jan Kees patted her shoulder and went back inside.

She was checking the contents of her small duffle bag – her torch, compass, woollen hat and gloves and the small zipped-up bag containing essential medicines and bandages – when Will appeared at her side and slipped his arms round her waist. She twisted round and took his face in her hands. By the look in his eyes she could tell that he didn't want her to go, but he didn't say it, just locked her in a tight embrace.

'Come back safely,' he whispered close to her ear.

'I will,' she breathed, grateful that he trusted her.

The muted thump of another explosion somewhere in the distance told her it was time to go.

She swung her duffle bag onto her shoulder and blocked everything else from her mind, stepped out into the dark night and ran for the protection of a nearby wood. She knew it would be a longer route. Drimmelen was only a mile or so along the road where they'd been dropped off, but it was too exposed and there was the risk of being seen.

She took out her torch and shone it around, noting that the vegetation under the trees was sparse, with no discernible path.

She knew she could easily get lost going this way, but also that she was less likely to come across anyone.

Setting off at a run, she darted through the trees. It didn't take long for her eyes to adjust to the darkness. She ran as lightly as she could to avoid making any sound in the deathly quiet wood. Occasionally, a twig cracked like gunfire underfoot, but she didn't let that concern her.

Then, through the trees something glistened. Pausing to catch her breath, she was surprised to see she'd reached the water so quickly. Her spirits lifting, she took a few steps, expecting to find a network of streams she could jump over to reach dry land, when she was brought up short. In front of her was a lake, and a large one at that. She peered into the darkness. How on earth could they all be expected to get across that? Quickly, she scanned the shallows to determine where the shoreline ended and the lake began. Thick clumps of tall bulrushes made it hard to work it out. The sound of gently lapping water did nothing to allay her fears that getting across would be anything but easy. She had to find a way. Thinking hard, she wondered if she should keep going and find where the lake narrowed. Perhaps she'd find a bridge.

She set off, keeping her eyes glued firmly ahead.

She almost missed the boat hidden low down in a thicket of rushes, and it was only when she heard the soft lap of water that she peered more closely and realised what she was seeing. The rowing boat looked like it had been abandoned or deliberately left. It was almost entirely surrounded by tall reeds. She took a few tentative steps down the bank to avoid slipping into the water – there inside the boat were two oars lying flat. Gripping onto the side, the boat wobbled. She hurled herself into it. Crouching, she felt around for leaks and, to her relief, found it was dry. Although the boat was large enough to take several people, she doubted they would all fit in. They would have to go across in two groups.

Elated by her discovery, she quickly retraced her steps back through the wood, ignoring the rustle of her footsteps through the leaves and the pop of twigs underfoot. Twice she stopped, convinced she could hear someone close by. She crouched low behind a tree until she could be sure the coast was clear.

She darted from her hiding place and ran lightly all the way back to the barn, where the men were waiting out of sight just inside the entrance.

'Back already?' said Ed with a dismissive cough.

Freddie ignored him. 'We need to leave right away. Beyond the woods, I've discovered a lake we need to cross to get to Drimmelen. I found a rowing boat in the reeds. It's big enough for four of us, so we'll need to go across in two trips.'

'Good work,' said Jan Kees. 'That'll belong to one of the line-crossers. Did you see any other boats? The Germans are known to patrol these waters in motorboats.'

Freddie felt herself tense up. She hadn't considered this. 'I didn't hear any, but we have to chance it. Anton will be waiting for us on the other side.'

It took two men to drag the boat free; it was firmly wedged in the rushes and caught up in a tangle of weeds, suggesting it hadn't been used for a while. Once it was on the open water, four of them were selected to climb on board.

Freddie went with the first group, with Will rowing, and directed him towards the opposite bank. There was a nervous moment halfway across when an engine could be heard starting up in the distance.

'Stop rowing a moment,' Freddie warned Will.

He lifted the oars out of the water and let them drift sound-lessly, barely moving.

The noise of the engine faded. 'It's just a car,' Freddie said with relief.

Will carried on, the only sound in the still night the splash of the oars as he pulled them through the water. Thankfully, there were no bulrushes to prevent them from making a landing on the far bank.

'Over there,' instructed Freddie, spying a dilapidated wooden landing stage. She and the others got out and Will rowed back for the others, disappearing into the darkness.

Only when they were all safely on dry land could Freddie breathe easily. She looked around and saw the dark outline of houses a little way from where they were standing.

'Well done, Freddie,' said Jan Kees. 'We've made it to Drimmelen thanks to your quick thinking.'

'Well, let's not wreck things by us all turning up at once. Wait here while I go on ahead and tell Anton we're here.'

The address she had was a modest house in a quiet street. After checking all around her, she went up to the door and rapped out the first bars of the Dutch national anthem, which many people knew to use as code to prove they weren't unwelcome German visitors. The door was opened by a middle-aged woman in a faded floral apron.

'Willem had a big moustache,' Freddie quickly recited – it was a nonsensical sentence she'd been given by the resistance to prove she was one of them.

The woman nodded and stood aside to let her in.

Freddie told her she was with a group of six English pilots who needed to evacuate that evening. 'They're waiting down at the water. Is Anton here?' Her heart pounded – what if the woman was about to tell her he wasn't in. Then she remembered the woman wouldn't know who she was. 'Jan Kees Akkerman is leading the group.'

'Ah yes. Anton's expecting him,' the woman said with the flicker of a smile. 'You'll find Anton in the back room.' She led the way down a dark passage and opened a door at the far end. Two surly-looking men were sitting smoking at a table. They were both dressed in black with woollen hats pulled low on their foreheads.

'They've arrived,' the woman said to them. 'This is...?' She turned to Freddie.

Was it her imagination, or were they surprised to see a woman turn up? She quickly dismissed the thought. 'Freddie. I'm helping Jan Kees Akkerman, who's in charge of this operation. We're not too late, are we?'

Anton, she guessed, stood up and scraped his chair back. 'No, but you're running it a bit fine. We'll need to leave right away.'

'We came as quickly as we could. Is it safe to go to the river? We've been hearing explosions all evening.'

He scoffed. 'It happens every night. If it's not the Germans, it's the Allies retaliating. Or vice versa. It's been going on ever since the Allies liberated South Brabant, but we can't let that stop us.' He pursed his lips into what seemed to Freddie like a grudging smile. 'I'm Anton. This is Erik.'

The other man, who had been watching silently, lifted his hand up in greeting.

Anton went on, 'Erik's just returned from taking another group to the crossing. Americans, or maybe they were Canadians. Messy business it was, but we think they all got across.'

Freddie was shocked. 'You mean, you don't know if they made it?'

He shrugged. 'Once they're picked up by Allied boats, they're no longer our responsibility. You won't believe how many want to escape. Who can blame them?'

These weren't the words Freddie wanted to hear, but she had no reason to believe he was exaggerating. And what choice did they have but to put their faith in Anton and Erik, hardened line-crossers, who were no doubt paid good money for doing so? She realised this was just another job for them.

THIRTY-SEVEN

Anton hadn't mentioned that their group was only one of several who were due to evacuate that night. It only became apparent they weren't the only ones after they had completed an exhausting slog through a cold muddy swamp, which sucked at their feet with every step, swirling weeds dragging at their legs. They had to stay close to the water's edge where they couldn't be seen, trying to avoid drooping branches lying in wait ready to slap them in the face.

When they finally heaved themselves onto dry land, they found Anton staring intently into the darkness. He swung round and sucked in a breath. 'Right in front of us is an open field. We have to get across it to reach the wood leading to the river crossing. There is no other way. The problem is the Germans have caught on to what we're doing. Every night they have their machine guns trained over the field looking for men escaping.'

Will exchanged a worried look with Freddie. 'If we get across, won't the Germans be waiting for us on the other side?' he asked.

'Not if we run to the safety of the wood before they get us.

Unfortunately, it's a risk we have to take if we're to escape. Rest assured, Erik and I have taken many Allied airmen across and we haven't lost a single man.'

Freddie stared in the direction he'd been looking, trying not to dwell on the danger that lay ahead. She could just make out a number of dark shapes lying motionless on the ground. She refused to believe they were dead bodies.

Anton went on, 'We'll wait to see how this lot get on, then it's our turn.'

'How many men are out there?' asked Jan Kees.

'I don't know exactly. At a guess, a hundred?'

Freddie felt a shiver run through her. So many men trying to escape. What chance did they have of making it without being shot dead?

'This is madness. We're dead men walking,' Alan said, voicing what everyone must be thinking.

'Dead men crawling, more like.' Ed's attempt at a joke was lost as the field was suddenly illuminated by a flare of bright white light. Immediately the tat-tat-tat of gunfire started. In the short moment when the field was visible, Freddie glimpsed prone bodies everywhere. Shocked, she tried to count how many – ten... twelve – before it went dark. The bodies lay so still, Freddie could not help fearing the worst.

Anton divided the group into pairs and told them to stay together, one following the other. Freddie was briefly consoled to find herself next to Will. They would go after Anton, then came Jan Kees and Ed, Alan and Derek, and finally Erik and Stan.

'After the next flare and burst of gunfire, get ready to go,' Anton said. 'We'll be crawling all the way on our bellies. Whenever there's a flare, stop dead, lie flat and keep perfectly still.'

For several tense minutes nothing happened. Suddenly, out of nowhere another flare crackled into the night sky, bathing everything in a ghostly white glow. Freddie forgot to count how many men were still ahead of her, but that was probably just as well. She couldn't allow herself to dwell on the possibility that they were all about to be caught in the gunfire. Almost immediately, the explosion of light was followed by a tat-tat-tat, so deafening that it seemed to come from right next to her.

'Get down and start crawling,' Anton commanded and dropped to his belly. Freddie felt Will tug her hand and pull her down with him onto the hard cold ground.

'You go first. I'll be right behind you,' he said. She felt his breath close to her ear.

She began squirming forward on her front, lifting her head every so often to look for Anton, but he was moving away faster than she was able to keep up. Desperate not to lose sight of him, she whispered to Will over her shoulder, 'I can't keep up with him. You go ahead.'

Will crawled by her side. 'Are you sure?' he said hesitantly.

'Yes, please just do it.' She had no idea if it was the right thing – what if she lost sight of him too?

'I'll keep looking back for you,' he said softly, as if reading her thoughts. He crawled past and for a short while she was able to breathe again.

'You've got to keep up,' she kept telling herself as she slithered slowly and painfully, her arms aching from the effort of dragging her body along the unforgiving ground; she tried to ignore the small sharp stones digging into her body.

Whoosh! The night sky lit up again. Instantly, she flattened her cheek to the earth, scarcely able to breathe as she waited for the gunfire to start up again.

'Keep still. It'll be over soon,' she heard Will whisper to her close by.

She sucked in a shaky breath; then she heard the crackle of gunfire, bullets peppering the ground and bouncing up right by her head. The firing seemed to go on for ages, then it stopped as suddenly as it had started. Suddenly, Freddie found she was too petrified to move.

'Freddie, you have to keep going. We're almost there,' Jan Kees called out to her.

'All right,' she said in a small desperate voice and tentatively raised her head to look for Will, but unbelievably he was no longer there. Panicking, she said, 'I can't see him.'

'He'll be there, just hold on.' Jan Kees's voice was calm, but she wasn't reassured.

The only thing propelling her forward was fear. Using her elbows to wriggle faster, she was stunned to find she'd reached the edge of the field that fell away in front of her. She rolled towards it and down a slope into dense tangled undergrowth seconds before the next flare exploded. There was no time to think, even hesitate, as others tumbled after her.

'Christ, that was close.'

'How do we get out of here?'

'Where's Anton?'

Freddie tried to make sense of what was happening from the confusion of voices. 'Where's Will?' Her voice trembled. She desperately wanted to retrieve her torch from her sodden duffle bag strapped to her back, but the firing was still so close.

Erik took charge. 'Come on, we have to keep going. It's always crazy at this point. We're bound to catch up with them soon.'

On all sides men were crashing through the undergrowth in their panic to get away. Some were moaning, some limping, all moving. As she stumbled after Erik, Freddie didn't dare think about those who hadn't even got this far.

She'd almost given up all hope when through the confusion she heard Anton calling Erik's name.

Erik pushed past her, sounding relieved. 'I told you we'd find them.'

Freddie hurried to keep up with him, her heart thudding painfully.

Erik got there first. 'Is he wounded?'

Anton was crouching beside Will, who was bent double and in obvious pain. 'Don't worry about me,' he said in a strained voice.

Freddie was next to Will in an instant, untying the straps of her duffle bag and getting out her medical kit. Her instincts as a nurse kicked in. 'Let me take a look,' she said in a shaky voice.

'He didn't know he'd been shot till we were almost clear,' Anton said, pointing to the lower part of Will's leg.

Freddie gently rolled up his trouser leg and could see he'd sustained a flesh wound to his calf. As far as she could tell, there wasn't too much damage, which suggested the bullet must have glanced off his leg. She asked Anton to shine a torch while she cleaned and bandaged it as best she could. She knew that the adrenalin would be masking his pain for now, so helped him to his feet. He took a few tentative limping steps and said he was fine to carry on.

When they got into the wood, Anton gathered everyone round to tell them that they needed to get to the river quickly because the Canadian army were bringing in boats at midnight to take the men across.

Anton led the way, with Erik bringing up the rear. The wood was filled with shadowy shapes all creeping in the same direction. All around them was the sound of gunfire and mortars exploding, but none was close enough to impede their progress.

The woodland thinned out and they came to a road running parallel to the river just visible beyond it, where they found dozens of men waiting for a lull in the firing before they crossed.

'We're all going over together. Keep close,' urged Anton.

Freddie slipped her hand into Will's and he squeezed it. When Anton gave the signal to run, they all dashed over the road, and had barely reached the other side before there was another burst of gunfire. From behind her, Freddie heard screams, but she held tight to Will's hand and kept running.

After all the turmoil, they huddled shivering in a thicket of trees on the riverbank, waiting for the boats to land. There was a pause in the shooting, but everyone was on tenterhooks in case it should start up again. Anton kept his eyes fixed ahead, saying he knew exactly which boat would be theirs and would give the signal for the men to go. He indicated a white tape line the Canadians had laid out on the ground. They would need to keep to it in order to avoid stepping on mines.

Freddie and Will sat close together holding hands, keeping their eyes fixed on the water for any signs of movement. She laid her head on his shoulder. She was worrying about his leg wound and whether it would slow him down, but couldn't bring herself to say so. Instead, she said, 'The bandage is only temporary. Get someone to change the dressing as soon as you get to safety. Promise me you'll do it.'

He kissed the top of her head. 'I promise. And as soon as we're on the boat, you must leave with Jan Kees. No looking back.'

She closed her eyes and pressed herself against him, knowing he was right. When she opened them, she glimpsed a red light on the river, blinking on and off as it glided towards them. All around was perfectly quiet, not even the sound of a motor. She gripped Will's hand hard, not daring to speak. Then, as the shape of a boat came into view, they turned to each other, their lips pressing together in a last urgent kiss.

Anton was on his feet, and swung round. 'That boat is yours. Are you ready?' He looked at Will, who nodded. 'You're on your way to freedom now. Good luck.'

Will stood up, stumbling slightly, but once he started

running he easily kept up with the others. One after the other, they kept to the white tape all the way to the shoreline. Only when they had all clambered aboard did their rescuer switch on the engine and swing the boat round. In seconds, they were swallowed up by the darkness.

Freddie kept watching the spot where the boat had disappeared, listening to the fading sound of the motor. She was only vaguely aware of men moving all around her, dashing to the shore to other boats that had now turned up.

A sudden burst of gunfire and several explosions sent the river water spurting up into the air. It was impossible to see if any of the boats had been hit. Freddie dropped to her knees, her eyes blurring with tears, her heart clenched in fear.

'Come on, Freddie. There's no point staying. We need to get out of here,' said Jan Kees, who was at her side. Then she remembered Will's words – *no looking back* – and made herself leave without having any idea if he had made it.

THIRTY-EIGHT

Will

Will felt his legs buckle as he stumbled onto dry land. His wounded leg didn't hurt as much now but had grown stiff from trying to stay hidden in the boat during the hour-long crossing. He'd had time to reflect on the extraordinary events of the past days and the number of times he'd been so close to being caught by the Germans. It was only now they were separated that he appreciated how much of his escape had been down to Freddie. She had repeatedly and fearlessly got them through the most difficult of situations without a moment's thought for her own safety. His heart ached as he remembered their last tender kiss, a poignant reminder of what she meant to him.

An officer in army uniform rushed forward and caught Will moments before he fell to the ground. 'That looks a nasty leg wound. Come with me. The jeep's just over there. I'm driving you straight to the hospital.'

English, Will thought in relief, realising how tense he'd been feeling. He was about to thank the officer when he was hit by a wave of nausea. Swallowing hard, he leaned on the man's arm and concentrated on hobbling to the jeep. He eased himself into the front seat, where he had room to stretch out his wounded leg. He heard the others scrambling in behind him.

'Major Hibbert, but you can call me Tony,' said the officer, getting into the driver's side and slamming his door. 'At the hospital you'll be checked over and given something to eat and drink.' He bent over and picked up a bottle from the footwell. 'This should keep you going till we get there.'

Will was first to drink from the bottle of whisky. His nausea eased and he relished the burning sensation that filled his chest up with warmth. He was about to lift the bottle for another swig when there were protests from the back.

'Steady on. You're not the only one in need of a drink. Leave some for us.' Ed leaned forward to grab the bottle before the others could get to it, but it was all good-natured stuff. Despite his discomfort, Will allowed himself a smile.

'Are we ready to go?' said Tony with a chuckle.

The jeep burst into life and roared away. Tony had to shout above the din of the engine as he told them how he'd been picking up evadees every night for the past few weeks. 'I've never seen anything like it. Some nights so many turn up we have to put them up in tents before we can get them to the hospital. We have the Dutch underground to thank for organising the whole operation. It feels like a small victory after what the Jerries did to us at Arnhem.'

'What happened?' asked Will. 'We've had virtually no news about the war since our planes came down. And we've had hardly any contact with anyone on the British side. We've all been in hiding,' he added in case Tony hadn't known.

Tony quickly glanced at Will, then back to the road. 'Details are still sketchy, but the Germans caught wind of our operation. They moved thousands of their troops to Arnhem ready to pounce on our men as they dropped close to the key bridges. The First Airborne Division bore the brunt of the casualties and we're only now beginning to understand just how many of our men died, let alone those who were captured by the Germans. We won't know exact numbers till all those who survived make it back to England. It could take months.'

There was silence in the back. Will wondered if they hadn't caught Tony's words, which were hard to make out against the drone of the jeep's engine. His thoughts turned to his best friend Jack, then Sam and Nick, all trusted colleagues who'd been prepared to go to any lengths to protect one another. As far as he knew, they'd all died; he had to question why he, out of all of them, had survived. He knew he should be grateful, but right now, having left Freddie and not knowing if he'd ever see her again, he felt hollowed out, knowing that everyone dear to him was gone.

Tony drew up to the entrance to the hospital behind several other jeeps. They waited their turn as nurses and hospital assistants with wheelchairs came out to help the men from the vehicles – most were able to walk unassisted, but some were too weak or wounded and had to be taken in by wheelchair. When it was their turn, Tony leaned his elbow on the open window and instructed the orderly to bring a wheelchair round for Will. Will was about to protest, but when he was helped out he found his legs failed him and he fell heavily into the chair. He hung his head over his chest, embarrassed not to be able to do something as simple as walk through the doors of the hospital.

'Hello, I'm Mabel,' said the nurse attending to him. 'We'll get your leg seen to straight away and you'll soon be as right as rain.'

'You're English,' said Will, lifting his head to look at her.

'That's right. There's a few of us here. We've been brought in to help care for the returning troops.'

Ed and Alan moved over to him. Ed touched his shoulder.

'We'll see you after they've done our medical checks. Then we're off to the field kitchen. There's talk of bangers and mash and more Scotch.' He grinned.

'Take care of yourself, old chap,' said Alan. 'You'll be home before you know it.'

Will took heart from their words. While the doctor X-rayed his leg and gave him the all-clear that there were no broken bones or bullet fragments lodged in his flesh, he allowed himself to dream of getting home in time for Christmas. He would allow his mother to fuss over him and nurse him back to health. And when he was well enough he would find a way to get back to Freddie. It was all he could think of for now.

'A few questions about what happened after the plane crashed,' he vaguely heard the English doctor say.

'Sorry, could you repeat that?' Will said, and realised he'd been daydreaming.

Frowning, the doctor peered at him for a moment, then tapped the end of his pen on the notepad he was holding. 'Do you remember anything about the crash?' He waited for Will to reply, but try as he might he found he couldn't bring the details of the crash to mind. Only one thing was he sure about – Jack.

'My co-pilot – my friend – didn't make it.' Will closed his eyes. The last clear image he had was of the two of them side by side in the cockpit and how they'd joked about getting back to base to drink beer and whisky. The rest of it – the moment the plane's engine was hit, losing height, crashing in a field – he'd been told what had happened but it was all still a blur.

'I understand. I just need to know if you spent any time in hospital. Perhaps you were taken to the one in Arnhem?' the doctor gently probed.

'Yes, that's right. It was Arnhem. How could I forget?' Will began to smile as Freddie's concerned face swam across his vision, and he was relieved that this latest lapse of memory was only fleeting. 'I had concussion,' he said, knowing that much was true.

The doctor knitted his thick brows. 'I'm not surprised to hear that,' he said and wrote something on his notepad.

'I'm fine now. It's just all been a bit much,' Will said weakly.

'You've been through a lot.' The doctor nodded as he continued to take notes. 'It can take several weeks, even months, to recover from concussion, and sometimes there can be a relapse. Plus we'll need to keep an eye on that leg of yours.'

'I can't stay here all that time,' Will protested. 'I need to get back home.'

'You're better off staying here and resting until you're well enough to travel.'

'How long will that be?' Frustrated, Will straightened himself in his chair, wanting to give the impression he wasn't as bad as he looked.

'I can't say until you're thoroughly checked over. We'll let you know then.'

THIRTY-NINE

It was another two weeks before Will was deemed well enough to undertake the long journey home. The prospect of another rough ride in a jeep to the military airfield at Brussels, where planes had been requisitioned for the evacuation of British army personnel, and the bumpy flight to Kent and onward travel home, was a daunting one. He knew he wasn't up to it, however much he pretended. Despite this, he was aware that he wasn't nearly as badly off as some of the other patients who had life-threatening injuries. All of them had made the perilous river crossing in the days and weeks before Will arrived.

One morning, Will was sitting in a chair by the side of his bed when a skinny young man was wheeled in and transferred to the bed next to his. Both his legs were encased from top to bottom in plaster.

Will waited till the nurses had left before introducing himself. 'Hello, I'm Will,' he said, giving the young man a sympathetic look.

'Bertie,' said the young man in a croaky voice; he managed to crack a smile. He looked Will up and down. 'Looks like you got off lightly,' he said jokily, and something about his manner reminded Will of Jack.

Will gave a scoff. 'They're not keeping me here because of my leg, but because of this.' He tapped the side of his head. 'I was knocked out when my plane came down. I thought I'd got over it, but I'm apparently suffering from the after-effects of concussion. What happened to you?'

Bertie didn't reply at first as he stared in dismay at his legs, which lay straight out in front of him. 'I can't even blame this on the Jerries. Our boat had just landed and I was so excited to make it onto dry land. Our jeep was full up, so I volunteered to sit on the bonnet and shout out directions to the driver. Thought it was a bit of a lark until we went slap into another jeep coming in the opposite direction. I managed to pull my legs up just in time else they would have been chopped off from the knee down. Even so, they're so bust they say it'll be months before I go home.' He clicked his tongue. 'Hey-ho. Could've been worse, couldn't it?' he said bravely and gave a half-hearted chuckle.

'Bad luck, but just think, the bloody war will probably be over by then.'

'Yeah. Bloody war.' The young man sighed.

After a moment, Will said, 'Did you see fighting at Arnhem?'

'Did I?' Bertie exclaimed. He proceeded to tell Will that he was a corporal with the Oxford and Bucks Light Infantry and that he'd been parachuted into Holland on the Sunday before fighting began. 'There was a group of us and we were preparing to launch an attack on the bridge. First thing we saw was a couple of armoured vans at the side of the road with bullet holes in the sides. We couldn't take anything for granted, so we searched them – and found two German soldiers hiding in the back of one of them. A couple of our men captured them and marched them back to our HQ and handed them over. After that, I was ordered to take up a position in a nearby building with Coxy, a friend of mine. We had our machine guns trained on the bridge and waited for the Jerries to turn up. From our position we could see the major get into his jeep – he'd fixed a machine gun on the roof. The plan was to drive across the bridge and break through the German line. He was waiting for the right moment to go when a convoy of German troop carriers turned up. All of us opened fire, but our machine guns were pathetic against their superior firepower.'

'But you obviously got away. How did you manage it?' said Will.

'I was hiding three storeys up in that building. We weren't the only ones. All the buildings close to the bridge were manned. And then this shell came flying through the window and Coxy was blown clean out. I don't know what happened to him, but that was the last I ever saw of him.' He winced as if in pain, and Will knew it wasn't his legs that were bothering him.

'I know how hard it is,' Will said carefully. 'I lost my best friend when our plane crashed. And Sam, our wireless operator. I thought Nick, our navigator, had been killed too, leaving just me, but I saw him later. I keep asking myself, why not me?' He felt a wave of self-pity compounded by pain at not knowing if Freddie had even made it back through the Biesbosch without getting caught, or if she'd even got home alive. But the last thing Will wanted was for anyone to feel sorry for him, especially Bertie, who didn't know if he'd ever walk again. He didn't expect him to answer, knowing he had his own demons to contend with. Stories like his had become so commonplace that they'd lost their power to shock. There was nothing more either of them could say.

. . .

A week later, the doctor signed Will off and said he was well enough to travel. The doctor was satisfied he had recovered well from the concussion, and told him that his initial concerns over his leg being infected proved to be unfounded. He gave Will instructions to keep an eye on the wound and get the dressing changed regularly once he was home.

Will's initial joy at hearing that he would be allowed to leave was tempered by the irrational thought that Freddie would come looking for him and might turn up at the hospital at any time. As unlikely as that would be, his heart jumped every time a nurse came into the ward, only to feel bitter disappointment that it wasn't Freddie, the girl he loved.

He walked back to the ward and began to pack the clothes, razor and toothbrush he'd been supplied with into an army-issue holdall. He looked up to see a nurse pushing Bertie in a wheelchair with his legs elevated straight in front of him. She helped him back onto his bed and made him comfortable.

'Off to Blighty now, are you?' Bertie said after the nurse had left.

Will heard the bitterness in his voice despite his jocular tone. He sensed that it couldn't have been easy knowing he still had months ahead of him in this place. 'Yeah, there's a C-47 waiting at Brussels that's leaving this evening. Then it's on to RAF Manston for a debrief. I don't expect I'll get home for a few days yet.'

'What then? Will you go back to flying?' Bertie looked at him intently.

Will suddenly felt sick as he thought of getting behind the controls of a plane. It was what would be expected of him and if he refused he knew his career as an RAF pilot would be as good as over. He swallowed. 'I shall have to. It's my job.' He smiled through pursed lips. 'Look after yourself, Bertie – and don't go riding on jeep bonnets any time soon.'

'As if. I'm done with the army. From now on, it's the quiet

life for me.' Bertie gave a hard dismissive laugh, as if he didn't actually believe his own words.

Will laughed too and gave him a friendly slap on the shoulder. He picked up his bag and walked away; the slight hitch in his step the only indication that he wasn't fully recovered.

FORTY

DECEMBER 1944

Freddie

However many layers of clothing Freddie put on it never seemed to be enough against the persistent cold. Every morning, she was reminded of it when she pushed her nose above the blankets and saw her breath rising up into the frigid air. The ice crystals formed intricate patterns on the windows, a pretty but terrible reminder that all was not right. Some days she could hardly get out of bed. It was tempting to huddle under several blankets with her woollen hat pulled over her ears. She told herself it was just the cold, but knew it was more than that. Each day she had no news from Will, a small part of her seemed to shut down.

Six weeks earlier, Freddie had been called to assist Dr Akkerman on an operation to remove shrapnel from the back and legs of a young Canadian soldier. She had scrubbed up and was waiting for him when he arrived, slightly out of breath, at the operating theatre.

'Good morning, Freddie. I was just leaving the house when Jan Kees came—'

At that moment a nurse turned up and asked if he had a couple of minutes to discuss an urgent matter. Freddie was left anxiously waiting in case the doctor had been about to impart bad news – every day she'd had the same churning feeling in her stomach that something terrible must have happened to Will – but when the doctor returned he was smiling.

'Sorry about that. I'd better be quick.' He glanced at the wall clock, which showed it was two minutes to ten, then lowered his voice. 'I'm sure you'll be pleased to hear that all the men made it back to England in one piece.'

Freddie let out a long shuddery breath. 'Even Will?' She needed him to confirm it.

'Yes. Jan Kees said that all the men from the Biesbosch evacuation were flown from Brussels a week ago to an RAF base in the south of England.'

She forced a smile, desperate for him to tell her more. 'Where are they now?'

'Jan Kees didn't say. Listen, we can talk later, but we really must get on.' He gave her a kind smile and pushed open the swing door, waiting briefly for her to follow him.

Freddie's initial relief at hearing that Will was safe gave way to a new feeling of anxiety – why hadn't he written like he said he would? Had his leg injury worsened… or maybe he'd had a change of heart now that he was back home? Refusing to believe any of it, she quickly went after the doctor into the operating theatre.

Three weeks later, she was called into the matron's office with Inge and several other nurses to tell them that they were no longer needed in Arnhem after the British had taken back control of the hospital and brought in their own people to deal with the wounded on both sides. There were fewer Allied patients now and all the extra Dutch nurses who had been dealing with the aftermath of the invasion were surplus to requirement.

Freddie had been half expecting it, but wished she could stay on a few days in case word arrived from Will. Under the circumstances, though, she had no choice but to leave. Dr Akkerman kindly promised to let her know straight away if Will got in touch. She was consoled that she had Inge for company on the return journey. Inge, who was the only person who truly understood what it had been like to work in a military hospital under German rule, and who'd worked tirelessly to stop patients from being seized by the Germans and taken to the concentration camps. Together with Dr Akkerman, they had saved countless lives, not only through their medical skills but by smuggling men out of the hospital with the help of the resistance. But many injured Allied airmen weren't so lucky and their fate was decided even before they'd made it through the doors.

Freddie left Arnhem with a heavy heart and a nagging feeling that she could have done so much more to help the men who hadn't made it.

Instead of moving into the nurses' accommodation in Haarlem, Freddie opted to stay with Trudi, who was renting a room in a house that had a vacant room. Almost straight away, winter set in, with polar winds sweeping from the east, causing temperatures to plunge and freeze over canals and rivers at the precise moment that the Germans imposed an embargo on the transport of food and other basic essentials. The sisters consoled each other that it couldn't last, and Freddie found it a comfort to be with her sister and spend long evenings chatting together to distract themselves from the bitter cold. Talking to Trudi about Will and how much she missed him gave her some solace and Trudi encouraged her to write to the address Will had given her in London. But with no contact name or department, Freddie had no idea if the letter she'd sent care of the RAF would even be read. She very much doubted she would get a reply. Trudi was sympathetic, for she was also missing Piet, the man she loved and a resistance fighter like herself, who was working in different parts of the country on dangerous sabotage assignments.

But it wasn't long before serious issues began to occupy their minds. The Germans were still running the country and determined to keep the Dutch in their place. On one of the coldest days so far, when the thermometer plunged below zero, the Germans cut off gas and electricity supplies, leaving most people without the means to heat their homes or cook. In desperation, people were left to break up their furniture for fuel, their only means of boiling a kettle or heating up a bowl of soup. Freddie and Trudi didn't have that luxury as the only furniture they had belonged to their landlady, Mevrouw de Jong, and they knew she would throw them out if she discovered they'd been burning her chairs. The only alternative was to go foraging for wood, but everyone else had the same idea. Park benches, wooden fences, trees of every description, large and small, were cut down and sawn into logs for firewood. Amsterdam's Vondelpark was closed to the public because so many trees had been razed to the ground and the wood sold by enterprising individuals on the black market.

Freddie hadn't yet gone back to work at the hospital – nothing could be further from her mind than working a long shift. Each day was a struggle for survival to find enough fuel and food to see them through until the following morning.

One day, Freddie and Trudi were out searching for scraps of wood when a man approached them, offering to sell them a small bundle of firewood for fifty guilders. They almost refused; the meagre amount seemed hardly enough to light the stove, even for one meal. And fifty guilders – it was a small fortune! As they deliberated, the man turned his back on them and began to walk away. It was neither here nor there to him, for there would always be someone else desperate enough to pay up. Freddie ran after him and quickly handed over their hard-earned cash. That evening, they were able to cook a pan of soup, which they ate standing up next to the stove for warmth. A few days later, having eked out the wood as much as they could for cooking, they found they were down to their last sticks and back to square one – they had no idea where they could go for another source of fuel.

Freddie suspected she'd be able to cope with being cold if she only had enough to eat. There was virtually nothing left to eat in the shops due to the embargo of food by the Germans. Or maybe it was just another excuse for the Germans to steal from them, Freddie thought. The Germans had already raided all the local grocers, greengrocers, bakers and butchers in order to feed themselves, and had left so little on the shelves for everyone else that even a loaf of bread had become a scarce commodity. Some days, Freddie and Trudi came home empty-handed after scouring every shop in their neighbourhood and had to make do with a watery soup made from a single potato and the remains of an unappetising wilted cabbage. For fuel, they now burned old newspapers and pages torn out of books, which were hardly fit for purpose and flared to nothing in an instant.

And yet despite these difficulties, the two sisters continued to work on assignments provided by Frans. It was mainly courier work these days, delivering packages to contacts in The Hague, a good thirty-five miles away by bike along the coast. Frans was grateful for their continued willingness to work, for his group was dwindling in numbers as more men took the decision to disappear and become *onderduikers*. The Germans knew that their latest demand for more male Dutch workers to plug the gap of their own diminishing workforce wasn't working, and they set about tracking down any men under the age of forty-five who hadn't registered for forced labour with a renewed vengeance.

Since the weather had worsened, they took it in turns to go out to work on assignments. It was Freddie's turn to work today, which meant she'd have the luxury of a whole slice of bread with a scrape of margarine for breakfast. It was barely enough to sustain her, but she promised Trudi she would try to get hold of some firewood and maybe call in on a farmer she knew and see if he was prepared to sell her a couple of eggs and a bottle of milk.

Before venturing outdoors, she wound her woollen scarf round her head to protect her ears and mouth and buttoned her threadbare winter coat up to the neck. She put on two pairs of gloves, for she would be cycling her bike along the exposed coastal road into the unrelenting bitterly cold wind that penetrated her whole being.

Trudi put a coat and scarf on to come to see her off. She opened the flap of Freddie's saddlebag and looked inside. 'Is that all you're taking today?' she said, taking out two small wrapped items and examining them with an air of disdain. 'This seems to be happening more and more.'

Freddie sighed. 'I know. It hardly seems worth it, but Frans told me this delivery is urgent.' She glanced sideways at Trudi. 'Apparently, these packages were handed to him by someone high up in the resistance.'

Trudi scoffed dismissively and hugged her arms tightly against her chest. 'I'm not convinced something that small can be of any importance. It would help if we knew what we were carrying.'

'You know that's never going to happen,' said Freddie, putting the packages back and securing them underneath the hidden flap at the bottom of her bag. 'At least I'm not going as far as The Hague today. I should be back by early afternoon.'

Trudi seemed to soften. She walked over and kissed her sister with tenderness. 'I've had a tip-off about potatoes at a farm out towards Bloemendaal. It means I'll have to dig, but I'll bring back as many as I can fit on my bike.'

'How did you know I've been dreaming of a big plate of potatoes with melted butter?' said Freddie wistfully. 'But seriously – please make it happen.' She gave Trudi a sad smile and wheeled her bike onto the icy street.

FORTY-ONE

Freddie turned left onto the long straight road along the dunes and was immediately battered by a blustery arctic wind. It was hard going and before long it began to snow. The snowflakes felt like sharp needles piercing her face and blinding her eyes. She gripped the handlebars tight and had to stand on the pedals to get her bike to move forward against the force of the gale. By the time she arrived at her destination she was almost in tears from cold and exhaustion. She only hoped that Mr Engels, the recipient of the parcels, would allow her to come inside and warm up a little before setting off back home.

She leaned her bike at the gate. Her hands were so cold that she could hardly pick the packages out of her saddlebag. Her face hurt and would be red raw from the cold – she knew she looked a sight, but was beyond caring.

She walked up the path and rapped on the door. It creaked open to reveal a scruffy middle-aged man with a half-smoked cigarette hanging from the corner of his mouth. 'Who is it?' he asked suspiciously, with not so much as a smile.

Undeterred, Freddie gave him her best smile. 'The bus is arriving late,' she said, reeling off the code she'd been given for this assignment. After he nodded, she continued, 'I've come from Haarlem with packages for Mr Engels. Is that you?' She stamped her frozen feet to try to get some feeling back into them.

'I'll take these. Wait here.' He shot out a hand to grab them from her and closed the door in her face.

'Excuse me! Can I come in out of the cold for a minute?' she shouted and banged on the door, almost screaming in frustration. The cheek of it – had he no idea what she'd gone through to get here, and all for two measly packages? She heaved in a breath to calm herself down and made herself wait.

After a short while, the door opened again. The man pressed a twenty-five-cent coin and a handful of cigarettes into her palm. 'For your troubles,' he said, not quite meeting her eye.

She stared at the coin and the cigarettes – one was half crushed – and then looked up at him. 'Is that all I get for cycling twenty miles in this weather?'

The man frowned, then shrugged. 'It's your job, isn't it?' And he shut the door firmly, before she had a chance to say anything more.

Furious, instead of riding home she took a detour to Frans's house to complain about the situation and demand to know what was going on with all these small packages that needed delivering so urgently.

Frans was surprised to see her, but immediately invited her in and offered her a cup of tea. 'It's the best I can offer you, I'm afraid,' he said, taking her into the kitchen. 'But I have managed to get my hands on a little sugar, so please take a spoonful.'

She felt close to tears at his generosity, especially after the cold reception she'd received earlier. It was such a welcome relief to be invited in out of the cold that, by the time she'd finished her drink and warmed up, Freddie had almost forgotten how angry she'd been at the way she'd been treated earlier.

'I'm glad you came because the packages are coming thick and fast.' Frans chuckled.

Freddie pursed her lips and sighed. 'That's what I came to talk you about. Every day, Trudi or I cycle over to The Hague. It's exhausting in this weather, and we're permanently hungry. I don't want to complain, but we can't even get hold of any firewood to light the stove, and even if we do, we have no food to cook.' She wiped a hand across her eyes, which were watering, annoyed with herself for appearing so pathetic.

Frans leaned across the table and took her hands. 'Freddie, why didn't you come to me sooner? I should have realised.'

She shook her head and managed to pull herself together. 'Why would you? Trudi and I aren't the only ones. Everyone's got it hard these days.'

He nodded. 'But there's no need to be going out on your bike in these conditions. I'm sure some of these packages can wait.'

Consoled by his remark, Freddie went on to tell him about the cold reception she'd received from the man out on the dunes, and all for a couple of tiny packages. 'Do you even know what they contain?'

Frans looked surprised. 'No, I don't. Most of the time I'm not told. But that man shouldn't have been so rude to you. I'll make sure you don't deliver to him again.'

He got up, went over to the dresser, opened a drawer and took out several packages wrapped in brown paper and secured with string, which he put on the table. 'I promise these will be the last ones. They're for a different contact in The Hague – I think you've been to him a couple of times recently. I agree the situation has got out of hand – I won't accept any more.'

Freddie was barely listening as she picked up one of the packages, turned it over and shook it against her ear. It felt and sounded suspiciously like a packet of cigarettes. Before Frans could protest, she slid off the string, tore open one end and pulled back the brown paper. 'So this is what I cycle seventy miles a day for,' she said, gazing at Frans as she held up a packet of Lucky Strike, an American brand she'd heard of. 'I thought as much.'

Frans stared at her. 'Believe me, no one told me this was going on. And with such blatant disregard for the danger you put yourselves in to deliver something so worthless. It's an utter disgrace.'

Freddie pursed her lips grimly. 'Looks like we've both been had.' She eyed the other packages – two more were like the one she'd opened; the third was a long rectangular box. 'Shall I open the others?'

Their eyes met, and Freddie went on, 'Because if you won't, I will.'

FORTY-TWO

Freddie had returned from talking to Frans, her heart lighter than in ages, with her saddlebags filled up with firewood, a smoked sausage and a twist of greaseproof paper containing just enough butter to fork into the mash she was so looking forward to. She hadn't expected such generosity from Frans, but he'd insisted on sharing what little he had with her.

'It's the least I can do,' he'd said and had given her a clumsy hug, the first time he'd ever shown her any kind of emotion. This small gesture had meant more than anything to her, confirmation that he valued her loyalty and readiness to put herself through such difficult situations.

Trudi squealed when Freddie walked through the door carrying an armful of wood.

'Where on earth did you get all that from?' she exclaimed, relieving her of several pieces before placing them in the stove.

'Frans gave it to me.' Freddie's cheeks were flushed from the cold, but also from sheer delight that she was able to give her sister a little joy.

Trudi stood up straight, firing questions at her. 'You went to Frans? What did you have to do to make him give you this?'

Freddie laughed. 'Hang on. Can't we eat first? Then I'll tell you everything. I'm starving.' She took the sausage and tiny package of butter from her pocket and placed them on the kitchen table.

Trudi's eyes widened. 'To go on the potatoes?' she gasped.

'Of course. What else?' said Freddie, then suddenly narrowed her eyes. 'You did manage to find potatoes, didn't you?'

Trudi nodded and told her about her find. 'I managed to fill my saddlebags with enough to last us for at least a couple of weeks. And as I was leaving I found a turnip lying by the side of the road, which I slipped into my coat pocket for good measure. They're peeled and ready to boil. I'll cook.' Trudi draped an arm round Freddie's shoulders and sat her down.

That evening, Trudi and Freddie ate their first proper cooked meal in several weeks.

'That was heavenly.' Freddie laid down her fork on her empty plate with a sigh. 'I wish we could eat like this every evening.'

'We wouldn't appreciate it as much,' said Trudi drily, and got up to put a small log into the stove. It was the first time in ages that they'd dared keep the fire going longer than they needed to. She turned back, her cheeks rosy from the unaccustomed heat. 'Come on, Freddie. Tell all. I'm dying to know what was in those packages.'

Freddie enjoyed keeping Trudi in suspense and had been eking out her story bit by bit. She'd got to the part when Frans had brought out the latest packages for her. 'It was just too tempting, so I picked one up and opened it. And do you know what was inside?'

'No.' Trudi's eyes were bright with anticipation.

'American cigarettes.'

Trudi stared at her for a moment, then said, 'Why would

anyone send you all that way just to deliver a single packet of cigarettes?'

Freddie made a derisive noise in her throat. 'I asked myself that too. It all became clear after I'd persuaded Frans to let me open the other two packages. They both contained jewellery – expensive jewellery. One of them was a long pearl necklace and the other a pair of diamond earrings. I can't imagine how much they were worth.'

'So, all this time we were unwittingly running errands instead of doing worthwhile work. But who would use our couriers to deliver that kind of thing – surely nobody who works for Frans?'

'We couldn't understand it either, until it dawned on Frans who it was. Apparently, Frans has been so anxious to build up numbers that he agreed to join forces with the leaders of other local groups, but without first checking their credentials. He thinks it must be someone inside the group who was always boasting about his many girlfriends. It's hard to believe anyone can even think of taking advantage of the network Frans has set up to shower gifts of jewellery and cigarettes on women.'

'I hope you told him that's the end of it,' Trudi said sharply.

'Of course I did. I spoke for both of us and said we wouldn't be doing any more courier work, at least till he can sort things out. I told him that in future we won't take on anything unless we're told exactly what it is. He wasn't happy about it – you know how he likes to keep things secret in case we're stopped by the Germans and interrogated. It took some persuading, but he did eventually agree.'

'It's for the best.' Trudi sighed. 'I'm glad you confronted him. With any luck, the war will be over soon and then we won't have to worry about such piffling things.'

·   ·   ·

Trudi was wrong. The Hunger Winter, as it had become known, dragged on through January and February with no signs of any let-up. They stuffed newspapers into the windowframes in a vain attempt to prevent icy draughts from permeating the unheated flat, not that it made much difference. She and Trudi were often too exhausted, hungry and cold to undress for bed, so slept in their clothes under a blanket and eiderdown, but it was never enough.

The biting cold was relentless and there was no food in the shops. Working was unthinkable at the present time. Each new day was a challenge for the two sisters, who would venture out on their bikes and ride around town in the hope of finding a shop open for business. Most remained firmly shut, a potent reminder that the Germans were still very much in charge. Occasionally, there were rumours of a shop opening for a few short hours, but however early they set out there were always long queues outside, and all for the hope of obtaining a few gnarled turnips or the slight possibility of finding a loaf of bread made from dried-pea flour. Often they would arrive at a shop rumoured to be open only to find people huddled round expectantly, waiting in vain for the owner to arrive. Everyone knew of someone who was too ill to get out of the house themselves, but it was the talk of men, women and even children dying of hunger that was most shocking. How could it have got to this, thought Freddie, angry at how the Germans had done nothing to help her people in their hour of need. The very least she could do was to look after her own, as did Trudi, and they devoted their time to helping their relatives and close neighbours.

One morning, Freddie cycled across town to a butcher that was allegedly open after receiving a delivery of meat. Her elderly neighbour had been told about it and asked Freddie if she could bring her back some, however little and whatever it was. Freddie was happy to oblige and hoped the butcher would

give her extra for her parents, though she suspected the uniden-
tified meat would have come from a dubious source. She dared
not consider what kind of meat it was, but was sensible enough
to know that any meat was better than none. And she wasn't
going to turn her nose up at it.

She arrived at the butchers and took her place in the queue
behind two women who were conversing about the merits of
tulip bulbs as food.

One of the women spoke in an excited whisper. 'Did you
know you can eat them? They're meant to be as nutritious as
potatoes and you can make soup from them. You can even dry
them out and grind them to make flour.'

'You're joking! You won't catch me eating a tulip bulb,' said
the other woman with a dismissive sniff.

'I bet you won't say that when there's nothing else to eat, not
even potatoes. What else is there? Listen, people are helping
themselves to tulip bulbs out in the bulb fields. They're going
there with bags and pushchairs and filling them right up.'

'You mean, they're stealing from the farmers?' She stared at
her friend in disbelief.

The queue shuffled forward; the woman who'd suggested
digging up tulip bulbs stared at her feet. 'I wouldn't call it
stealing as such. And it is in a good cause. I mean, look at us
standing in a queue hoping for a few scraps, when we could be
getting plentiful food for free.'

'I suppose so.' The other one sounded doubtful.

'Listen.' Her friend glanced over her shoulder and
happened to look straight at Freddie. She turned back and
lowered her voice. Freddie leaned a little closer. 'My Len says
he's going to take the handcart first thing tomorrow', said the
woman. 'I can get him to bring you back some bulbs if you like.'

Freddie didn't catch the other woman's answer. She mulled
over what she'd just heard. In springtime, when she'd ridden
through the vast colourful fields of tulips that the farmers sold

for export, she'd had no idea that the bulbs were edible. She didn't much fancy the idea of eating them, but if it were true and they were such a good food source then she'd be mad not to join others and dig them out of the ground before they were all taken. At any other time, she would have considered stealing from the farmers immoral, but these were desperate times.

And she had another reason. Only the day before, Freddie had seen a man stumble and fall down in the street. She'd rushed to his aid, saying she was a nurse, but there was nothing much she could do for the painfully thin man, whose clothes hung off him. She knew at once that the reason he'd collapsed was because he was dying from starvation. She wasted no time in helping him back to his freezing cold house, where he lived on his own, and told him she'd be right back with some food. Racing home, she found the only thing she could offer him was the thin soup she'd made from a potato and a handful of dried beans for hers and Trudi's lunch. The man had been so grateful for her kindness, insisting he would repay her, but Freddie would hear nothing of it. She resolved there and then to do whatever it took to help him, though at the time she'd had no idea how.

And now the answer was staring her in the face. Who would have known that the humble tulip bulb would keep them all from starvation?

FORTY-THREE

During the early months of 1945, the two sisters regularly cycled out to the fields and filled their saddlebags with tulip bulbs, bringing back enough for themselves, their parents, the elderly neighbour and the man who'd almost died of starvation before Freddie had taken him under her wing. She had the unappetising gnarly bulbs to thank for staving off her feeling of perpetual hunger, even though she never quite got used to their bitter taste and mealy texture, which was impossible to disguise with salt or pepper. She couldn't think of any other kind of flavouring, simply because the cupboards were bare.

Gradually she felt her strength return, though to her dismay she found that her clothes now hung off her and she had to wear a belt to stop her skirt from falling down. She only had to look at Trudi's hollow cheeks and the way her blouse looked two sizes too big to realise just how bad the situation had become.

Although life was still hard, Freddie didn't worry so much about where the next meal would come from. The evenings were getting lighter and when the sun broke through the grey clouds and warmed her back, however briefly, life seemed just that little bit more bearable.

And yet the war raged on. There were rumours that the German occupiers would soon be defeated, but Freddie found this hard to reconcile with the menace of German soldiers still patrolling the streets. And then there were the horrifying reports in the illegal press of the lengths they were prepared to go to root out Jews in hiding and forcibly remove them on transports to the concentration camps.

It had been several weeks since Freddie and Trudi had undertaken any courier work for Frans when he contacted them with an unexpected request from the Swedish Red Cross. As a gesture of solidarity towards the starving Dutch population, the Swedish government had shipped in a large consignment of white flour, which was being distributed to bakeries across the country. The Red Cross needed volunteers to deliver loaves and distribute them to the elderly and infirm. The sisters didn't hesitate in accepting and rushed to their local Red Cross depot in Haarlem to sign up. When they turned up in the villages with their saddlebags bulging with the freshly baked white loaves, people came pouring out of their houses, curious to see what all the commotion was about. It was rewarding to see the joy on their faces, but there was only enough flour for a single loaf per household and people's happiness soon evaporated.

It was mid-March, and Freddie was only too aware that she'd heard nothing from Will. Ever since they'd parted, she'd been counting the days and weeks, and was unable to understand why he hadn't been in touch. It just didn't make sense after everything that had passed between them; he'd been so adamant that he would write to the hospital in Arnhem as soon as he was home. But every time she'd written to Dr Akkerman for news his reply had been the same, though he always promised to contact her as soon as he heard anything. Now, as she thought back to how long it was since she'd been back in Haarlem, she was shocked to realise that almost four months had passed. How could that have happened, she thought with a stab of despair. Spurred into action, she wrote Dr Akkerman a letter, almost begging him if there was anything he could do to help.

Two days later, she received his reply. But as she read his letter, her eyes filled with tears.

Dear Freddie

It gave me great joy to receive your letter. I was so relieved to hear from you. I've been wondering how you've been coping during these terrible cold weeks, though I can't imagine what it must be like to live off tulip bulbs. The hospital feed us as best they can. It's better than nothing, although it's a far cry from the meals we used to get.

I'm all too aware you are still waiting for news from Will, but the truth is I've heard nothing. I did ask Jan Kees if he could find out for you, but he's no longer working locally and has moved to Utrecht, where his skills are needed. I'm afraid I haven't had much contact with him recently. I'll leave it up to you to guess what he's doing.

I've been thinking about your request. There may be a way for you to get some information on Will's whereabouts. A friend of mine told me that the RAF has set up a service for missing British airmen to help people who have received no news from loved ones after the Battle of Arnhem. It's called the 'Missing Research and Enquiry Service'. They help trace airmen listed as missing, presumed killed, but please don't jump to any conclusions. We know that Will did make it back home alive. I'm sure the RAF will know of his whereabouts. I believe the headquarters are in London, but I'm afraid I don't have an address for them.

I'm sorry I'm not much help. Please write back soon and tell me how you get on. It may not be the right course of action, but it's a start.

Your ever affectionate friend,

Hans Akkerman

Freddie wiped away her tears, not fully understanding what had brought them on. Perhaps it was the doctor's concern for her situation or the relief of having something positive to cling on to after all this time. After she'd allowed herself to have a little cry, she realised she did feel a bit better.

Straight away, she set about carefully composing a letter to the RAF. She guessed that they wouldn't be prepared to release information to anyone who wasn't a relative, so she made out that she was Will's Dutch cousin and gave his name and rank from the dog tag she still wore round her neck. She wrote her address at the top of the letter, then, referring back to the doctor's, wrote on the envelope:

RAF Missing Research and Enquiry Service, London, England

She hoped it would be enough to reach the right person. But as soon as she let go of the letter and heard it land inside the postbox, she regretted including her address in case it fell into the wrong hands. But it was a risk she had to take if she was to have any chance of tracking down Will. It was too late to worry. She knew she just had to sit back and wait.

FORTY-FOUR

Two weeks later, Freddie and Trudi returned from a long day at the Red Cross headquarters. They had been packing food and clothing parcels for an orphanage run by nuns, who were finding it hard to provide for children who'd been orphaned in bomb attacks.

Freddie put her key in the lock and pushed open the door. Straight away she saw the letter postmarked 'London WC2' lying on the doormat. Her hand shook as she picked it up. 'It's from the RAF,' she said with a catch in her voice.

'You go and sit down and I'll boil the kettle and make us some tea.' Trudi smiled sympathetically.

Freddie hadn't known what to expect, but when she slit open the thick envelope she found several sheets of paper inside. The top sheet was a letter that barely acknowledged her enquiry and just told her she must provide as much information as possible on the enclosed forms about Flight Lieutenant William Cooper.

Freddie quickly flicked through the pages of the question-naire. 'I'm not sure if I can do this. There are questions here asking the number of his last flight and the date he went missing. How am I supposed to know that? All I know is he made it back home, so he probably doesn't qualify as missing. Tell me what you think.' She pushed the sheets of paper over to Trudi, regretting how little she actually knew about Will. Why had she never asked? It was probably too late.

'Let's not jump to conclusions,' said Trudi. She took her time studying the forms, pointing out the questions that Freddie couldn't be expected to answer, such as positions held by the missing person in question, dates and length of time served in the air force. 'I'm sure the RAF are used to relatives not knowing all the answers. It sounds like they need as much information as possible to allow them to do their searches. Show me the tag Will gave you.'

Grateful that Trudi hadn't dismissed her efforts to trace Will out of hand, Freddie untied the string of the dog tag and deciphered the letters and numbers, just as Will had shown her. '"W. Cooper." That's William Cooper. "Offr" means officer and I know he was the pilot of the plane,' Freddie explained.

'I presume 137499 will help the RAF find him on their records. What is CE?' asked Trudi.

Freddie had to think a moment, then remembered it was to do with his religion and it came to her. 'Church of England,' she said.

'This dog tag is for a reason. I imagine it will give them the information they need.' Trudi spoke encouragingly. 'I'll help you fill in the forms and you can send them off.'

Freddie was still unconvinced even after she'd signed her name and date at the bottom of the final page. It reminded her of coming to the end of a school exam paper knowing that she hadn't done enough revision to pass. Still, she was relieved to seal the enclosed envelope containing the half-completed forms, and hoped it was enough to bring her closer to finding him.

'There, it's all done,' said Trudi. 'Try and forget about it for now and come out for a walk with me. I've been meaning to see if the café on the market square is open. I haven't had a cup of acorn coffee for weeks,' she said drily and wrinkled her nose.

Every day, Freddie woke with a feeling of anticipation that this would be the day that a letter would come from Will, saying that he'd never forgotten her and still loved her. The feeling never lasted any more than a minute before she was fully awake and aware that the reality was quite different: Will was not coming back.

And yet, a small part of her wasn't ready to give up hope.

She was lying in bed willing herself to get up when she heard the soft click of the letter box. Instantly, her heart gave a jolt and she jumped out of bed, hurried onto the landing and leaned over the banister, from where she had a view of the front door. There was a single white envelope on the doormat. It had to be for her. With her heart in her mouth, she took the stairs two at a time, and stooped to pick up the thin envelope, reading the now familiar London WC2 postmark, noticing how light it was. Good news or bad? She was unable to guess as she climbed the stairs, more slowly now, and returned to her room and closed the door behind her.

She was sitting on the edge of her bed, the letter in her hand, when she heard a knock.

'Come in,' she said flatly.

It was Trudi. Freddie gazed up at her but didn't register her standing there.

'Is everything all right?' Trudi came and sat next to her.

'Yes, I suppose so.' Freddie felt tired. 'Read it yourself.'

Trudi took the letter and read aloud, stumbling over unfamiliar words.

Dear Miss Oversteegen

Further to your letter and provision of information on the completed forms, we are pleased to inform you that Flight Lieutenant William Cooper has returned to duties at RAF Saltby after a period of convalescence.

Please address any further correspondence as follows:

RAF Saltby, Sproxton Road, Grantham, Leicestershire, England

Yours faithfully

M. Weston

Missing Research Section, Air Ministry, London

Trudi lowered the letter and smiled. 'This is good news, isn't it?'

Freddie smiled weakly. 'I suppose it is.'

'So what's the problem?' Trudi's voice came out harsh, impatient.

Shaking her head, Freddie frowned. 'Can't you see? Will's fine. Absolutely fine. He's recovered – of course I'm pleased about that, but he's back at work flying those deadly machines.' She made a gulping sound as she imagined what terrible dangers he was flying into, yet again. 'It's obvious he's forgotten all about me. And after all the things he said – about how much he cared for me. And I believed him... how could I have been so stupid?'

FORTY-FIVE

Freddie, delivering Red Cross parcels in town, was wheeling her bike down a side street when she saw Inge ahead of her, walking quickly and purposefully. She was dressed in her nurse's uniform and looked as if she was in a hurry.

'Inge!' Freddie cried out and broke into a run.

Inge stopped and glanced over her shoulder. 'Freddie! Where have you been hiding yourself all this time?' She beamed.

Freddie came alongside and leaned over to kiss her friend on both cheeks, one, two and three for luck. 'Are you off to work?'

'Yes, and I'm late. Walk along with me. I'm dying to hear your news.' She glanced at Freddie's pale blue dress with the Red Cross emblem on the pocket and sleeve. 'Since when have you been working for them?'

Freddie couldn't help but smile at the implied slight. 'Trudi and I signed up for volunteer work and we've been helping pack and distribute aid parcels. I wasn't intending to stay long, but they're always short of helpers.'

'Hmm,' said Inge, looking askance at her. 'I was wondering

where you'd got to. We're also short-staffed. It's sometimes just me on a busy ward of thirty.'

It sounded like a rebuke, but Freddie knew her friend better than that. She felt she owed her an explanation. 'I did intend to come back, but when the weather turned so cold and the gas was turned off it was such a struggle to keep warm. Trudi and I spent all our time looking for food and wood to cook it on. How have you coped?'

'I'm sorry you've had it so bad. We didn't have any heating either, but I'm grateful for a roof over my head and the hospital always makes sure we're fed. You know, if you'd come back, the hospital staff would have helped you. Everyone's been so supportive of one another.'

They arrived at a main crossroads and waited for a pause in the traffic. Inge turned to Freddie and searched her face. 'Have you heard anything from Will?' she said gently.

Freddie shook her head, and suddenly felt her eyes prick with tears. 'I know he managed to make it across to England and that he's piloting planes again. Who knows, he might even be up in the skies over Holland right now.' She looked up, which helped to stop tears from spilling down her cheeks.

'Oh, Freddie,' said Inge and put an arm round Freddie's shoulders, giving her a squeeze. She inhaled sharply. 'But you're so thin,' she said, drawing back in surprise.

'I'm fine, really I am.' Freddie pulled back and quickly wiped the tears from her cheeks.

Inge took hold of her hands. 'Don't give up on Will. He's bound to be part of the Allied efforts to liberate Holland, and the news is so much more positive. They say the war will be over in a matter of weeks. I must go, but please say you'll come back to work.'

Freddie had a sense of déjà vu as she remembered running into Inge all those months ago and how she'd persuaded her to get into nursing. They'd been through so much together and it wasn't over yet. She would go back, even if it was just to take her mind off Will. 'Yes, Inge, I will.'

Inge's face lit up. 'Thank goodness. I was convinced you'd say no. I'll put in a word for you and make sure you're on my ward. God, have I missed you.' And she quickly gave her another hug.

Being back on the ward gave Freddie renewed purpose, not least because she had no time to dwell on Will and where he might be. The long hours meant it was surprisingly easy to forget. She soon got used to the variety of work and the constant demands of a busy general ward again. Often it was just Inge and Freddie working a shift, which meant they had to turn their hands to everything from administering the correct medicines to mopping the tiled floors several times a day. Freddie never complained, but it was a far cry from the camaraderie of Arnhem, where the medical staff all pulled together whenever there was an emergency. She realised how lucky she'd been to assist in operations and how much she'd learned from Dr Akkerman.

Freddie was nearing the end of her shift and going through the list of new patients when her eye was caught by the name of a young man who was awaiting surgery for a complex fracture of his right leg. She knew about such injuries, having treated airmen whose parachutes had failed over Arnhem. This man's name was Harry Taylor, not a name she knew, but she guessed he must be English, or maybe Canadian. She had a pang of nostalgia for Arnhem and all the Allied soldiers in her care – not least Joe, the cheerful American from Michigan who was looking forward to getting back home and seeing his fiancée, and whose life had so cruelly been snatched from him.

She went over to the young man who was sitting up in bed. Inge was standing over him taking his blood pressure and listening to his heart through a stethoscope. 'Everything is fine. Do you need more pain relief?' she said, writing down his readings.

'Aw, would you, Nurse? My leg's killing me.' English, though he spoke in an accent Freddie hadn't heard before, quite different from other airmen she'd met.

Freddie touched Inge's arm. 'Let me stay with him while you fetch the tablets.'

'He's a parachutist with the RAF,' Inge whispered. She winked and left Freddie with the patient.

'Hello Harry,' said Freddie to the young man. 'So you're with the RAF. What happened to you?'

'I was on sorties dropping food parcels over Holland. I was a crew member on one of the Lancasters – huge beasts they are – but instead of bombs, our cargo was food. Hundreds and hundreds of bags with tins of food and bars of chocolate. We had to fly so low it didn't look like we'd make it, but the pilot found the target and the lads and I worked like billy-o throwing shedloads of the stuff out. You should have seen all those people down below waving and cheering us.' He chuckled at the memory. 'But he had to fly out of there fast before the Germans started firing at us.'

She said, 'I didn't see the air drops, but it must have been quite a sight all those food parcels dropping out of the sky. You can't imagine what it feels like after having no food for so long. Everyone's so grateful for your help. But how did you break your leg?'

He gave her a toothy grin. 'We made three more sorties that day. Back to base to pick up the next load and then straight off again. The Germans knocked out one of our engines on the last sortie. I was down in the hold throwing out the parcels. I stupidly lost my footing and fell out of the plane just before it came down with an almighty thump. My leg got smashed up, but I suppose it could be worse. I've got no one to blame but myself.'

'What happened to the others?' Freddie felt her mouth go dry.

'Everyone was fine except me. We got picked up sharpish. And I was driven straight here. I hope they let me out soon. I want to be home in time for the celebrations. There are huge celebrations planned.' He grinned at her again.

Freddie felt something shift inside. Could this young man be part of the same squadron as Will? Surely it would be too much of a coincidence, but she couldn't let it go. 'Do you mind me asking... what's the name of your air base?'

He frowned and looked as if he wouldn't answer, but then he said, 'You won't have heard of it. It's somewhere in the middle of England.'

'I might have. I was working in Arnhem last September and met an RAF pilot whose plane came down. He was the only survivor.' Even after all this time, saying it brought a painful lump to her throat.

'I'm sure you won't heard of it,' he said, shaking his head. 'RAF Saltby?'

Freddie caught her breath as if she'd been winded. 'That's the one,' she said. 'And what was your pilot's name?' Could Will really flying overhead without her knowing it?

He was looking at her strangely. 'John Jackson. Is that the bloke you met?'

'No,' she said, almost in relief. That seemed to settle it. She told herself he wouldn't know him. 'His name is Will. Will Cooper.'

'You know Will? Now that's a surprise. No one expected him to come back to work after what he went through at Arnhem, but he turned up at base a couple of weeks ago. We don't work in the same squad, so I can't tell you any more than that.'

Will was safe! Freddie's heart began to race at this unexpected turn of events, at the confirmation from this man that he'd seen Will so recently. 'I just want to be sure you're talking about the same man. He's an officer, tall with fair hair and blue eyes.' She smiled as she imagined gazing up at Will in her arms.

He gave her a puzzled look and nodded. 'That's him all right. Ah, Nurse. At last,' he said, turning his head as Inge approached. 'I thought you'd forgotten me.'

'Now, would I?' Inge said with a smile. She gave him two tablets and a glass of water and waited till he'd swallowed them down.

Freddie was still standing there, her mind in complete turmoil as she tried to process his words. After all this time not hearing a word from Will, she couldn't just walk away without asking for this man's help. 'Harry, would you pass a message on to Will when you get home?'

'Course I will. What do you want me to tell him?' He was now staring curiously at her.

'I'm not exactly sure. I'll write something and bring it to you after your operation. Before you leave the hospital.'

'That'll be tomorrow then, won't it, Nurse?' He winked at Inge, who was quietly listening.

'Maybe the day after,' she said. 'Now you get some rest. You've got a big day ahead of you.'

Freddie was still hovering close by, elated at the prospect that she and Will would find each other again. 'Thank you, Harry,' she said. 'You boys are doing such a wonderful job.'

FORTY-SIX

ONE MONTH LATER: MAY 1945

As the days began to warm up and colourful spring flowers came into bloom, there was an air of optimism out on the streets that hadn't been experienced in many a long year. People had been behaving as if the war had ended, even though the Germans hadn't formally surrendered. Each evening, there were blazing bonfires burning brightly right in the middle of the streets. Men, women and children danced round them with abandon, cheering loudly, waving red, white and blue flags and singing patriotic Dutch songs.

'It's over, it's over!' they chanted.

Freddie smiled as she weaved through the crowds on her way home from work. She didn't begrudge these people their enjoyment, but wasn't ready to celebrate until she had the certainty of an official announcement that the war was over. And yet, she wasn't averse to a little treat. Her bag was satisfyingly heavy with the food she'd just bought from the grocers two streets away, open again for business after many months. She was looking forward to surprising Trudi with some real food she hadn't had to forage or barter for.

Retreating inside the quiet of the house with relief after the party noise, she thought she heard a man's voice coming from the sitting room. Trudi hadn't mentioned having a visitor. Frowning, she went to see, and found Trudi on the floor with her head close to the wireless set, which they normally kept hidden under the floorboards.

'Quick, you're just in time.' Trudi frantically beckoned her in. 'The rumours are true – Hitler really is dead!'

Shocked, Freddie dropped her bag and went to sit beside her sister. She was just in time to hear the announcer confirm that Hitler had committed suicide while hiding out in his bunker in Berlin. This meant that the war was effectively at an end, he said, as the Germans had no choice but to surrender.

Freddie held her breath as she let the words sink in. 'After all this time… can we really believe it?'

Trudi was crying. 'Yes, we really can,' she said, laughing through her tears. She took Freddie in her arms and they hugged each other tight, rocking back and forth. And when a loud cheer went up from the street, it was all Freddie needed to believe that the war was at an end. Tears cascaded down her cheeks.

When she had recovered herself she laid out their celebratory feast – cheese, tomatoes, bread, and gherkins from a jar Trudi had found languishing at the back of the kitchen cupboard.

Freddie stood back to admire the table, then realised there was something missing. 'We've got nothing to toast ourselves with.'

'Yes, we have. Just wait here a moment.' With a cheeky smile, Trudi disappeared from the room, leaving Freddie to guess what she'd been hiding. From outside the room, she heard the cellar door open and Trudi's footsteps as she descended the stone stairs. After a few minutes she came back holding a bottle of wine.

'That's not ours to take,' said Freddie in mock reproach, but she was unable to keep the smile from her face. 'Where did you find it?'

'Right at the back behind some boxes. I noticed the bottle when I was looking for somewhere to store the tulip bulbs. And there's more than one. And before you say anything, I doubt Mevrouw de Jong even knows what's down there.' Trudi strode to the dresser and rummaged in a drawer for a corkscrew. She tugged at the cork, which came out with a satisfying pop, and filled two tumblers with the rich dark red wine.

Freddie took a tentative sip and pulled a face that made Trudi laugh. 'It's very sour,' she said, and coughed.

Trudi agreed but said she was sure it would taste better after the first glass.

'And after we've eaten,' said Freddie, slicing the crusty bread and cutting chunks of creamy cheese for them both. The first few mouthfuls of real food tasted wonderful, but she quickly felt full up and pushed her plate away.

Trudi did the same. 'It's strange, but I've dreamed so often of food like this, and now I can't seem to eat it.'

'We don't have to eat it all in one go,' said Freddie, taking another sip of wine, which did indeed taste better now that she'd had something to eat.

Trudi refilled their glasses. 'I think we should have a toast to absent friends.'

Freddie nodded and chinked her glass against Trudi's. 'To absent friends,' she said.

'No, you're doing it all wrong,' said Trudi, slightly slurring her words. 'I meant we must toast each of them individually. Starting with Hannie.'

Freddie shivered as she thought of their dear friend Hannie, locked up in a prison cell on the dunes at Scheveningen. She'd been arrested just a week ago when she'd been out on a fairly low-key assignment. It seemed so unfair that she'd been stopped on this occasion when she'd managed to evade the Germans so many other times. Hannie had been carrying illegal newspapers and might have got away with it had they not searched her saddlebags more thoroughly and found she'd been hiding a gun. This is what made them realise they had finally caught the woman they'd been after for years. Freddie shivered again. She knew that Hannie wouldn't be celebrating – maybe she hadn't even heard about Hitler's death.

She touched Trudi's glass with her own. 'To Hannie, the bravest woman I ever met,' she said with a lump in her throat.

'And who made me braver than I ever could have imagined,' said Trudi ruefully.

'And me,' echoed Freddie.

They stared into their wine glasses, swilling the ruby liquid round and round.

Freddie cleared her throat and raised her glass again. 'I'd like to toast Piet, for staying loyal to you through thick and thin.' She smiled and chinked glasses.

'To Piet,' said Trudi with tears in her eyes. 'I can't wait to see him after all this time. He's promised to come back for the celebrations.'

'Has he?' Freddie reached for the bottle and divided the remainder between their two glasses. 'That's wonderful news,' she said, trying her best to sound pleased.

'Freddie, I know things haven't worked out the way you'd hoped, but it doesn't mean they won't. You just have to give it time. It's not even a month since you wrote to Will.'

'I know, but I'm tired of waiting around for a letter that may never come. And now I wish I'd never sent that last letter, in case I've made a fool of myself and he's completely forgotten about me.' Maybe it was the wine, but she was now feeling sorry for herself.

Trudi spoke slowly and deliberately. 'From what you've told me about Will, I don't believe he would forget you. I'm sure there must be a perfectly reasonable explanation. Personally,' –

she stood up unsteadily and put her hands on the table – 'I think he's madly in love with you. Do you want me to get another bottle of wine?'

Freddie let out a joyful laugh. Maybe they were both feeling just a bit too tipsy, but she wanted to believe that Trudi was correct and that Will did love her. 'No! I think we've had more than enough – I don't want to be completely hungover for tomorrow.'

'All right.' Trudi sat back down heavily and leaned forward on her elbows. 'Freddie,' she began, and blinked several times.

'You're drunk.' Freddie giggled. 'Now you listen to what I have to say.'

Trudi gave an exaggerated nod.

Freddie sat back in her chair, composed herself and gazed into the middle distance. 'I've been thinking about what I want to do with my life. I want to get more qualifications. Perhaps get a job in the teaching hospital in Amsterdam or even study to become a doctor. It'll give me a purpose.'

When Trudi didn't answer, she glanced back at her and saw she'd fallen asleep, her head resting on her arms. Smiling, Freddie leaned forward and planted a kiss on the top of her sister's head.

FORTY-SEVEN

Inge came for them early the next morning, pressing on the bell repeatedly until Freddie opened the door.

'Inge... hello. What time is it?' Freddie stood there, rubbing the sleep from her eyes.

'It's nearly nine o'clock and if we don't leave right away we won't get a good position before the Canadians start arriving.' Inge spoke breathlessly. She pushed past Freddie and began pacing up and down in the small hallway. 'People are going mad out there already. Did you hear the church bells pealing? It's the same all over town. Isn't it wonderful?'

Trudi appeared, yawning, on the landing. 'What's the hurry?' she called down the stairs.

'Why aren't you two up and dressed?' said Inge impatiently.

'Trudi found a bottle of wine in the cellar last night,' said Freddie with an embarrassed grin.

Inge rolled her eyes. 'Well, there's no time to waste. You'll never guess who we're meeting in town.'

'I can't possibly guess. Just tell us.' Freddie was starting to feel overwhelmed by Inge's enthusiasm.

Inge beamed. 'Hans Akkerman. He came over to the

hospital yesterday looking for you. You must have just missed him. He seemed quite disappointed.'

'That's a shame,' said Freddie, covering up a yawn. 'I hope you told him I'd finished my shift.'

'Of course. He said he'd stay on for the celebrations and said they're bound to be better than in Arnhem. He didn't take much persuading.' She waited eagerly for Freddie's reaction.

'It'll be nice to see him. Trudi!' Freddie called up. 'Let's get dressed.'

'Hurry up and be sure to put on your best summer dresses,' said Inge. 'It's going to be a wonderful celebration.'

Linking arms, the women skipped three abreast down the middle of the road, carried forward by the joyful mass of people, all with one purpose in mind. The Canadian tanks were due to start arriving at ten o'clock and no one wanted to miss the spectacle. As more and more people joined the procession, they were forced to walk more slowly, sometimes coming to a complete halt. Each time they stopped, a roar went up from the crowd and someone would start singing a song and everyone joined in. Men threw their hats in the air and some people hoisted small children onto their shoulders. All along the streets, orange streamers and Dutch flags fluttered from upstairs windows.

The noise was deafening. Car horns sounded and bicycle bells were rung, children cried and groups of people broke into spontaneous song.

The sun beat down on their heads and Freddie was glad she'd remembered to wear her sunhat for the first time that year. She held on tight to Trudi on one side and Inge on the other, till the Amsterdamse Poort came into view.

Suddenly, Inge let go of Freddie's arm and started waving

frantically to someone walking a little way in front of them. 'Hans! Hans!' she shouted.

The crowd slowed to a halt and Freddie took the opportunity to bend down and fasten the strap of her sandal, which had come loose. 'I'll catch you up,' she called out. But by the time she stood up she could no longer see Inge or Trudi. Shielding her eyes against the sun and scanning the backs of the heads in front of her, she finally recognised Inge by her neat fair hair that shone brightly in the sunshine. 'Inge! Wait for me!'

Inge swung her head round and shouted something excitedly, but her words were carried away by a roar that went up from the crowd.

Distracted by the noise, Freddie turned to where the commotion was coming from, and heard the low growl of the first tank as it came rolling noisily along the street. People were applauding, crying out and waving flags. Women rushed forward and ran alongside the tank, raising their arms to be lifted on board by Canadian soldiers, who encouraged them with laughs and banter. Soon, a procession of tanks came trundling through. Soldiers sat on top with their legs dangling over the sides, whooping with laughter as they threw sweets, chocolates, packets of cigarettes and nylons into the eager crowd. Everyone was laughing, crying and shouting out their thanks to the soldiers for liberating them from the Germans.

Freddie laughed and clapped, mesmerised by the spectacle, and forgot she'd been trying to keep an eye out for Inge and Trudi. And then she saw the doctor, who stood out above the crowd, tall and bespectacled with his shock of white hair.

'Dr Akkerman, it's me, Freddie!' she attempted to shout above the crescendo of noise, but he didn't turn his head. She had to push through the throng to get to him.

'Excuse me, excuse me,' she kept saying, trying to keep her eyes on the doctor, who moved in and out of her vision and was eventually swallowed up by the crowd.

There were so many more people now that Freddie barely had room to move. She could no longer see over the heads of people towering above her. Hemmed in on all sides, she gulped for air, and felt a wave of panic.

'I can't do this,' she thought, stumbling and crashing against a man, who looked round at her angrily. 'Sorry,' she mouthed, and had just thought she was about to faint when she had the sensation of someone grabbing her elbow and an arm supporting her round her waist.

'I've got her,' said a man's voice in English.

The angry man's expression changed to a smile when he heard the other man speak. He tipped his hat. 'Thank you for all you've done,' he said in accented English, and others turned to stare and smile at the man supporting Freddie, and give their thanks too.

It can't be... Freddie almost forgot to breathe. She turned to get a better look and was instantly lost in the familiar smiling blue eyes she had thought she'd never see again. 'Is it really you?'

'Yes, it's me, beautiful.' Will laughed.

Freddie had only a moment to take in his immaculate dark blue RAF uniform, his cropped blond hair when he removed his cap and his mesmerising blue eyes, before he kissed her full on the mouth.

'*Hoera!*' yelled someone close by. One by one others joined in, shouting their approval.

Will whispered against her ear, 'That's for us.'

'No, it's for you, Will,' Freddie said, hot with embarrassment at this outpouring of emotion. Will became more than a little red in the face himself as each person came over to shake his hand.

'Dr Akkerman's waving at us,' said Freddie, still scarcely able to believe what was happening, and she led Will to a less crowded spot where they could talk. She stopped and took a good look at him. 'I never thought you'd come,' she said, letting her eyes roam over his handsome face, still not believing he was real. 'I thought you wouldn't come.'

'Didn't I promise?' said Will, then swooped in for another kiss. 'I've missed you so much.'

'You took your time,' Freddie said, laughing, thrilled at his words.

Dr Akkerman appeared at their side. 'You found her. Thank goodness, I'm so pleased,' he said, pushing his glasses up his nose. 'Inge went off with Trudi to meet Piet. They should be back any time soon.'

'I don't understand,' said Freddie, turning to Will. 'Did Dr Akkerman know you were coming?'

Will exchanged a quick smile with the doctor. 'I was one of the crew organising food drops, and after the last one I stayed on and went straight to Arnhem. I thought you'd be there.'

'It was my idea for us to come to Haarlem,' said the doctor with an apologetic shrug. 'I arranged it with Inge.'

'I wanted to come and see you straight away, but...' said Will.

'Inge said it should be a surprise and that we should wait till the morning. For the celebrations,' said the doctor. 'I hope we did the right thing.'

Freddie looked from one to the other, amazed at how the three of them had plotted this without her knowing.

The doctor's attention was diverted by someone he knew in the crowd.

Freddie stood with Will, still in awe that he was actually here, but something was bothering her. 'Will, I've tried so hard to get in touch with you, but it was hopeless. I wrote letters to the RAF giving all the information from your dog tag.' She paused to finger the tiny memento that still lay against her skin and had sustained her all these months. 'But they were useless. They wouldn't tell me anything except that you were back at work after convalescing. I even gave a letter to a patient called Harry Taylor. He said he served at RAF Saltby and knew you.'

Will looked puzzled. 'I know of him, but he never came to me with any letter from you. I thought you'd forgotten about me —'

'Will, wait,' Freddie interrupted. 'You promised me you would contact the hospital in Arnhem, but you didn't. I was convinced you'd forgotten about me.'

Will looked uncomfortable. 'I'm sorry I didn't write.'

'So, you admit it?' she said, disappointed by his weak apology.

'It wasn't like that, Freddie.' He put his hands up. 'Please listen to what I have to say. I was in a bad way when I got back. I started getting nightmares of that night of the crash. Everything came back to me in my dreams, which were so vivid. It was all I could do to get through each day. My little brother, Freddy, helped me get over it.' He smiled, with a distant look in his eyes. 'I remember when you told me your name was Freddie. My brother Freddy isn't so little now. He's seventeen and I owe him everything. He got me to talk about the good things about my time in Holland. And you. And even though I hadn't heard from you, he said I should go back and find you.'

'I'm so sorry. I wish I'd known.' After all he'd suffered, she should have known better than to doubt him.

She reached for his hand. He kissed hers. 'It's all in the past now. I'm here now and I've no intention of going anywhere.'

Inge came pushing through the crowd, her face radiant with heat and exhilaration. 'We're all here now. Isn't it exciting?' She swivelled her head and beckoned to Trudi and Piet to join them, then rushed to Will and hugged him. 'It's so good to see you. This girl has been going mad waiting to hear from you. I hope you have a good excuse.'

Will responded by squeezing Freddie round the waist and dropping a kiss on the top of her head.

'Yes, he did,' said Freddie, glowing, and leaned in for a proper kiss. 'Trudi, come over and meet Will.'

'I've heard a lot about you,' said Trudi, with an approving look, and held out her hand.

'Don't forget Piet,' Inge chimed in, and arranged them all in a circle so they could make their introductions. She put herself between the doctor and Trudi.

'Oh look, we've missed the last of the tanks,' Inge said suddenly, as she strained to see over the tops of heads. 'Never mind, it's time we went and celebrated with a proper drink.'

'Good idea,' said Trudi. 'Let's go back to the house. We've got a cellar full of wine.' She caught Freddie's eye and they both laughed.

'And I've got hold of some bottles of jenever,' said Piet, with an affectionate glance at Trudi.

'Perfect,' said Inge, her eyes sparkling with laughter. 'You'll join us, Hans, won't you?' she said, turning her face up to the doctor, and Freddie suddenly realised there was something more than friendship between the two of them.

People were beginning to disperse in their groups. There were plenty of couples too, the men in uniform and their sweethearts clinging on to their arms as they strolled away.

Still chatting and laughing, the little group set off, leaving the crowds behind.

Freddie and Will dropped back so they could carry on their conversation and catch up on what seemed like a lifetime apart, their arms firmly round each other's waist, as if their lives depended on it.

A LETTER FROM IMOGEN

Whether you have read all three books in 'The Dutch Girls' series or you have discovered them for the first time via *The Wartime Nurse*, then I would like to give you my heartfelt thanks for taking the time to read these stories. If you would like to keep up with all my releases, please sign up at the following link. Your email address will never be shared and you can unsubscribe at any time.

www.bookouture.com/imogen-matthews

I am always fascinated by little-known or forgotten stories of ordinary Dutch citizens and the extraordinary courage and determination they showed in taking on the occupying Germans and refusing to be trod all over by them.

Two years ago, I was researching ideas for new books and came across the stories of three young Dutch women who joined the resistance and were passionately determined to help those less fortunate than themselves in standing up to the Germans. All three were just teenagers at the outbreak of war in the Netherlands in May 1940, when the German occupation turned everyone's lives upside down. As I found out more about their daring exploits as the only women in their local resistance group in Haarlem, I came to realise just how extraordinary these three women were. And yet, very few people outside the Netherlands have heard of the Oversteegen sisters and their fellow resistance fighter Hannie Schaft, let alone that they took up arms against Nazi collaborators and high-ranking officials in the German Wehrmacht.

The lives of these three teenagers made compelling reading and I was immediately hooked by the idea of writing a series of three novels based on their lives and heroic actions.

The Wartime Nurse features the third of the three young women. Her name was Freddie Oversteegen and she was the sister of Trudi, who is the main character in *The Girl from the Resistance.* The sisters joined the resistance at the same time and took part in many dangerous and daring assignments together, which threw up a concern for me – I could hardly write the same story for Freddie as I had for Trudi. So I came up with the idea of giving my fictional character a job as a nurse that was separate to her resistance work. As a nurse, she is brought right into the centre of the conflict in 1944, when the Allies staged a massive attack to take the bridges at Arnhem from the Germans. This historical event is well documented as the Battle of Arnhem, or Operation Market Garden, but the skirmish ultimately failed and resulted in another eight months of misery for the Dutch population.

Throughout the book, I have stayed as close to the character and actions of Freddie Oversteegen as possible, especially in regard to the dangerous assignments she undertook as a member of the resistance, as well as the hardship she and Trudi suffered during the Hunger Winter of 1944–45. Here, I was able to draw on my own personal family connections, and in particular my mother's own struggles to survive starvation when the Germans cut off food supplies to the Netherlands.

I have read widely on the subject of the Netherlands during the Second World War and have found much valuable source material, including original videos such as *Biesbosch*, a film by Rinus Rasenberg about resistance workers operating in the treacherous and inhospitable Biesbosch region of the Netherlands, which was one of the important escape routes used for Allied airmen. The film is available on YouTube.

You can read more about the extraordinary stories of Freddie and Truus Oversteegen and Hannie Schaft in:

- *Three Ordinary Girls* by Tim Brady
- *Seducing and Killing Nazis: Hannie, Truus and Freddie: Dutch Resistance Heroines of WWII* by Sophie Poldermans

If you loved *The Wartime Nurse*, I would be so grateful if you could write me a review. I'd love to hear what you think as it makes a real difference in helping new readers to discover my books for the first time.

I love to hear from my readers and you can get in touch via my Facebook page, through Twitter/X, Instagram or my website.

Thanks again for reading.

Warm wishes,

Imogen

www.imogenmatthewsbooks.com

facebook.com/ImogenMatthewsBooks

x.com/ImogenMatthews3

instagram.com/oxfordnovelist

ACKNOWLEDGEMENTS

I would not have even considered writing the Dutch Girls series of novels had it not been for the support and encouragement of my editors at Bookouture. It started when I pitched the idea of a new series based on three remarkable Dutch women resistance fighters to my then editor Susannah Hamilton, who enthusiastically encouraged me to write a three-book series inspired by these women. Thank you, Susannah, for getting me started and helping me shape the first book in the series.

I would also like to extend special thanks to Nina Winters, who started work with me later on in the project. She is Dutch, which is such a boon, as she has provided me with so many fantastic suggestions and ideas on how to strengthen my story and make it as authentic as possible. Her eagle eye has proved invaluable in ensuring the details I provided are correct and to put me right where I have gone wrong.

I could not have completed this project without the encouragement and professionalism of the incredible editorial, marketing, digital, publicity and sales teams at Bookouture who made it all happen.

On a personal level, I am grateful to Matthew, my husband, for his patience and support throughout the lengthy process of starting a book to its completion. Our shared love of Holland means we frequently travel over on the ferry from Harwich to the Hook of Holland for family cycling holidays. It's on these trips that I'm always on the lookout for the seed of an idea for another book.

PUBLISHING TEAM

Turning a manuscript into a book requires the efforts of many people. The publishing team at Bookouture would like to acknowledge everyone who contributed to this publication.

Commercial
Lauren Morrissette
Hannah Richmond
Imogen Allport

Cover design
Debbie Clement

Data and analysis
Mark Alder
Mohamed Bussuri

Editorial
Nina Winters
Imogen Allport

Copyeditor
Jacqui Lewis

Proofreader
Anne O'Brien

Marketing
Alex Crow
Melanie Price
Occy Carr
Cíara Rosney
Martyna Młynarska

Operations and distribution
Marina Valles
Stephanie Straub
Joe Morris

Production
Hannah Snetsinger
Mandy Kullar
Jen Shannon
Ria Clare

Publicity
Kim Nash
Noelle Holten
Jess Readett
Sarah Hardy

Rights and contracts
Peta Nightingale
Richard King
Saidah Graham

Printed in Great Britain
by Amazon

53098765R00158